I0668877

da sticks

by
Rich Kisielewski

WOLFSINGER

PUBLICATIONS

Wolfsinger Publications Security, Colorado

ISBN 978-0-9816233-9-9

Printed and bound in the United States of America

Chapter 1

Eighteen years old. Only eighteen years old. You're just beginning to really get a feel for the world around you, how it works, what it can give and how much it can take. It grabs you, sucks you in, and you're off to the races. Life's got you by the short hairs with no way out. But, and it's a huge but, you're hanging on for dear life and loving the ride for all it's worth. Then someone turns on the fan and life gets the upper hand.

"Harry, it's me. I need your help."
"Tom, I already left."

Maybe I should jump back a few steps and let you in on what's going on here. My name is Harry because I'm told an aunt promised to lay some bread on me if my mom named me Harold. I don't believe it one little bit because I didn't see a single dime, and to my knowledge, neither did my moms.

Oh yeah, it's Harry, or should I say Harold Mickey Shorts, which wasn't my given name when I was ushered into this wonderful world of ours. My original name didn't cut it in my eyes, and the Mick, Mister Mantle, is my all-time favorite ballplayer. Plus, my original last name was way too long. I believe wearing tee shirts and shorts is how God intended us to dress, so that's how I came up with my new and improved name, 'Shorts', which just happens to be a great conversation topic for the ladies.

By trade, I guess you would call me a private investigator. But I'm not your ordinary run-of-the-mill, every day private dick. Kismet Incorporated is what my card would say if I had one. I owe what I am today to Tom, the guy who called me. He taught me the business for no reason whatsoever, never asked for squat in return. Squared my shoulders, showed me where my balls were, and taught me how to use them. When I had learned enough to be dangerous, he kicked me in the ass and sent me packing. That's why I'm headed to Central Pennsylvania to do whatever it takes to help Tom, my friend.

And so the story begins…

Chapter 2

"The kid could screw up a wet dream, I swear he could," was how Tom had endearingly described his son to me on more than one occasion. Tom Naughton that is, and his son Cam, short for Cameron. Six years ago, when he was twelve, I spent some time around Cam. He was a handful back then and he only got worse as he got older, and stupider. Cam's mom died when he was five. Tom gives it all he has, but his very best wouldn't begin to be close to enough with that kid. Cam doesn't run with the wrong crowd, they run with him.

And run they damn well do. Tom wasn't around near enough for a two-parent try at Cam and his posse, never mind going it alone. Two-day absences without even a phone call were common practice for Cam. When he'd show up again, Tom would just take him back in and love him even more.

School was ancient history for Cam. The local Police Chief and Tom spoke regularly, for all the wrong reasons. There were several close calls, but somehow Cam had managed to keep his ass out of jail so far. Unless I'm mistaken, Tom may have had a lot to do with it.

* * *

"He's never been gone four days," were the words that greeted me when I got to Tom's house. No 'How the hell are ya,' or 'How they hanging.' Just those six words and the sad eyes Tom gets—like his puppy dog just died. I knew we had a problem.

"Mind if I come in for a minute?" I asked.

"Oh man, I'm sorry, Harry. Drag your bones in here and cop a squat. I'll get us a few cool ones. Give me a sec."

"Take your time old man."

He hates it when I call him that. Loves it, too. No better human being on the face of this earth as far as I'm concerned. I don't have to let him know that's how I feel—we've been there, done that together.

"Harry, it's real good to see ya again," Tom said as he came back into the living room.

It wasn't much of a house to speak of, but Tom never needed much. I got the feeling Cam was getting in the way of Tom's work more and more every day. Probably more when he wasn't around than when he was.

"Yeah, yeah. Gimme a rock, will ya?"

Tom still loves his Rolling Rock, even chooses it on somebody else's nickel. Me, I love my Magic Hat. Just to be sociable, I'll suck down some Rocks to keep him company.

"What's the deal?" I asked.

"Cam's been gone four days with no word at all. I got this case that's a bitch, getting pretty heavy. Maybe I got threatened, maybe I didn't. Depends on how you see it."

"Hey, Tom, it's me, Harry. Cut the crap and spill it, okay."

"I got a call last week suggesting a vacation might be in order. Didn't recognize the voice; it traced back to a phone over at the Silver Spring shopping center."

"What exactly did the voice say?" I asked.

Tom took a long pull on his beer before speaking again. "The caller told me to go away for a while and find another case to work on when I got back. Said my kid's more important than that place. Something along those lines, I think."

"Hum," is what came out. When my brain can't come up with anything better to say, that's usually what comes out. Had to cogitate on this one for a few minutes.

"What's the case and how's Cam connected?" I finally asked.

"Cam has nothing to do with it. You know I never involve my kid in my work, never did and never will. Ever. It's a rule I live by and nobody is gonna make me change it."

"I know that, Tom. Forget I mentioned it. Now, how about the case?"

Tom sat back and thought for a few minutes. When he gets into that 'thought process' stage, you let him go until he comes out of it and is ready to talk.

"The reason I called you, other than I wouldn't trust anyone other than you with my work, is the case involves a local insurance company. It's kinda complicated. I'll get some more refreshments and we can get down to talking."

"I'll hit the head." It was gonna be a long night if I had this story pegged right.

Chapter 3

A little history lesson might be in order right about now. Tom found me when I was lost and confused. I had hacked around the East Coast a bit, doing a lot of nothing, none of it good. He was straight with me and me with him. Went something like this...

"Want a job?"

"Yeah."

From the very start, I broke his balls every chance I could and he gave me every crap job that came along. Like in the Karate Kid, I didn't know I was learning anything at all, never mind how to be a private dick. Learn I did, though. He even let me do some investigating on my own. I knew he was watching me, he knew I knew, and I knew he knew I knew. Get that? Now you know, too.

The moral to the story, if there is one, is he pushed my ass so hard I became something in spite of myself. I succeeded and he was, and is, as proud of me as he is of his own kid. I went on my merry way and didn't even say thanks. Didn't have to, Tom knew. I'll never figure out how, but Tom always knows.

Enough already. If it's okay with you, let's find out what's going on.

Chapter 4

We were now set for the evening. Tom's old beat-up hunting cooler was in the middle of the two of us, stocked with Rocks on ice. Fresh one in hand, Tom proceeded.

"This guy had more money than God him/herself (old habit we both seem to use—no sense in taking chances) and couldn't help making more in everything he did. Bought a small insurance company about three or four years ago, proceeded to grow it into a big one. Next he builds a building on Carlisle Pike in Mechanicsburg just past the KFC on Route one fourteen, heading toward Carlisle. Big company needs BTIE's, so he dumps the crew running the show and brings in a whole new management team to make him millions."

"Excuse me for interrupting, but what's a BTIE?" I asked.

"Big Time Insurance Executive was the nickname the old company people made up for the new guys running the circus they created," Tom said.

"Oh," was all I could muster, so I didn't say anything else.

"Gimme the dead one, grab another and shut up and listen for once. Can you do that, Harry?"

"Sure, Tom, you got the floor."

"Anyway, Swindle puts this team in place and tells them to go light the world on fire."

"Sorry again, Tom, but who's Swindle?" I asked.

"That's a good question, Harry. Swindle is the nickname Cam hung on Mister Moneybags. His real name is Windel, Ralph Windel. I hear he splits his time between New York and California running his conglomerate from both coasts. He also has a place in Martinique, wherever that is. One thing is for sure, he's no Mechanicsburg guy. He spent a few hours here a while back, never came back again."

"Cam have a reason for taggin' him with a name like that?" I asked.

"No, just Cam being Cam."

"Okay, go on," I said.

"Anyway, the company kept getting bigger and the guys on top kept getting richer. I heard there was a bundle being thrown around every

Christmas, enough to set me and you up for life. Don't get me wrong, Windel was the real winner."

"So, where do you come in?"

"I'm getting to that, Harry. You never could just sit still and shut your trap, could you?"

"Okay, it's zipped," I promised.

"It seems last year didn't meet with Windel's idea of continued progress. Company lost some money, how much I'm not really sure. It pissed Swindle off big time. Rumor has it the BTIE's got shafted come bonus time and they didn't take too kindly to it. They only came to Mechanicsburg for one reason, to make lots and lots of money. Plus, the President got his nuts in a ringer since he owed the current owners a bundle to close the deal on the Harrisburg Senators sale."

"I didn't hear about that, Tom. The Senators are getting sold?"

"Yeah, right after the end of last season. Very hush, hush. Probably seeing the likes of you in a Bayport Schooner uniform convinced them they needed to get out of the baseball business. Plus, they got top dollar from the New York yahoos looking to play big shot baseball team owners."

"Thought you said the president bought the team?" I asked.

"He was the primary guy. Takes a lotta green to buy a team, Harry. I heard through some guys that two other MechInsCo senior guys went in with him as minority owners to get him to the number they needed. Major payment was due last week, I think. Collins, the prez, he didn't have it, and he had to borrow big time from some New York guys to keep the deal alive."

"Why didn't he let it die?" I inquired.

"Big man from New York, he shot his mouth off in all the papers when the deal was struck. To save face, he ponies up the nut like there was no problem. I hear tell the two other guys are shitting bricks."

"So, where does your case fit into this circus?"

"The company went into a nose dive, spiraled to the point where they were puking red ink. The State Insurance Department is nosing around and the rating agencies are looking at lowering their rating if it continues—whatever in Sam hill that means. I was hired to find out what the hell happened and who caused it. Only problem is, I don't know who hired me."

"Tom, have you gone plain loony? Where's the brains behind that?

What did you teach me—don't ever never work for a man behind a man. I took it to heart and always know who is pointing the finger and paying the tab. Most important, I know why."

"You're right, Harry, I plain screwed up. Maybe I'm getting too old for this. I'm in deep though, and I need to find Cam and figure out what's going on. Can you help, Harry?"

"You know better than to ask a question like that. Let's get something to eat and go from there."

Chapter 5

There's no feeling like being behind the wheel of a true driving machine, all out balls to the wall. I had my Mustang Mach One at a hundred and ten, flying down the road watching the scenery stand still. Gives a guy the opportunity to think clearheaded when he has nothing to do but watch the bugs hit the windshield for several hours. That's what I was doing while I was trying to figure out a game plan to get Tom out of his jam.

Here's the way I see it. Just guessing mind you, but I get paid to guess sometimes. As I often say, keep wandering around bumping into shit. Sooner or later the shit is gonna bump back, or you step in a pile so big you find a clue buried down deep. Private dicks do that, they really do.

Now, where was I? Oh yeah, Tom's problem. Why did the company go into the dumper almost overnight with no explanation? Somebody did something at MechInsCo and covered their tracks pretty well so far. Time to renew my insurance career. And that my friends was a classic Shorts QAS—Question, Answer, Solution. Get used to them, they happen.

* * *

"Hey, Tom, how are ya, my man?" I said into my cell phone.

"Harry, you left here an hour ago. Do you think things could have changed that fast? You better get with it, bud," Tom said.

"Just thinking about what we discussed and wanted to let you know I'm with ya man, until the bitter end."

"I know, Harry, I know. And thanks."

"I'll call you in a day or two when I get it together and I'm ready to head back down. Gotta set up a few things in New York so I can be gone for as long as I need. Cam will turn up any minute now and you can kick his ass. Then be sure and hug him one for me, too. Stay tough."

Chapter 6

"Morning big guy. How's the world's greatest real estate mogul doing on this fine day?" I said.

"Stick it, Harry. You staying for a while, or just stopping by to make my life dog turd miserable? I'm getting used to the peace and quiet around here without you making my life miserable all the time."

"My, my, aren't we in a pleasant mood this morning. A few more outbursts like that and I won't consider you my favorite ex-brother-in-law any longer. My psyche needs stroking to survive in the dark channels I travel through. You're the rock that holds me up in times of need, the cove that shelters me in the worst storm. You're…"

"I'm the guy you owe the rent to, asshole. That's all you should be thinking about right now. And don't run that EBIL bullshit by me again today, or any time this week for that matter. You only have one ex-brother-in-law and your ex-wife is all over my ass because you missed Saturday with the kids. Forget again, did we?"

"For your information, big Mel (oh how he does hate when I call him that) I called the house and talked to the kids on Friday. They were cool with moving it to next Saturday. Ex-wifey pooh was out, which saved me a severe ass-chewing from her royal bitchness. Now, say you're sorry, and make nice, or I'll pout all day."

"You can stick it," Big Mel said looking less than soundly told off.

"I accept your apology," I said. "By the way, what do you know about MechInsCo out of Mechanicsburg, PA?"

"Mech what, from whereburg?" he asked.

"MechInsCo. I think its short for Mechanicsburg Insurance Company. It's located in a little town in Central Pennsylvania not too far from Hershey Park. Bought about four years ago or so by a guy with lots of expendable cash named Ralph Windel."

"Windel of Windel-Woodburn Enterprises?" he asked.

"Don't know for sure. What do you know about the guy?"

"If it's him, he and Jock Woodburn were venture capitalists who hooked up about eight years ago so they would stop banging their heads together trying to grab the same pieces of choice meat. They decided to beat the rest of the world at the buy, build, rape, sell game. The SEC has been after their butts since day one but can't seem to nail them on anything. They make money and crush people's lives, plain and simple."

"You cashing in on their success?" I asked.

"The only people profiting from those two scum buckets are those two scum buckets. By the time working stiffs like me manage to get a sniff they have already completed the strip and burn, or else they pop the IPO and only the institutional insiders get in on the ground floor. Poor little guys like me can only watch and admire their brilliance once again."

"A small favor almighty one; can you check and see if they are the guys who are transforming MechInsCo into a big player. And why?"

"You into something here?" he asked.

"Maybe yes, maybe no. Maybe I dunno. Let's just say I'm returning a long overdue favor."

"OK, I'll check around a bit. Now, fork over the rent"

"Death, taxes and big Mel's rent. Where did I go wrong? Oh yeah, how could I possibly forget about the ex-wife," I said in partial disgust.

Chapter 7

If you watched any of the Crocodile Dundee flicks, you probably heard that cool Aussie guy talk about taking a little 'walk-about'. Translated into our language, it means you hit the road and don't come back for a long time. When my ass got kicked out of baseball for being an A number one fuck-up beyond all belief, I skipped out on my family and took a little walk-about 'round the states. Turned out to be a long walk. The kids don't know any better and don't care. Seems the ex-wife has a different slant on the matter and she has a memory like an elephant.

It was in Arizona that I hooked up with an insurance company, stayed just over a year. Insurance companies are weird places, man. I'd bet the average Joe has no clue what goes on inside an insurance company. An agent sells you a policy that you may, or may not need, and you pay premiums for years. If you're unlucky enough to have a loss—God help you. Getting a claim paid at all is tough enough—getting it taken care of quickly is a pipe dream. It's a game of gimme your dough and I'll hang onto it as long as I can to make investment bucks on your money. A shell game that's legal.

There's a reason I'm wasting your time with this drivel, in case you're wondering. The reason is I'm guessing I'm about to renew my friendship with the world of insurance, and MechInsCo be the place. Strap in kiddos, you ain't seen nothing like the ride we are about to take. If I'm right, and we know I'm almost always right on target some of the time, we are gonna find some interesting things within the confines of MechInsCo's walls. When I turn on the fan, those execs in question had better be wearing brown suits.

Chapter 8

"What's up, Max?" I said to my favorite son. The fact he is my only son doesn't come into play here. "How you doing, and how's that sister of yours?" I continued.

"I'm good, Briande's good, and if I may make the assumption you just forgot to ask—mom's good too. Where are you?"

"Be careful little one. You know what happens when you ASS-U-ME! And for your information, I'm here in town. Got back last night. We still on for Saturday?"

"You bet your lazy-butt we are. Me and Bri have it all planned out, from start to finish."

"That's what I was afraid of. How about a little hint for your lazy-butt dad? Could be worth your while if you come clean up front."

"Nah, don't think so. Spoils all the fun watching you try to guess what we have planned and then trying to weasel out of it. I think I'll pass for now."

Not your typical little wise-aleck kid's response, but he learned a bit too much from the master, I think. Maybe I should have kept him in the dark as to the ways of devious minded sneaks like me. Wait till he gets to be a full fledged teenager. I'm in for a rough ride.

"OK squirt, see ya on Saturday. How's nine o'clock sound?"

"Nine's fine. Can't wait to see ya again. Bye," and he was off.

* * *

The kids get to choose what we do on our once-a-month Saturday excursions. It gives me a chance to spend some 'quality time' with them, whatever that is supposed to be. There's no definition for it I could ever find. For me it just means I get to have fun with the kids I neglected for a real long time—make it up to them in a small way. They get it, and appreciate it, when I make the effort. Least a past dead-beat dad can do.

Question is—what am I in for this time?

Chapter 9

"Tom, it's Harry. Anything happening?"

"Harry, man, thanks for calling. I don't understand why he hasn't called yet. Just like you said, I put the word out on the street that I was off the case. Did it yesterday morning with a couple guys I trust and I've gotten feedback already. The man in front of the man gave me a ration for backing out on the deal."

"Did you run down the Reader's Digest version of our plan to him?" I asked.

"Yeah, and he said he had to get the okay from the big guy. Harry, I hope you got this pegged right, cause if you don't, we both could be in big trouble. I just wish Cam would call already."

"Tom, you know I can't give you any guarantees. If I was still a betting man I'd take the odds on this one. Not a six to five favorite, but way short of a long shot, too. Don't worry, Cam will roll in the front door any minute, and just like I told ya last time we discussed this, you can kick his ass but good. And, like I said before, give him another of them big hugs for me, too. Trust me, okay?"

"Harry, I don't have much choice, do I?"

"Well, Tom, I guess you don't. Unless some brainstorm invaded that thick head of yours overnight, we go with what we discussed and agreed on. I'll be heading down on Sunday morning. Gotta do the kids thing on Saturday and get myself together for a long stay-away. Remain cool kiddo, it's gonna be fine."

* * *

All I have to do now is convince myself as well. If anything happens to that kid Tom will never survive. Save the kid, save the man. Boy, am I in a tough spot; but that's why I get the big bucks. Trouble is I ain't getting paid for this gig, and never would have taken the job if it wasn't for the man that straightened out my miserable life.

I feel bad for the assholes who are gonna be sorry they ever messed with Tom and his friend for life.

Chapter 10

"You look particularly fetching this morning my sweet little thing," I said to Ms. Bunny Malone, secretary make-believe and newly named assistant to big Mel.

"Harry, I'm glad to see you again. We miss your silly face when you go away. And I miss some other things, too," she said blushing.

Ms. Malone's skills as they relate to her position in the working world are, to put it mildly, in question. I don't believe I have ever seen her type anything of any substance and her filing skills could be matched by a drunken one-armed chimpanzee. Transposing numbers, if she remembers to give you a phone message at all, is commonplace, with absolutely no chance of the name having anything to do with the person who called. I can hear you asking. 'What in the world is she doing there?'

At the very moment you were thinking that very thought, Big Mel got off the phone and yelled over to Bunny to get him some folders and paper clips.

I present Exhibit One for the defense of her employment, your honor—Ms. Bunny Malone bending over to get the folders and paper clips from the bottom drawer of the filing cabinet. If your honor will notice, the filing cabinet is strategically placed equidistant between Big Mel and myself for our perfect viewing pleasure. Exhibit Two, your honor, is a close up of Ms. Malone's long shapely legs leading to a fine looking ass, if I do say so myself. Speaking as an expert witness for the defense, one who has personal and rather intimate knowledge of afore-mentioned personal attributes, it is no optical illusion, but the real deal.

Your honor, need we go on? I thought not. The defense rests, but not for long if lead counsel has his way.

"Hey, Bunny, I gotta go outta town for a while and was wondering if you could look after my place for me while I'm gone?"

"How long you going for this time, Harry? It seems like you just got back from your last trip."

"Don't know for sure yet, but it looks like it could be a long one. Perhaps we should stop by my place so I can make sure there isn't anything you aren't familiar with."

"Harry, from my last spin through your place, I'm as familiar as I can be with everything that happens in your place. But, no reason to take any chances, if you catch my drift," Ms. Malone said.

The defense would like to request a continuance your honor to allow counsel the proper time to thoroughly interrogate this witness. And trust me your honor, if your honor was present during this particular interrogation, you would no doubt be drop-dead mouth open astonished.

Thank you your honor, counsel is in your debt.

"Bunny, permit me to show you the way."

I knew full well she didn't need any showing, but it sounded like the thing to say.

Mel just shook his head in continued wonderment.

Chapter 11

Manhasset, New York was still my home base, but lately I seem to find myself away from home way too much. The reason I hightailed it back from parts unknown was to get back with my kids and try to give them a father to kick around when they needed. The plan was working, and would be cool, if I could just stay in town a bit more often.

Away from home was where I was presently headed again, probably for an extended period of time. Funny what you do to pass the time when you're stuck in your car with four hours and nothing but road ahead of you. It was Sunday morning, and like it or not, I was headed back to Nowheresville, Pennsylvania to get Tom's butt out of hot water. My mind was wandering over the past four days of activities. Real funny what you remember when you're not trying to. Not ha-ha funny, but odd funny—you know what I mean.

Exploratory endeavors aside, Bunny's cool with watching my place while I'm gone on my extended assignment. Unfortunately, I missed seeing my neighbor Mrs. Taylor, or Sandy as she prefers I call her. She and I have this mutually beneficial agreement that satisfies our needs and requires no strings attached. Same place, same time kinda arrangement. Gonna miss her a little.

Plus her kid, who happens to be home from college, is looking foxier every time I see her. Mother and daughter together—gotta put that one in definite memory storage for future use.

Hey, I said my memory storage, not yours. Picture your own weird fantasy world stuff if you don't mind.

Even though he can be a real dick, big Mel understands I love my kids and will watch out for them and my ex, their mom. Kinda weird relationship he and I have, but it works for us, so we're not about to break it. As long as I pay the rent that is. No rent and I'd be the same as any other dead-beat schmuck.

My mind flashed on yesterday and my day with the kids and I couldn't help but smile. Same routine as always; they have become true creatures of habit. Sometimes they are just creatures, but not on our Saturday excursions.

I picked them up exactly at nine in front of their house. I actually got a wave from Sherry, the mother of my kids and ex-sweetie to yours truly. At least I think she was waving. She could have been giving me the finger now that I think about it. Either way, I didn't get yelled at and it didn't cost me any money.

We were on our way.

"Where to, oh wee little ones? And, by the way, you guys ain't so little any more. Maybe you should be contributing to some portion of these fantasy island jaunts once in a while."

"Try that one again when you hit the pillow tonight, dad," said little Max. "Sounds like you're dreaming while you're still awake."

The day went uphill all the way from that point on. My favorite daughter Briande got her wish and ice skating at Rockefeller Center was our first stop of the day. Max really wasn't psyched about that part, but he was cool and he had some fun when this small group of honey-buns about his age showed up. He's gonna take after his old man I think, which hasn't always proved to be a good thing. Oh well, a teenager has to do what a teenager has to do.

"Hey Max, keep it in your shorts," I kidded him.

"Oh yeah, I saw you chatting up their moms over there. Didn't see the banana in your pocket when you picked us up. Must have come with the rental skates."

"At least I have a shot. All you'll get is your mom yelling at you to get out of the shower," I chided.

The rest of the day included a trip to FAO Schwartz, where the three of us ran around like kids in a candy store with a fistful of quarters. Even me. I just love the place. Dinner at the ESPN Zone was Max's choice. Briande was the hit of the rich kid's birthday party she somehow got herself invited to ten minutes after we arrived. The kids are definitely growing up way too fast. Or maybe I'm just enjoying them so much I don't want them to ever grow up. Anyway, we had a blast of a day as usual and they got home right on schedule.

Gonna have to hold me over, cuz I'm off on my mission to save my friend and his only son.

Chapter 12

My everyday car is an ancient Datsun B210 HoneyBee that actually has a HoneyBee painted on the side. I think it's totally cool. The kids hate to even be seen in it. Too bad on them. The Mach I wouldn't be the right wheels for some shit bum nobody working in the finance department of a nowhere Insurance Company. The HoneyBee is a cool ride if you enjoy low-end get where you need to go transportation. And, which I might add is most important, the chicks think its way cool, too.

That was what I was driving as I tooled into beautiful downtown Mechanicsburg, Pennsylvania early Sunday afternoon. Wanted to get a good look around before I went by Tom's place and started this job for keeps. If you worked as hard as you possibly could, you might spend an hour getting acquainted with the surroundings. After fifteen minutes, you know you ain't seen nothing and won't be increasing the load any time soon. Local folk place for Central PA local folk. Tom fits in real well.

"How they hanging old fella?" is how I started my conversation with Tom as he opened his front door. He did have that relieved look on his face one gets when the world finally gives you a break and the 400 pound gorilla jumps down off your shoulders.

"Harry, you are the man. Get your ass in here and let's wet our whistles."

Tom reminded me, as I have often stated, "It is always cocktail time somewhere in the world."

As we headed for the kitchen and a few whistle-wetters, Cam came from the back of the house and gave me a, 'What are you doing here?' look. He didn't seem fazed one bit. I needed to get the lowdown on what, where and the rest, but it could wait.

"Cam, good to see ya, kiddo. How you been?" I asked him.

"All's cool with me, Harry. Been away a bit hanging with some new dudes, just got back. Dad's bummin' me and I told him to ease up. You ain't gonna do me hard too, are ya?" Cam asked.

"Hey kiddo, we're buds. Buds don't rock. We're cool," I answered.

With that Cam was off and me and Tom sat down to get our bearings straight. I needed to know where Cam was while he was missing and who he was with. I needed to know where Tom backing out of his deal stood and what the word on the street was. I needed to know how I was gonna get into MechInsCo and how Tom had managed to fix it. I was in possession of a boatload of 'need to knows' and didn't want to know any of them right now.

No choice, so we got it going from right where we had left off. As we talked, or as Tom talked and I absorbed, the old I-don't-give-a-damn attitude was gone from his voice and probably from his life. You could just tell he didn't have it in him anymore. Maybe it was Cam, maybe it was this case, and maybe it was the accumulation of all the cases and all the years, but something or someone had beat Tom down for the last time. His investigating days were kaput and I had the feeling he knew it.

As I listened, I hoped I would never come to this point, never have to admit I didn't have it in me anymore. What does a washed-up private dick do when his spying days are over? Not much he can do. Ever wonder who the old guys doing the graveyard shift in some hell-hole of a warehouse are—that's right—washed up private dicks. Not me, man. No way, not ever gonna happen.

Like Tom does with Cam, I'm gonna have to take him for what he is and love him even harder.

Chapter 13

The entire army done hopped on my face, pried open my pie-hole, and marched down my throat, dragging their mangy dogs along with them. The inside of my mouth tasted like crap and some real bad heavy metal rock band was doing their thing inside my head with the volume pumped up big-time. Slowly the prior day and night came back to me and the reason for feeling like I did became very clear. Tom and I had tied on a doozy and I don't even remember how I got back to the apartment I was renting.

Not good, my kiddos, not good at all.

A long alternating hot and cold shower, what seemed like a gallon of scalding black coffee, plus a half dozen Advil didn't help. I still felt like warmed-over dog puke. No problem though, I wasn't planning on going anywhere today. I needed to replay the events of this case over and over through my mind to make sure I had all the facts straight. When that's done, I do it all over again. Makes me concentrate on each event and period of time as if it was happening in my head at that very moment.

Weird you say. You're right. But it works for me and I'm the guy with his ass on the line. One small detail forgotten, however seemingly insignificant at the time, can blow your chances of cracking a case. Plus, it sharpens the mind and hones the keen P.I. skills I possess.

Enough you say—okay, I'll stop.

Say thank you.

You're welcome.

When all is said and done after running what I know multiple times in my mind, I still don't have a clue what's going on. No brilliant deductions came from my mental gymnastics, just more pounding in my already damaged cranial area. Tomorrow, I'm off to start my infiltration of MechInsCo.

See ya then.

Chapter 14

I was up bright and early and ready for my new position in life—some meaningless little job in the finance department of a questionable insurance company. Jumped into the HoneyBee and off I went. While motoring down Silver Spring Road towards the Carlisle Pike, I figured a recap might be in order. Good to know some details if asked.

Tom's connection got me the spot as a favor to a friend of a friend. Didn't give me much to work with, and I figured I'd play it that way— friend helping out a new guy in town. Sooner or later I'd get a handle on who the inside connection was and that might help. Or maybe it wouldn't—for now, I'll just improvise and see where it leads me.

Made a left onto Carlisle Pike and kept on going across Route 114. A little bit later I made a right into the MechInsCo entrance and parked in the visitor's parking lot. I hadn't started yet, so I was technically a visitor—plus the spots were right by the front door. Why hoof it from the back of the lot when you don't have to.

The MechInsCo building was impressive, but didn't compare with the other local insurance company's palatial digs I had just passed at the corner of Carlisle Pike and Route 114. Philco I think it's called. I'll have to settle for second best for now—but I'll have to check that place out before long. No good reason other than curiosity, of which, as you already know, I possess copious amounts.

* * *

Upon entering the building, my day brightened immeasurably. The main lobby was designed to impress and sitting at the main reception desk was a thing of beauty. Long blonde hair and the cutest face you ever saw. The closer I got, and the more I saw, I realized the whole package was worth ogling over.

"Morning," finally came out of my mouth when I realized I was standing in front of Miss Goldilocks, staring and not saying anything.

It's not like Harry Mickey Shorts to be mesmerized, but this one had me.

"Good morning to you, sir, and welcome to MechInsCo," she said. The smile fit the face perfectly.

"My name is Harry Mickey Shorts. I have an appointment with Mister Millwood in the Human Resources department," I said.

"I do have your name here, Mister Shorts. Please sign in and have a seat. I'll let Mister Millwood know you're here."

"Thank you Miss…" I let hang in the air as I looked down to put my John Hancock in the sign-in log. Unfortunately, the phone rang at the same time and Miss Shall-Remain-Nameless answered it.

I wandered over to the reception area and sat down, picked up the new Sports Illustrated off the end table, and waited for Mister Millwood.

Chapter 15

My mother always told me patience was a virtue, and to the best of my ability, I try to relax and enjoy life if I am required to wait. After enjoying forty-five minutes of my life, and relaxing less and less as time went by, my patience was quickly running out. Without having met the man, Mister Millwood had managed to piss me off royally.

"Mister Shorts, Mister Millwood will see you now."

Seems his assistant, who I later learned was Nancy Cross, was sent to fetch me.

"If you will follow me, I'll show you to his office," she said.

"I'm right behind you, and please call me Harry," I said. "May I ask you a question?"

"Surely, Mister Shorts. What can I assist you with?"

I gathered she didn't hear my offer to call me Harry.

"The young lady at the reception desk looks very familiar. Would you mind telling me her name?"

"She has that affect on most young men who come into our building. They all seem to think that she looks familiar for some reason. She is a very popular young lady, indeed. And for your information, it's Crissy, Crissy Metzger."

Unless I was mistaken, and I don't believe I was, Crissy wasn't one of Ms. Cross' favorite employees at MechInsCo. Didn't faze me none, she was one of mine, or at least I hoped she would be real soon.

"Mister Millwood, Mister Shorts is here to see you," she said as I entered Millwood's office.

"Have a seat, Shorts. Mind if I call you Harry?" Millwood asked.

No "I'm sorry to have kept you waiting," or, "Were you waiting long?"

"Harry will be just fine, Mister Millwood," I replied as cordially as I could be. No reason to jump ugly with the guy the first time I meet him. Plus, I didn't know who was on which side of the good-guy bad-guy fence and he might prove to be useful down the road.

"I don't know why the additional position was created while we have a hiring freeze on, but it was. I was told to create it and give it to you, no questions asked. The job is budget analyst working in the finance department for Joe Stoner—his third damn budget analyst by the way."

"That so," I said.

Millwood looked at me with a gaze that could kill. "You know anything about budgets or insurance finances, Shorts?"

"That so," I said just to piss him off.

Guess calling me Harry went out the window with his manners.

"I don't need this, I just plain don't," he said to himself, shaking his head, looking totally disgusted.

"Nancy," he yelled, "tell Stoner his new budget analyst is on the way up and then point Shorts in the general direction."

When she was gone, he turned to me. "Now get your ass out of my office."

I did as instructed and didn't even get a smile from Ms. Crissy Metzger as I followed Nancy passed the reception desk to the elevator bank.

Don't let anybody ever tell you Harry Mickey Shorts doesn't know how to make a killer first impression.

Chapter 16

"He's not normally like that," Nancy Cross said to me as we waited for the elevator.

"I hope not. Tough attitude for somebody who's supposed to be in the people business," I said.

"Things were fine when we first got down here from New York. Timothy's usually a fun person to be around and a consummate professional. This last year has taken its toll on him," she said.

So, all things point toward Millwood being one of the New York yahoos brought in to run the company.

"May I ask you a question …?" I was starting to say when the elevator door opened and Ms. Cross walked away without saying another word. What set Millwood off would have to wait for the time being. I'll have to explore the Timothy, not Mister Millwood, angle as well. Another piece of the puzzle with lots of detecting needed.

The building was three floors, not including the basement. The finance department was on the second floor, and if the company was set up like most corporate offices, the executives would be on the third.

Out of the elevator, a turn to the left, then all the way to the end of the hall. A right turn, then straight ahead brought me to my destination—Mary Ann Williams, Stoner's assistant. Following directions isn't always my strong suit, but I managed this time.

"Hi there, I'm Harry Mickey Shorts. I believe Mister Stoner is expecting me," I said.

She gave me the deer-in-the-headlights look. "Mister Stoner has someone in his office at the moment. If you will have a seat, he will be right with you."

I didn't know why, but Mary Ann seemed pretty flustered at that moment. Also, having a seat was gonna be a problem, since her desk was surrounded by several cubicles and a small bit of open space. There were no chairs anywhere to be seen.

Now, hanging out in front of a twenty-something chickamarita normally doesn't bother me much, but you could just feel the electric tension in the air. The reason was soon very apparent when Stoner's door suddenly burst open.

"And you better get your act in order, pronto. Don't make me have to come down here again to clean up your mess, or next time it will be your ass I kick out the god-damn door. You can count on it, Stoner!"

"Move, asshole," was my initial introduction to Dominick Phillips, MechInsCo's Senior Vice President and Chief Financial Officer, as he stormed past me and disappeared around the corner.

"Sure thing, big guy," I said as he blew by, but I don't think he heard me.

Stoner appeared in his doorway, his face white as a ghost. Mary Ann Williams was frozen in place at her desk, her face looking like she had probably just shit herself. Harry Mickey Shorts, world class ace detective, was wondering what he had gotten himself into.

All in all, not a bad first couple of hours on the job.

Chapter 17

After about ten minutes, Joe Stoner's face had recovered the majority of its color and his hands were barely shaking. Mary Ann had cleaned up the puddle of water off his desk—seems the act of getting the glass of water Mary Ann had given him from the desk to his lips proved too much for him to handle. Mary Ann wasn't walking funny, so I guess she hadn't shit herself after all.

"I can come back later if you would prefer," I offered.

I had been sitting in front of his desk while he attempted to recover from Phillip's verbal assault. Joe was somewhere in his late thirties or early forties, and I hoped like hell he wasn't gonna have a heart attack and die right there.

"No, Harry, that's all right. Just give me another minute. Mister Phillip's has a way of upsetting me, and I guess no matter how many times it happens, I'll never get used to the New York way of dealing with things. You would think going on twenty years of dedicated service to the company would mean something. It is Harry, isn't it?"

"Harry it is," I replied.

"Thanks," Stoner said.

"Why don't you let your assistant point me toward the person I'll be working for. That way I can let you have some more time to regroup, and we can talk later," I offered.

"Under any other circumstances I would accept your kind offer. Unfortunately, in the midst of 'cleaning up my mess' as Mister Phillips so aptly put it, he fired Barb Mueller, the supervisor you would have been reporting to."

Joe Stoner was visibly upset, either by the actual firing of his employee, or his embarrassment at having to relay that fact to me. Plus, I witnessed the tail end of a nasty episode with Phillips. Add it all up, very bad scene for Joe Stoner, especially in front of a new employee.

"How's this sound? Mary Ann points me to my workstation, or cubicle, or whatever you call it here. You have time to get it together, Mary Ann goes back to her desk and gets herself glued straight, and then I go get a cup of coffee and wander around staying out of everybody's hair for about an hour or so."

"That will work, Harry. Sorry for the initial impression you must have of me and this company. A little more time will probably do me some good. I'd offer to take you to lunch, but I think I have to unruffle a few feathers and soothe some nerves in the department. Let's get together again this afternoon. OK?"

"Good deal," I said.

"Mary Ann," Joe called. "Would you please show Harry to the desk next to Larry and then come back here for a minute?"

"Yes sir, Mister Stoner," Mary Ann replied.

Mary Ann showed and I followed, and if you did have to follow somebody, Mary Ann would do any time. Wheels weren't bad and she had that back and forth wiggle to her ass. She was no Crissy Metzger, but since I hadn't had the opportunity to follow Crissy anywhere yet, I'll reserve final judgment on the issue.

This place was getting wackier by the minute, and I had the feeling it would get much worse before it got better.

Chapter 18

That night we were sitting in Tom's basement sucking down some suds as I recapped my first day at MechInsCo for him. I started with my meeting with Millwood and went on from there.

"'Move, asshole,' was exactly what this sucker Dominick Phillips said as he blew past me. Never met him before and I don't think it would have mattered if I had," I told Tom.

"I didn't run into him while I was looking into things. I did jaw with Joe Stoner for a while. Of course, I already knew him from the lodge."

"Opinion? Lodge?" I asked.

Tom thought for a few seconds. "Don't really think he could be a player in this game. Local guy who worked his way up from the bottom—small potatoes compared to the New York schmucks. Not the sharpest tool in the shed, either, if you catch my drift."

"That came across when he and I got back together later in the afternoon," I said. "He had calmed down, but he was royally pissed at the verbal brow-beating he had taken from Phillips. Wasn't the first time either from the way Stoner lovingly referred to him as 'That Prick' Phillips."

Tom just nodded.

"What about Millwood. Ring any bells?" I asked.

"Name sounds familiar, but I didn't have any direct contact with him, or talk to anybody that mentioned him," Tom said.

"Ever hear anything about this Phillips dude?" I asked.

"Just saw the name on the list of executives I was given when I first started the case."

"Do you still have the list?" I asked him. "Would be helpful to know who the rest of the New York players are should I run into them."

"It's around here somewhere," Tom said. "I'll have to look. But I can run down a few of the big honchos for you from memory if you want."

"That would help for starters," I said. "I'll get us a few more cool ones while you rack that brain of yours for the top couple of guys. Don't strain yourself now."

"Fuck you and the HoneyBee you rode in on, Harry," he said with a laugh.

Got four cold Rocks from the fridge Tom had in the other room and sat down to go over the names he had scribbled on a paper napkin.

"The president's name is Paul Collins and he's supposed to be one tough sonofabitch. Phillips you met and you already know he's an asshole. Don't know if it meant anything, but his name was listed second after the top guy's name. The two other guys I remember are the marketing guy, Bob Givens, and the head claims guy, whose name is Randy Hobbers, I think. The lawyer chick's name I can't remember, but I think she's local material."

"That's great, Tom. It's a start and gives me a heads up as I snoop around the company."

"I'll find the full list and get it to you," Tom said.

"Good man. Also, it's about time I sat down with Cam and got his story straight. His little trip may come into play in this fiasco, and I better be prepared for anything."

"Sure, Harry. I may not like involving him any more than I have to, but I understand. How about some dinner tomorrow? Then you can catch up with Cam afterward."

"Sounds like a plan, Tom," I said. "I'll drop over around six and we can chow down then."

The food was gonna be good. Tom had learned how to put a decent spread on the table when he wanted to. Cam was gonna be another story, and I wasn't sure at all what to expect.

Driving back to my temporary home, listening to some old Jethro Tull to cheer me up, a Shorts QAS that had been meandering around inside my head finally crystallized. How am I gonna get the inside dirt at MechInsCo that I need to point me in some kind of a direction? Identify the person who has the best source of info within. Use the old Shorts charms to get it, as only Harry can.

Chapter 19

"Good morning, Crissy. How are you today?" I inquired as I approached the reception desk at MechInsCo for my second day of fun and games. Who better to know all the goods and the bads at MechInsCo than my current favorite receptionist, of course.

"You decided to come back after yesterday's activities, Mister Shorts?" Crissy asked.

"First, it's Harry, not Mister Shorts. Shame on you. Second, and most important of all, you're here, aren't you? Of course I'd come back. And third, lunch at noon; you get to pick the place."

Was that utterly charming, or what?

"First, Harry it is, and shame can be a real good thing at times. Second, I am here, and I had no doubt you'd come back. And third, lunch at twelve-thirty, and you bet your ass I'm picking the place, that is if I hear a pretty please," she said with a smile.

"How's pretty please with sugar on top?" I tried.

"That will do, and sugar sure does like it on top!" she smiled.

Harry Mickey Shorts was on a definite big-time roll and loving every minute of it. Unfortunately, somebody got in the way.

"Hey, Shorts, what the hell do you think you're doing?"

"And a good morning to you, Tim babe," I said in reply.

"Did I hear you right? Did you refer to me as 'Tim babe' just now?" Millwood said in obvious amazement.

Crissy was doing all she could not to piss her pants behind the reception desk.

"That would be correct, and in answer to your question, I was saying good morning to the company receptionist, Crissy. Have you two met?"

"Don't wise-ass me, Shorts. And, it's Mister Millwood to you."

"Sure, Tim, and you are going to have to learn the good morning thing. Everybody does it you know."

As the steam seeped out of Millwood's ears, I took off for the stairs as fast as I could. The sound of Crissy's laughter filled the halls as I made my getaway to freedom, and continued employment, I hoped.

I had no doubt lunch was gonna be a blast.

Chapter 20

Joe Stoner was in his office when I got to the finance department. He had probably been there since 7:00 am like he always was, from what I heard.

"Morning, Mary Ann. Joe available?" I asked.

"Morning, Harry." She smiled. "He's just finishing up a call and said you should go right in when you got here."

"How is he this morning?" I asked.

"He's still smarting over Barb getting fired. He doesn't know who's going to do her work, and Mister Phillips already gave him 'what for' this morning. Other than that, he's just great, I guess."

She wasn't smiling any more.

I went into Joe's office and copped a squat while he finished his call. We had started to go over what I was gonna do yesterday afternoon, but he got interrupted by somebody from the third floor who needed something immediately. Too bad, cuz he didn't have it, and a bad day got even worse for him.

"Morning, Harry. Sorry about yesterday afternoon. When the big guys yell, we all scoot like hell, no matter what," Joe said.

"How'd it go?" I tried.

"Oh, as usual, I caught holy hell for something that wasn't due until next week. It doesn't matter to Mister Collins if it was supposed to be ready or not. You didn't have what he wanted, so, you're a shithead. His favorite word, only it normally follows dumb, fucking."

"Phillips set the date?" I asked, although I already figured the answer was gonna be yes.

"Ah, what?" Joe said, somewhat confused. "Oh yeah, he did," he said when he realized what I was asking.

"Okay, let's forget Phillips, Collins and the rest of the big guys. What can I do to help?"

"Harry, how much do you know about budgeting, forecasting and management reporting?" Joe asked. He had this 'please say you know something' look on his face.

"Well, I could tell you I'm a dumb, fuckin' shithead who knows nothing about budgeting, forecasting and management reporting and I'm really here to accelerate your downward march into hell. I won't now, but I might add it later. I actually spent some time doing just that for an Arizona company; and, I might add, got pretty good at it."

"Don't play with me, Harry," Joe said.

"Hey, I'm not playing with you, Joe," I told him. "After yesterday, I'd have to be a real prick to mess with your head."

"Sorry, I'm still a little defensive, I guess," Joe said. "I'll hook you up with one of my people and they can give you the lay of the land, show you how we do things up here. Feel free to offer suggestions and let's get you in the flow right away. We can use all the help we can get."

"Done," I told him. "Just point me toward your problems and I'll get right on them. I specialize in figuring out stuff that baffles the normal human being and maybe I can *whodo* some of the same magic here."

"I hope you can Harry, I hope you whodo can, or whatever the hell you're talking about."

Chapter 21

Same old shit, in a same old accounting department, in a same old insurance company, in a different same old town. My initial introduction to MechInsCo's accounting world didn't shed any light on what was causing the problems they had encountered, or where they came from. Maybe tomorrow, maybe the next day, but sooner or later I'd find it.

* * *

Lunch, my friends, was a whole different story—no same old at all. Ms. Crissy Metzger, receptionist and looker extraordinaire, proved to be a trip unto herself.

"Twelve twenty nine and thirty seconds. You were almost right on time," she said as I ambled on up to the front desk.

"I would have been here fifteen seconds ago, but I didn't want to seem too eager to be in your company, Ms. Metzger," I answered as I handed her a single white long stem rose.

"Let's get a few things straight, Shorts. One, Ms. Metzger is the General Counsel at MechInsCo and Crissy Metzger is me—call me Crissy. Two, white's nice but I prefer red in roses and wine. Not blush— I very rarely do. And three…"

I waited.

She waited.

I figured it out and said, "Let's go find out what three will bring."

"Yes, let's," she replied, and we proceeded to do just that.

Ruby Tuesday's proved to be the place of choice for an amazing hour that seemed to go by in an absolute flash. Her mom actually is the General Counsel at MechInsCo. She got Crissy the job after she had traveled the country and abroad for a while after graduating from high school. No obvious burning ambition meant no college, no job, and a bit of a 'walk about.' It was like déjà vu all over again for me—two kindred spirits being tossed together by a smart-aleck God to relive a past gone by. We laughed and laughed until the people around us started laughing even though they didn't know why. Real light stuff on a who-you who-me lunch that made me remember there is fun in this world, and shit doesn't always have to happen. A beautiful thing was beginning to unfold in the life of one Harry Mickey Shorts.

* * *

And the preacher raised up his arms to the heavens above, his booming voice heard by all near and far, as he proclaimed for all who would listen, "And the Lord brought forth to this earth on a glorious day, one child of the heavens and universe, so as to bring joy and happiness to one man—and he called her Crissy Metzger…"

Could have happened you know.

Chapter 22

Tom does this veal and peppers dish he knows I'd kill for. He made it that night and had some dynamite garlic/cheese bread to go with it. I brought a case of Rocks and we ate and enjoyed some time like we used to. Even Cam seemed to go with the flow. When we were done, Tom started to clean up while me and Cam went out on the back deck to hang for a while. It was time to find out what was going on from a different perspective.

"So, how you been?" I asked him.

"Been good, been bad, been," he said. "Dad keeps pushing me to get it together and do something, but I don't know what I wanna do, man. It's like I gotta let it happen to let it happen the way it should. You know, Harry?"

"Yeah, I know, Cam. Been there and done that, and it comes to us all sooner or later. He's just worried you've been drifting for too long and running with the wrong dudes. You're gonna get your ass in a sling once too often and he won't be able to bail you out. You know, kiddo?"

"Can't see it yet, Harry. Gotta keep doing what I'm doing for now."

"You will, Cam, you will."

It was kinda cold, but not so we couldn't hang for a bit longer. It was time. I figured the best way was to leave it open ended and started by saying, "Tell me about the new dudes you hung with for a couple of days."

"Just some oddies that happened and we hung," Cam said.

"Oddies?" I asked.

"Yeah, odd dudes who shouldn't a been where they were. Older than us and never been to the pool hall before. Odd, man. We talked, they said they were gonna party, we split."

"They say where they were from?" I asked.

"No, never asked and they never spilled. Just jumped in the van and headed for the mountains to get down. Kicked it with some heavy hemp and never stopped for couple of days, man. Don't know if I was stoned, or drunk, or both half the time. Some chicks showed and we got down, I think. Kinda all blurry like, you know?"

"How many guys?" I asked.

"Three first, and then one at the cabin who brought the chicks. Weird dude taking pictures all the time, not partying down much. Older, big guy, not like the other dudes. Chicks were all dynamite though, round my age."

"Catch any names?" I asked.

"Nah, just hey man and party on dude. Weren't from around here— sounded like you, and talked about heading back north. They fronted, I partied. Nuff said, man."

"That's cool, Cam. Your dad just wants to know where you are and that you are all right. If you think of anything else, yell at me, okay?"

"I'm down, dude," he said.

* * *

With that, Cam split, and I went back inside to warm up and cool down with a Rock. Interesting approach. All this would have added up to trouble for Cam and Tom if Tom hadn't decided to heed their warning and shut down his investigation. Weed, booze, and whatnot, most likely underage girlie-girls with lots of pictures to show what went down. Stuff Tom doesn't need to know or be bothered with right now. Maybe never, I hope.

We hung for a bit, had a few cool ones, and then I split for home. With the new information I had gathered from my conversation with Cam, I think I may need to re-evaluate the level of competition a little. Better safe than sorry, but better never sorry.

Chapter 23

"Morning Crissy." I strolled into MechInsCo the following morning, struttin' and flashing the famous Shorts smile. Never pass up an opportunity to dazzle and score points. "You are looking especially lovely this morning."

"Aren't we in a good mood," she answered with a smile.

"Just the pleasure of seeing you could brighten up anyone's day," I said.

"The pleasure will really begin when you pick me up at seven tonight," she whispered.

Not again! Out-one-lined by a young damsel is not what the master is used to, rendering Harry Mickey Shorts temporarily lost for words. But not for long!

"The pleasure will be all yours before the night is done," I said as I walked down the hall.

Minor save, but it will have to do.

* * *

Mary Ann caught me as I strolled into the accounting department with that, *'Sorry to have to tell you,'* look on her face.

"What's up, kiddo?" I asked.

"Harry, the eh…you have to, eh…she wants to see you, eh…" she stammered.

"Mary Ann, who is the she and where is this she? Am I supposed to go see the 'she' now?"

"She's up there with the executives on the executive floor. It's the General Counsel, Harry. Ms. Metzger."

"No problem, Mary Ann. I'll go up there to the dreaded executive floor right now," I told her. "And Mary Ann, take a deep breath and don't worry, I'll be fine."

Crissy's mom, big time General Counsel of MechInsCo, wants to see Harry Mickey Shorts, low level accounting putz. Couldn't be the old 'Mom watching over the young daughter trick,' now could it? Only one way to find out.

"Harry Shorts for Ms. Metzger," I announced as I appeared at the desk of the General Counsel's executive assistant.

HMS observation if I may. Nobody's a plain old secretary any more. We have your executive assistants, your administrative assistants, your assistant to the president, vice president, assistant vice president or assistant to any other version of a fake executive you can muster. But, no 'secretary' to be found anywhere. Thanks, I needed that.

"I don't know who you are, and I absolutely didn't call and ask for you," was the indignant reply from one Candy Anderson, EA to the GC.

For your information, that was hip Harry Shorts with the happening insurance lingo.

Now, the vision that popped into my head was The Rock standing over her desk, glaring that menacing glare he does, saying, "Get your Candy-Ass outta my way before I lay some Smack-Down Whoop-Ass on your sorry–assed butt!"

Me, Harry Mickey Shorts, reserved and dignified private detective in disguise, I just smiled.

"So," she said with a scowl as I continued to smile.

"So," I said, "please get up, walk over to the GC's door and tell her I'm here. If not, I'll just walk right on in and you can explain to the GC why I barged into her office unannounced. Now, pick one, kiddo!" I calmly replied.

Nice shade of red. A Candy-Red you might say. A face that showed mondo indignation and a bit of, 'Who do you think you are and how dare you,' to go along with it.

"That will be fine, Candy. I'll see Mister Shorts," came a voice from the door to the GC's office.

I went in.

Chapter 24

In a word—WOW! Momma Metzger made Crissy look like the ugly duckling in the family. On the tall side, long blond hair down to her ass done up in a French braid. Legs that wouldn't quit. The kind a blind man couldn't help but notice as she sashayed back to her desk after we shook hands at the door. Funky little design on one of her well-manicured fingernails, and a tiny rose tattooed on her ankle. Observant private eye doing his observing thing. And, before I forget to mention, a body that could end a war. And legs, did I mention the legs? Yeah, I think I did—but they absolutely deserve a second mention.

"Thank you for coming up so promptly, Mister Shorts," she said.

"My pleasure, Madame General Counsel," I replied.

The look I got for that comment was one I couldn't place, but I know I'd seen it before, and it wasn't good.

"My name is Madeline Metzger. My friends call me Maddy. You will call me Ms. Metzger, not Madame General Counsel. Straight, Shorts?"

A mediocre start I'd say.

"And I didn't call you up here so you could compare me to my daughter, as you seem to have chosen to do."

A slight dip downhill I think.

"From top to bottom," she continued.

Oops crossed my mind at this time.

"That being said, it does a woman's heart good to know she can still turn an eye now and again," finished her thought. "Even in a young man such as yourself."

Reverse course, gondola to the summit was my new train of thought.

"Beauty is a thing to behold," I tried, "and I have been known to be holding now and then."

"Two things, Mister Shorts, in language you can understand," she said through the faint smile I seemed to have brought to her face. "If you 'be holding' Crissy, you be careful. Be very careful. She is very important to me."

"I hear you loud and clear," I replied.

"And two, Mister Trundle sends his regards, and suggests you remember to never underestimate the players in the game. Those you can see, as well as those you can't."

Before I could get a word out she continued. "And I'm quite busy, so go off and do something useful for the company. I'm sure we will see each other again, don't you agree, Mister Shorts?"

That Trundle remark floored me. Where the hell does she know Randy from? The Metzger family had me double teamed; I didn't know which way was up. All I could do was get up off the mat and head for the door, and add, "I'm counting on it, Ms. Metzger," to regain a small bit of cockiness I'm supposed to exude. "I am truly counting on it."

Round one to the GC.

Chapter 25

As long as I was up on the dreaded 'executive floor,' I figured I'd take a little stroll and see what I could see. Little bit of detecting, a little bit of just being nosey.

To break a few balls, I stopped by my new favorite fellow employee's desk. "So, Candy girl, where's the Prez's office?"

Shock, recognition, hatred. I do have a way with the ladies, you know.

"This floor is restricted, and if you don't go I'll have to call security and have you removed from the building," she said.

Before we could really give it a go, I found out the answer to my question, loud and clear. The voice that boomed from the corner suite could only be from one person.

"And don't you ever forget I'm the president of this company. When I fire somebody, their ass stays fired, and I don't give a damn what you or anyone else says. That includes lawyers, and every god damn outside agency that exists. Any questions?"

"No sir, Mister Collins, sir."

With that, my favorite human resources buddy put his tail between his legs, turned, and hit the trail double time. Millwood might be a New York guy, but he obviously wasn't the Prez's number one favorite guy.

"And while I'm at it, who the hell are you, and what are you doing up here?" Collins shouted in my direction.

As you know, bashful I am not. So, I strolled over to the door to the president's suite and said, "Harry Mickey Shorts—at your service."

"I know that name," he said. "Where do I know you from?" followed.

"I just started here, so I doubt my extraordinary work at MechInsCo's the reason."

I let that one sink in, and before he could put his extensive vocabulary to work, I continued, "But maybe it was when I played for the Bayport Schooners last season."

"That's it! Knew I knew you from somewhere. We need to talk some time about the game. I have some interesting things brewing, and maybe you can be of some value to me."

As he turned and walked back toward his office he said over his shoulder, "Make an appointment with Carol," and he was gone.

So, I did, and the game was on. Just not the one Collins was referring to, as he would soon find out.

Chapter 26

Some dudes spend way too much time trying to figure out what to wear when in hot pursuit of the young chickies. While I pondered my choices, I replayed my afternoon's activities with Larry, my cube neighbor, and current 'lay-of-the-land' instructor.

Insurance is really a very simple business. I learned this from a guy in Arizona who told me, "Insurance is very simple. You write business and you make money." He did go on to tell me it's what you write, how you write it, and what you do with it after you write it that makes the difference.

You're about to get a little 'Insurance 101' here, but it's necessary if you are gonna follow the story. Now listen up—don't skip any of this stuff and try and retain as much as you can. Yeah, you will have to concentrate for a bit, but you can do it, I know you can. Chocolate cake and beer as a reward for all the good little boys and girls who try real hard.

Buck up, here we go.

Larry gave me the royal tour of the accounting department, and the he-does/she-does as we went past each cube. It seems MechInsCo writes what's called standard Property and Casualty (P&C) business, both personal and commercial. The personal insurance, similar to your auto and homeowners policies you get from Allstate or State Farm, is just accommodation business to go along with their bread & butter, the commercial stuff. They write insurance on buildings in case they burn down, they insure companies in case people get hurt (workers compensation and general casualty), plus some other lines that don't add up to much, like Director's and Officer's (D&O) for when the big guys at companies mess up real bad. Just forget about the other stuff and we shall concentrate on the standard P&C business.

Now that should end your lesson for today, or at least one might think so. But, as usual, things ain't always what they look like. When an insurance company writes a policy, they assume what's called 'liability,' meaning they get the premium and they are 'liable' for the losses that occur. Not all insurance companies want to have the total liability responsibility, or position, nor do they have the cooleonies (my word—yours might be balls) to take that chance. So, they sell some portion of their insurance and liability to another company, and that is called reinsurance. They both share in the premiums and the losses, and the 'reinsurer'—the company that buys a piece of the insurance—pays a commission for it.

Confused? No harm in this case, since I understand this insurance stuff and it still confuses me at times.

Let's move on and finish up.

The last piece I'll fill your brain with is called 'fronting'. It's where an insurance company writes a policy and then 'reinsures' the whole premium and liability back to the company that bought the policy in the first place. It's called a 'front' and the insurance company gets a fronting fee to do it—to cover expenses and make a profit.

Enough already!

MechInsCo does all of the stuff I just explained, and Larry seemed to have a handle on most of it as we walked through the department and he pointed out who did what. I'm supposed to kinda free-lance around and fix problems, help people with stuff they are doing but can't get done. Jack-of-all-trades you might say. "'Nuff said already," you might also say. 'Insurance 101' is hereby over for now.

* * *

Had to wear something. So, I grabbed a pair of jeans and a not too wrinkled work shirt off a chair and headed out to meet the fair Crissy Metzger. Unlike some guys, took me a whole 30 seconds to decide, and I sure hoped Crissy was gonna be a whole lot more than fair when push comes to shove. Yeah, you know what I'm talking about, and I'm hoping to have lots to talk about when tomorrow morning rolls around.

Chapter 27

No pushing, no shoving, no Crissy Metzger, and no tomorrow morning conversation. Never even got close to picking her up for our rendezvous of a lifetime.

Something got in the way.

The something was a call from Tom on my cell. Got it in the car and changed directions immediately.

"How is he and what happened?" is how I started my conversation with Tom when I got to the hospital.

"Oh man, Harry, I really f'ed up," Tom said.

"Tom, no time for that crap now," I replied. "Squat and talk to me." I led him to a bench in the ER waiting room.

"I got no details, but they hurt Cam bad. My fault, my god damn fault, Harry, my god damn fault," Tom said.

"Who is they, and why?" I asked. "And why do you think you had anything to do with it?"

"Cam told me it was the dudes he partied with. For no reason, they just walked up and wailed on him. Two guys wailing away on a kid, my kid, Harry. Cam's all I got and I did this to him."

Tom was near tears and falling apart right in front of me.

"You did what, Tom? What did you do?" I asked.

"Harry, I'm sorry, real sorry. I let you down, and I let Cam down," he said.

"How?" was all I could think of to say.

"Just wasn't thinking, man. Had a few beers end of last week with a guy I've known forever, just talking and shootin' the bull. I didn't think nothing of it and asked him if there was any word on the street about MechInsCo."

Tom hesitated for a few seconds, and then he said, "The guy didn't say nothing, just got up, walked away, and left a few minutes later. Case closed, end of story."

"And," I said.

"It's tonight, couple days later, and one of Cam's buds calls and says, 'Cam is all busted up and you better come down real fast and get him.' I got him and brought him here. That's all of it, Harry."

"How bad is he?" I asked.

"Bad, Harry. Real bad, man. They took a baseball bat to him, Harry. Fucked up my kid with a baseball bat, cuz I got shit for brains," Tom said, and then he started to cry.

The price of poker just went up, big time.

Chapter 28

There isn't much to do in an emergency room when you are waiting for information on somebody you know. It gets much worse when your best friend in the world is sitting next to you, eyes red, feeling like the world is caving in all around him.

Welcome to my night.

"You Tom Naughton?" came from above us. Tall guy, heavy around the middle, shaved head.

"Me," Tom said.

"I'm Detective Strook." He looked at me. "Who are you?"

"A friend, here to help out," I said. "Name's Harry, Harry Shorts." No need to bring Mickey into this, I decided.

"Can we talk, Mister Naughton?" he asked.

"You talk to me, you talk to Harry, too," Tom whispered.

"Fine by me," Detective Strook replied.

Before we could get down to it with Strook, a doctor came striding toward us and asked for Tom Naughton.

"Me," Tom said.

"I'm Doctor Crow. I'm head of neurology here at the hospital. I've been in with your son Cameron, and let me tell you right up front, all signs point to a one hundred percent recovery."

"Oh, thank you, Jesus," Tom said.

Didn't think Tom was the religious type, but strange things can happen at times like this.

"Cameron has some serious injuries, but nothing life threatening. He has three broken ribs and one punctured a lung. We fixed that problem and it shouldn't have any lasting effects."

"Oh, thank you Jesus," Tom said again.

Crow looked at me, I shrugged, he continued.

"Some lacerations on his face and head required about thirty stitches, and he has a fractured wrist. They're nothing serious, nothing long lasting, and he should be out in a few days. Be about an hour before you can see him. He is a very lucky young man, Mister Naughton."

With that, Doctor Crow left, and Tom thanked Jesus, again.

Me, I had other things on my mind, and some guys I wouldn't exactly be saying thank you to.

Chapter 29

Detective Strook caught Tom and me after the doc left. We had an hour before we could see Cam, so a little chat with Mister Policeman was cool for now.

"Do you have any information on who did this to your son, Mister Naughton?" Strook started.

"It's all very confusing. I don't know why someone would want to do this to Cam," Tom replied.

That was detective speak for 'no chance I'm gonna tell you didly-squat till I know myself.'

"Can you tell me where it happened? You did bring him in, didn't you."

"Don't know for sure," Tom replied. "I found him by the pool hall over on Carlisle Pike. Got a call, don't know who, said Cam was there and I best come get him real fast."

"You can't identify the caller?" Strook tried.

"Just a voice, kinda scared, and he talked so fast I hardly knew what he said. I heard pool hall and Cam's name, so I high-tailed it down there and found him." Tom paused for a minute, looked up at Strook. "Who would do this to a kid?" he asked.

I was still a fly on the wall, watching from the outside in. I hadn't said a word yet. 'Bout time I jumped my way into the conversation before Tom got himself in any deeper.

"Maybe we can continue this tomorrow morning, Detective Strook? Tom's gotta see his kid and I wanna get him cleaned up some before we go in."

"Sure, I understand. Tomorrow is fine. Maybe Mister Naughton will be thinking a little clearer tomorrow and remember at least one fact that might help us get whoever did this. You can tell me your story then, too," Strook said.

He had that look in his eye that said he hadn't bought one word Tom said.

"I'll bring him in around noon, after morning visiting hours," I said.

"That's fine, I'll be waiting." Strook turned and left.

"You done good, Tom," I told him. "We can put a story together before we see Strook tomorrow; give him just enough to get the cops off our backs while we figure out what to do next."

"Okay, Harry. I'll leave it up to you, cuz my brain's fried, man. I wanna see Cam now." We went in together to start the healing process, in more ways than one.

Chapter 30

"Welcome to MechInsCo. I believe we may have met before, but we surely won't be spending any time together in the near future, so sign in please to refresh my memory on who you actually are."

She never even looked up.

That, for your information, was what greeted me on my arrival at my place of employment the following morning. Seems my failure to inform the lovely Ms. Metzger I would not be able to make our agreed upon rendezvous last evening was not to her liking. It could put a small crimp in Harry Mickey Shorts' love life if not corrected post haste.

"Ms. Metzger, you are absolutely correct, we have met before. And, if I might add, we would have spent a wonderful evening together last night if not for a very unforeseen and inescapable emergency that befell me on a moment's notice. Plus, and most important, in an obvious moment of Polish blockheadedness, I neglected to carry your phone number with me when I left to come and whisk you off your feet to hours of blissful delight."

She looked up and I had my opening.

"Your humble servant offers a hundred thousand apologies and pleadings for forgiveness from one as beautiful and compassionate as yourself," I said.

Lo and behold, a small sliver of a smile appeared, and all would be right with the world. At least I hoped so.

"Beat it Shorts, and don't think that stunt isn't going to cost you big time," she said.

"You don't have to tell me twice," I said and I was gone.

* * *

The morning consisted of reviewing production reports, claims reports, reinsurance reports, and you get the picture reports. It's what some people in accounting departments do, mostly because somebody has to do it. Most of the time it just confirms what was done matched what was supposed to have been done.

Three hours of eye-blinding, sleep-inducing tedium produced nothing more than what was done matched what was supposed to have been done. Bullshit work never excites me, plus my mind was on Tom and Cam most of the time, but I had the feeling there was something in the information I had looked at that was important. It'll come to me if there really is something there. After all, the Shorts brain works in mysterious ways!

* * *

Three interesting events occurred just before I took off to accompany Tom to the police station to see Detective Strook. The first was a phone call from the Prez's executive assistant who informed me my ass was to be in Mister Collins' office at 9:00 am sharp the following morning. Not exactly the way she stated it, but you get the picture. Event number two was a note I found buried under some papers on my desk that said, "Find anything yet?" Didn't recognize the handwriting, but the message made me believe I really did see something my brain had stored away in a safe place. Item number three—female receptionists should never be allowed to pinch your ass, sashay away without saying a word, cheeks swaying back and forth in perfect rhythm, leaving your balls in a flaming uproar.

She'll get hers, and if I'm not mistaken, she's looking forward to it as much as I am, if not more. Nope, couldn't be more now that I think about it.

Chapter 31

"Tom Naughton and Harry Mickey Shorts to see Detective Strook," I announced as we stood before the desk Sergeant at the station. Noon on the dot—we were the epitome of timeliness.

"Sit down, I'll call him," the Sergeant replied, the epitome of efficient desk sergeantness.

We sat and waited. And waited. And waited some more. If it kept up much longer, I would end up being late getting back to work, my title as 'epitome of timeliness' down the dumper. Can't have that, now can we.

"Desk sergeant, sir," I said. "Would you be able to inform Detective Strook our asses are getting sore from sitting on the hard bench out here, and our asses will be out the door real soon if he doesn't appear pronto. That is with a please, of course." I sat back down on my sore ass on the hard bench.

He didn't smile, he didn't like it, but he did call.

"Come on," was all Strook said when he appeared a few minutes later. We followed him into one of the interrogation rooms.

"Now that we are all comfy-cozy, let's hear your story, Naughton," Strook said as we entered the room.

"Strook, if I may call you Strook, or I could call you by your first name if I knew it, but since I don't because you haven't seen fit to tell us your first name, Strook, why don't you ask Tom some questions and he'll give you some answers," I said.

Harry Mickey Shorts, the epitome of accommodation.

"Shorts, shut your trap. Understand?" Strook replied.

"Naughton, what can you tell me about what happened to your son?" he tried.

"Nothing," Tom replied.

"Do you have any idea who did this to him?" Strook asked.

"No," Tom said.

"Do you have any idea why they did this to him?" Strook asked.

Tom shrugged.

"I take that as a no, Mister Naughton?" Strook said. "Do you know what obstruction of justice is, Mister Naughton? Do you know what withholding information in a criminal investigation can do to you, Mister Naughton?" Strook said. His attempt at intimidation was fairly obvious.

"Yes," Tom said.

"Are you going to answer any of my questions?" he continued.

"I have," Tom said.

What Tom didn't say was he was answering Strook's questions exactly as I had instructed him to. Yes and no, Detective Strook, nothing more. Never know the good guys from the bad guys, especially in little burg's like this one.

I thought this might be a good point for me to jump into the proceedings. But, before I could say anything, Strook looked at me. "I told you to 'shut up,' and I meant it."

He looked like he meant it, so, I shut up. Harry Mickey Shorts, the epitome of shutupedness.

"Naughton, if you have any thoughts of investigating this on your own, forget them. If you believe you and Shorts together can do a better job than the police of nosing this out, forget it. Go home, collect your thoughts, and call me when you want to cooperate, for Cam's sake and for your sake. Now, beat it, and take him with you."

With that, Strook got up without saying another word and left the room. We were right behind him.

Odd, he never turned on the tape recorder that was sitting on the table.

Chapter 32

There's this place called Grandpa's Growler on Route 114 in Mechanicsburg. I heard they had great wings and plenty of beer to wash them down. That night, in light of recent activities, as any respectable private dick would do, I investigated the situation. Some P.I.'s are slower and much more deliberate than others. In this case, I was real slow and deliberate, not as much with the wings as I was with the beer to wash them down. Their reputation proved to be well deserved, and I felt much better when I was done.

* * *

"Morning, oh light of my life."

I was attempting to get on Crissy's good side first thing in the morning.

"'Light of my life' my ass. Leave me hanging without as much as a phone call and, 'I light up your life?' Very funny. What are you, a comedian?"

"I have been known to be quite funny at times," I replied.

"Not today, Shorts," she said.

So much for a pinch your ass and sashay away.

"And get your butt up to Collins' office, now. His she-person called and said he wants you first thing."

"She-person?" I inquired.

"Shorts, you are pushing your luck way beyond where you should care to. And, oh yeah, my mom wants to see you, too. She must have nothing better to do with her time," she said, a small smile coming through on that one.

"Lunch?" I tried.

"I eat it," she said.

"With me?" I tried again.

"Not today," she replied.

"When?" I tried again persistently.

"Someday," she said. "Check your calendar and wait till 'someday' appears. That would be Monday, Tuesday, Someday…"

"Maybe Mister Collins will appreciate the goodness within my inner being and be nicer to me," I said and left.

I just love her laugh, which she happened to be doing to my back at the time.

* * *

"Good morning. Harry Mickey Shorts for Mister Collins. I believe he is expecting me," I told Collins' she-person.

"Sit and wait," she said without even looking up from her computer screen. New Yorker she-person I guessed.

"Love to," I said.

Didn't even get the seat warm before Collins came storming out of his suite. He didn't have just an office, he had an office, and a conference room, and a waiting area, all in one grouping behind the double doors to within, or so I'd been told.

"That little prick Millwood better be running down Carlisle Pike," he said as he buzzed by me with nary a glance in my direction.

"Do you think we should reschedule for another time?" I inquired of Ms. Iceness.

"I'll call you," was all I got.

Yep, didn't look up this time either. Harry Mickey Shorts, piece of budget analyst garbage not even worthy of a glance.

"I'll just scurry on over to the GC's office. Candy hates my ass, but at least she looks at me as she hates my ass," I threw in the EA to the Prez's direction as I scooted. No reason to get chewed out if you don't have to.

* * *

"Candy girl, how you doing?" I said with a smile.

"You," was all I got.

"Yeah, me, in the flesh, for all to behold. Ms. Metzger has asked for my presence I have been informed."

"Wait," Candy replied as she got up to see if it could possibly be true.

I bet her caboose would be worth jumping aboard with a little gym time. One Mississippi, two Mississippi, three Missis...

"Ms. Metzger will see you now, Mister Shorts," Candy said.

"Get in here, Shorts," the GC commanded from her doorway.

I obeyed.

"I'm busy," she said. "Three things—be nice and leave Candy alone; Trundle wants to know if you require any assistance at this time; and third, he says to do the most basic thing you should always do in your job." She waited a few seconds and I could imagine a dynamite tune playing in her very pretty head. "That's it."

"I'm busy," I said. "Three things—Candy should unpucker her ass and enjoy life; I'm good at the moment, but tell him thanks; and third, I'm trying and I will."

I waited a few seconds listening to Ian Anderson's flute playing in my mind's ear, then left telling her, "Looking good by the way," over my shoulder.

As I walked away, I thought I heard her say, "You better believe it," but I couldn't be sure.

Chapter 33

The rest of the day was a mix of crunching numbers, producing reports, and looking for anything that might point me in some direction. Frustrating when you know there has to be something there and you can't see it. It actually crossed my mind the company just flat out lost money through bad underwriting of business or bad claims handling, or both. It has happened to plenty before and there's plenty more to come, but I had the nagging feeling it was there for the finding if I could just catch a thread.

* * *

"Got a second, Harry?" Joe Stoner asked as he entered my cubicle.

"Sure, Joe."

"Let's go down to my office if you don't mind," he said.

"Cool, gimme a minute, and I'll be right behind you."

Didn't know what was up, but he had that 'just got my ass kicked again' look. Or maybe that was what he looked like all the time now. Whichever it was, I had to stir up his moxie to get him back to a normal hick town accounting guy again.

"Wazup, Joe?" I asked as I entered his office.

"Sit down, Harry. I want you to know that in the small amount of time you have been here you are doing great things. Lord knows we need the help."

"Thanks, Joe, glad to be of help," I said.

"Yeah, one thing though. If you could, stay focused on the work you are given, okay? I got word you were asking for some extra information from the Information Services group downstairs that doesn't go with what you are working on. Why's that, Harry?"

Interesting question. Who fed Joe the info, and who wants me off that info trail is something I will need to dope out.

"Sorry if I got your ass in hot water, man. I was just looking to round out a report and I thought the information might help it make more sense. Didn't mean to cause trouble," I said.

"No trouble, Harry. Please just stick to the assignments I give you so we can catch up and get back above water. I'll clear up this little misunderstanding," Joe assured me.

"I can take care of it if you want," I tried, hoping to find out who was looking over my shoulder.

"Harry, let it go, I'll handle it." Joe started to busy himself with stuff on his desk, which meant hit the road Jack.

I made like Jack and hit the road. Somewhere, someplace, somebody was watching for hits on specific data within the system. It was either that, or a person in IS was monitoring requests for the stuff, and passing it on to that somebody. I needed to know who they were, and why the data was too sensitive to have.

The note came back to me—"Find anything yet?"

Chapter 34

It was time to get the real skinny on the Crissy and Maddy show. Forget the nice kid and General Counsel stuff and get down to what I do best—detect. What happens will happen, can't worry about feelings and consequences some times.

"Crissy, grab your stuff and let's get out of here," I said as I passed the front desk around quitting time.

"Excuse me!"

"It's Harry, and hurry up, I'm thirsty," I replied over my shoulder.

Must have been a very quick 'Yes I will, no I won't' that ran through her brain. Before I hit the back door, she was right there beside me, stuff in hand.

"Good choice, kiddo. Let's eat, drink and be merry. The merrier the better," I said.

"As they say in these here parts, leave us be merry," she said and laughed that laugh I do love so.

* * *

We married it up big time down at the Growler. Wings, beer and shots all around till we had more than our fill. Some MechInsCo people who Crissy knew showed and we all partied down for a while. She could hold her own with the best of them and it felt good to just enjoy life, laugh and have a good time. Not enough good times lately.

We split and headed over to my place. Crissy did her usual bitching and moaning about having to ride in the HoneyBee, but I knew it was only her breaking my stones. Well worth listening to if the night played out the way I hoped.

I unlocked the door to my place and let Crissy go in first. I had cleaned the joint a little that morning, so it wasn't too much of a guy hellhole. Before I could ask her if she wanted anything to drink, she threw a lip lock on me that practically knocked me off my feet. A real free-for-all followed that would have killed most combatants. Luckily I'm in pretty good shape, cuz it seems Crissy was a gymnast in high school and hadn't forgotten any of her moves. We got into some positions and places in the apartment that surprised even Harry Mickey Shorts, man of the world and well-trained lover extraordinaire.

Quite by accident, we ended up on the bed as the festivities came to an end. Once I caught my breath, I said, "Excuse me, but what the fuck was that?"

"No excuses," she said, "and what I believe you really meant to say was 'what a fuck that was.'"

It took me a second to get it, but when I did, we both laughed ourselves silly. Take it from Harry Mickey Shorts, there's nothing better than lying next to a naked beauty laughing herself silly.

* * *

We laid there for hours, talking about stuff, periodically doing fun little things to each other. Not the big thing, fun little things, things that didn't quite lead to the big thing. Oh, the big thing was gonna happen again, just not yet.

"High school ended and you hit the road. How come?" I asked in the midst of our talking.

"A little family history," she said. "And if you ever repeat this to a single soul, that will be the last romp in the sack you will ever enjoy. Comprende, partner?" she said.

"Me comprende," I replied with a straight face.

"Mom, Ms. Madeline Metzger, General Counsel for MechInsCo, gave birth to Christine Metzger at the ripe old age of sixteen. Genius I.Q. with mediocre grades at Mechanicsburg High School, she had her good friends booze, drugs and sex to keep her company while her mom was gone. Good old granny, who had mom when she was seventeen, liked to disappear for days at a time. Granny never was sure who was responsible for mom entering this world, and mom was equally unsure of who my father was."

At that point, Crissy put her head on my shoulder and lay still for close to five minutes. She never cried, but I could tell she wanted to.

"Granny ran into the wrong guy right around the time I was born. Story was the guy was doing some nasty shit to her and she jumped out a window to get away. Only problem was, they were on the fourth floor, and the fall broke most of the bones in her body. The guy got away and mom was left alone, really alone this time. Me, I was three weeks old, and just about as alone."

"How'd you get to today, and your mom to where she is from that day?" I asked, mainly to break up her story and give her a second to catch her breath.

"Granny's brother from New York took us in. He threw mom into rehab and he and his wife took care of me. They didn't have any kids and she was thrilled to have us stay with them. The guy he worked for liked him, heard about it, had plenty of money to go around and fronted the whole thing, or so the story goes. This guy made it a priority to get mom straightened out and became her fairy godfather through high school, college at NYU, then NYU law school. She was tops in her class everywhere and he fronted the bills all the way. He saved her life, and mine," she finished.

"And you, what's your story?" I asked.

"Harry, I'm kinda tired," she said. "How about I finish mom's story and tell you my story another time. Okay?" she asked.

"Sure, no problem," I said.

We got to doing those little things to each other again, and before we knew it, the big thing was right there in front of us. Slow and careful, a pair of choreographed partners moving to the silent music we both heard, producing something I'll always remember. We slept like babies when we were finished, as if we had scared away all the bad out there and didn't have a care in the world.

Chapter 35

"Holy shit, get your ass up, Harry," Crissy yelled, a well placed elbow to my ribs for good measure.

"What the hell?" I cried now wide awake.

"What time is it?"

I rolled over and realized we must have knocked the clock off the nightstand the night before. I found it under a pair of very sexy lace undies that immediately rekindled memories of last night's endeavors. Luckily, the clock read a few minutes before seven, plenty of time before we were due into work.

"Relax, kiddo," I said, telling her the time. "We can get you over to your place to change before work without a problem. I'll start the coffee, let's get cleaned up and have something to eat, and then head to your place. Sound okay?"

"Fine, but let's get started, and no funny business. There's no time for any of your Shorts shenanigans, and I mean it," she said with a glare.

"It never even crossed my mind," I lied.

"Yeah, my ass," she said.

"If you insist," I teased, which was met with that same glare.

"While I get the coffee started and throw some breakfast together, why don't you jump in the shower. Everything you need should be in there. I'll get some sweats for you to wear on the ride over to your place," I offered.

"Okay," was all she said, and with a quick peck on the cheek, off she went.

* * *

The coffee was all set about the same time I heard the toilet flush. There was bread in the toaster and cereal in the bowls about the time I heard the shower go on. My tasks completed, and a need to clean up myself, I did what any red-blooded male would do; I proceeded to hit the showers. The fact I had a hard-on the size of a redwood was only a minor factor in the equation.

"Shorts, what do you think you're doing?" Crissy said as I stepped into the shower. "And what is that?" she continued as she pointed to the aforementioned redwood.

"Why, the same as you my dear, just showering for work," I replied. "And in answer to your second inquiry, I believe you became acquainted with 'that' several times last evening," I finished.

"That I did," she smiled, "that I did."

Generous amounts of soap and shampoo, a mouthful of this and a handful of that, a bunch of little things, all culminating in one more big thing. Which leads us to the age old question: If a single redwood is hidden in the forest, does anyone hear? Answer: Unless I'm mistaken, anyone alive in Mechanicsburg heard. Solution: There is no solution, and neither of us could have cared a bit. A classic Harry Mickey Shorts QAS if there ever was one!

* * *

We had a bite of toast, a sip of coffee, and off we went. The cereal would have to wait for another time, which I was surely looking forward to. Another time that is, not the cereal. From the smooch I got as we left my apartment, I believe the feeling was mutual.

I dropped Crissy off at her place and headed over to the MechInsCo building. As I approached the elevators on the first floor, the elder Ms. Metzger was coming around the corner from the cafeteria, coffee and yogurt in hand.

"Well good morning, Mister Shorts. You are looking very chipper this morning," she said.

"Good morning to you, too," I said warily.

"And it is especially gratifying to know that at least one of the Metzger ladies is probably feeling equally as chipper this morning," she said as she stepped into the elevator.

There I was, mouth open in amazement, as the elevator doors closed, the elder Ms. Metzger clearly relishing the moment.

Chapter 36

Unfortunately, you are going to have to endure another insurance lesson. Actually two lessons, or you won't be able to follow what I think I found. Pour through enough numbers, create enough reports from those numbers, analyze the reports you created from those numbers, and you know what you get? Numbers, reports and a headache. In the end, you hope to eventually make some sense out of the numbers.

Joe had me working on the quarter-end reports that go up to senior management. Doesn't take a rocket scientist, so I guess that's why he assigned them to me. It involved summarizing what happened during the past quarter and producing a few simple Profit & Loss (P&L) reports. Here comes lesson time:

You write a policy (gross premium) and give some of it to another company called a reinsurance company (ceded reinsurance) who pays your company a fee for the business (ceding commission), and the company ends up with what's left (net premium). Over the course of the year, you earn or take credit for the net premium (earned premium) and use the earned premium to pay losses and expenses. You develop a loss ratio and expense ratio (I'll skip that part of the lesson for now) which together equals your combined ratio. Insurance companies are judged by their combined ratio and how much money they make (profit) or lose (loss). Hence, you have your Profit and/or Loss Statements, commonly known as P&L's.

Lesson #2 is a quickie, and goes like this: the insurance company writes a policy and all too often pays a loss on that policy (gross loss), gives a portion of that loss to the reinsurance company that got a portion of the premium (ceded losses), and ends up with what's left (net losses). The company thus has a Gross Loss Ratio and a Net Loss Ratio. That kiddos is all you will need to know for the next portion of this enthralling tale, which I shall get to shortly.

* * *

I wandered down to the front desk after spending the majority of the morning crunching and analyzing mountains of information and numbers. My brain needed a rest and another part of my anatomy needed some excitement.

"Hello there, Crissy. How are we today?" I asked the fair young receptionist.

"Hello, yourself." Crissy looked up from the phone board.

"Rumor has it you still have a bit of a tale to tell. Lunch perhaps?" I inquired.

"Nope, sorry, can't do. Seems my mom wants to have our bi-weekly lunch today," she said.

"That's interesting," I replied. "We ran into each other this morning and she seemed to have knowledge of recent mutual developments. Any idea how that may have occurred?" I asked.

"Perhaps the fact she was traveling past my apartment building on her way to work this morning and saw me get out of an unnamed vehicle could have something to do with it."

"She did?" I asked.

"She did," Crissy confirmed.

"Oh," I said.

"Yes, oh," she repeated.

"I'll grab you after work and we can get a drink," I told her.

"We can get a drink after work and then you can grab me," she smiled.

"I could at that," I said and went off on my merry way.

* * *

The afternoon was more of the morning, more boring pages of more boring numbers and more boring spreadsheets. By the time five o'clock rolled around, I had had my fill of insurance. But, I had succeeded in making some sense of the gobbledygook, and was about ready to begin populating (a favorite insurance word) my P&L formats. Still no idea what the hell happened to make the company go in the tank, but if it's there I'll find it. Or so I keep telling myself.

Chapter 37

"Shorts, would you be able to stop by my office?" the GC asked when I answered the phone.

"I was just on my way out for an appointment," I replied. "But, if you need me, I can stop by before I split."

Man, two minutes and I would have been gone.

"That would be good, and thank you," she said as she hung up.

Before my ass was deep in hot water, I called Crissy to tell her I was going to be delayed and would meet her at the Growler.

"Shouldn't take long," I told her.

"Why does she want to see you?" she asked.

"Don't know, and she didn't say. Just said come on up," I said.

"Your ass had better be at the Growler soon, Harry. You hear me?" she said.

"Yes'm, I hear you loud and clear," I replied, and meant it.

"Good, Harry," was all I heard, and then I was listening to dead air.

* * *

"Ms. Metzger," I said as I peaked in the GC's doorway. "Candy girl seems to have left for the day and I didn't want to keep you waiting."

"Come in and sit, Harry. I need a few more minutes to finish this up," she said.

I copped a squat on her couch, which happened to provide a very nice side view of the GC at her desk. Legs crossed as she worked on her PC, her finely tailored skirt riding halfway up her finely shaped thigh.

"Read something, Shorts," she said without even looking up. Women just have a sixth sense about it. Men just don't care that they do.

She finished up whatever it was she was working on and took a seat at the end of the couch. Lucky for me, she brought the legs and thigh with her, skirt riding to about the same place.

"What can I do for you?" I asked.

The GC, Ms. Maddy Metzger, hesitated for a minute while she seemed to be running a few things around in her head.

"There are some matters we need to cover that are pertinent to this company, your presence here, my daughter and me. I am the General

Counsel for a fair sized insurance company that has fallen on some hard times. I am neither part of the cause for those hard times, nor do I possess knowledge of why it has fallen on hard times. Don't look at me for anything, it isn't there. But, if you are here to help the company, I will assist you in any way possible to determine if there has been any malfeasance perpetrated on this company."

She took a quick sip of water and then continued.

"I don't know what my daughter has told you about us, the Metzgers, so I'll give you the *Reader's Digest* version from my perspective. My mother had me young and I had Christine just as young, or younger. My past is private, very private, and anything Christine may have told you about me should remain private.

"Christine is a very special child who hasn't found herself yet. She will be going to Europe in the fall to study with an art master in Paris. She was a child prodigy who cares very little about her artistic ability, never has. That painting over my credenza was completed in her freshman year of high school and has been valued at one hundred thousand dollars in the private market. It was something she did for an art project over a weekend. Be very careful with her, Mister Shorts, Harry. She is special and very important to me."

I guessed she was done.

"Two questions?" I asked.

"Go ahead."

"If Crissy is twenty, that makes you thirty-seven? And second, our mutual friend was your benefactor?"

"Twenty and thirty-seven next month, you are correct, Harry. And second, Mister M. Randal Trundle was indeed my benefactor and the father I never had. For some reason he likes you a good deal and he also told me to watch myself around you," she smiled.

"Thanks, and with Crissy, I'll be careful. Any assistance you can lend toward my work here would be helpful and appreciated. Hopefully we will talk again soon," I told Ms. Metzger.

"You're welcome, Harry," she said.

As I got up to leave, the GC headed back to her desk. Just as I got to the door I heard her say, "We will see each other again soon, Harry, and we will do more than talk."

I kept on walking.

Chapter 38

"You are one lucky accounting department schmuck, Harry," greeted me as a sat down next to Crissy.

"And a pleasant hello to you, too" I replied.

"Several beers, please," I said to the cute little waitress who had appeared at our table.

"For the two of you?" she asked.

"No, for me. I'm thirsty, and I don't want you to have to hustle your buns around on my account," I told her.

"Forget him, Peggy. Just get us a pitcher of Molson, okay," Crissy told the cute little waitress. Did I already call her a 'cute little waitress'?

"As for you, the only buns you should concern yourself with are the ones I'm currently sitting on. Straight, Harry?" she asked.

"Straight as can be," I swore.

"What took you so long?" she asked.

I had to think about that for a second. An innocent little business discussion with the GC of the company I work for, or frank discussion on the Metzgers—past and present. Which one should it be?

"Your mom called to see me, and I popped up there before I left. Which reminds me, last night you promised to finish your story for me," I deftly threw out there to shift the discussion in a different direction. "Ready to spill it?" I asked.

"Let's have a few beers, relax and have fun for a while," she said. "I'll finish my story later on when we are in a more private location, that's if you plan on the two of us being in a more private location later on?" she asked.

"The cereal awaits, my dear," I said. We both laughed.

* * *

We were laying quietly, pillows propped up against the headboard, Crissy's head resting against my shoulder. Cereal had been consumed, after which two still hungry individuals had engaged in a wild romp through pleasure valley. Peace surrounded us. It was good to know I could still have a go with a wild-eyed youngin' and hold my own, not to mention convince the youngin' to hold it too. Must be all that good living.

Yeah, right.

"Mom's at peace with herself, I think," Crissy began.

No prompting, she just decided to start.

"You have a lady who finished high school on her own while in rehab after having given birth to a beautiful baby girl—that's me; started college at seventeen, and finished in three years. Breezed through law school and made a bundle on Wall Street as a venture capital analyst specializing in the insurance world. Quit, packed it all up, and moved back to Mechanicsburg, PA to be the General Counsel of some rinky-dink insurance company."

She got quiet and I let her.

"Some together lady after where she has been and what she went through," she finished.

"And you?" I asked.

"Me? Run of the mill? I don't know what to do, looking for the Promised Land, twenty-year-old wanderer, stuck in Mechanicsburg, PA. One thing I am sure of, I need to get out of here so mom can get on with her life and find a good man to love her," she said.

"That has the makings of a pretty good cowboy song," I said.

"The only thing cowboy going on here is us back in the saddle," she said as she proceeded to mount up and ride.

Life ain't all bad in Mechanicsburg, PA.

Chapter 39

MechInsCo had a series of reinsurance arrangements, called treaties, that automatically gave some of their business to other companies. If you remember any of our last set of insurance lessons you should be able to follow along. I was working on the Gross Premium to Net Premium calculations and separating all the reinsurance into the individual reinsurance companies.

Will God ever stop giving me only the best in life?

Anyway, as I was saying, the results over the past three years had gone from a 95% combined ratio, to a 102% combined ratio, and then a 113% combined this past year. That was the Net Combined Ratio picture after they ceded the business to the reinsurance companies. Out of curiosity, I looked at the Gross Combined Ratios for the same periods, which produced some interesting comparisons. It had taken me most of the day to put the Gross numbers together, but I had the feeling I needed to go back to the beginning to get to the 'right' end.

Here's what I found:

Year	Gross Prem.	R/I Prem.	Net Prem.	Gross Comb. Ratio	Net Comb. Ratio
2006	$200 M	$40 M	$160 M	97%	95%
2007	$225 M	$75 M	$150 M	98%	102%
2008	$275 M	$125 M	$150 M	100%	113%

Now let's look at what this means and what assumptions we might be able to draw from it:

Gross Premiums increased by $25 million in 2007 and then another $50 million in 2008.

Reinsurance Premiums given away to other companies increased even more from $40 million (2006) to $75 million (2007) and then $125 million (2008).

The result showed that even though the company was growing and writing more business, the Net Premiums were lower than 2006 in both 2007 and 2008.

The Gross Combined ratio remained fairly steady showing only a minimal deterioration of 3% from 2006 to 2008.

On the other hand, the Net Combined Ratio deteriorated much more showing an 18% rise from 2006 to 2008.

So, you might ask, "What does that mean to a person who doesn't know all that much about insurance, or insurance accounting, or care either." Don't worry, I'll spell it out for you. Or at least what I think I may have found, not being an insurance guru either.

The company decided it didn't have the nerve to take the chance they would have too much in losses as they wrote more premium, so they gave more premium away (ceded) to reinsurance companies to cut potential losses. Or, someone was consciously ceding more business to reinsurance companies from the new business the company wrote. Same result, different reason.

Next, while the business they wrote seemed to be about the same as past business from a combined ratio side (Gross Combined Ratio), the Net Combined Ratio was much worse. That would mean the business they gave to the reinsurance companies was better business, producing better results. MechInsCo's Gross business got slightly worse, yet their Net business got much, much worse? Somewhere, all things being equal, reinsurance companies were making money and MechInsCo was taking it in the shorts.

Rule number one in detecting, which I believe is what M. Randle Trundle was reminding me, is follow the money. And that is what I planned on doing.

Chapter 40

Things had definitely taken a turn for the better on several fronts recently and they took another unexpected turn with the phone call I got late on Thursday afternoon.

"Shorts, I'm heading down to Mexico tomorrow afternoon to see Mister Trundle. I have been asked to extend an invitation for you to join me on this trip. Randle wishes to speak with you on several matters of importance. Can I confirm your desire to come along?" the GC asked.

"Count me in," I said.

"Are you sure you can tear yourself away from your current entanglements?" she asked.

"Making sacrifices for the team is what I'm all about," I told her. "When do we leave, how we going, and when are we getting back?" I asked.

"A car will pick us up here at three o'clock tomorrow afternoon. I have cleared your early departure from work. The Trundle jet will take us down to Mexico and we will be returning via the same arrangements Sunday evening. Randle will be leaving early Saturday, so we will have a bit of R and R time through midday Sunday. Before you ask, bring a little of everything, and a lot of what you do best." She hung up.

There was a bunch of stuff going down right now, a tough time to split town, but sometimes strange developments produce amazing twists. Plus, there is the GC X-Factor to consider. What she meant by, "And a lot of what you do best," was a mystery, but one I would be more than happy to figure out.

* * *

"Cam, dude, you looking good, my man," I said as I entered his hospital room. It had been a few days since I had seen him, and he did look better. Good, no. Better, maybe.

"Harry, thanks for showin', man," he said.

"Should have been by before, busy with lotsa stuff," I told him. I didn't tell him all the stuff. We need to keep a bit to ourselves now and again.

"It's cool, Harry. When am I getting out? They don't tell me nothin', man."

"Your dad says a day or so. Doc said you are just about ready and the tests they are gonna run tomorrow will tell the story," I said. "They're good, you're outta here, kiddo."

"Not soon enough, you know?" he said.

"Cam, you remember anything yet about the dude who whacked you?"

"Harry, it was weird. All of a sudden he was standing there, using the bat like to lean on, and then he smiled. I said, "What's up, man," and before I could throw him a cool one, he up and wailed on my ass with the bat. I didn't do nothin', Harry. One thing I do know, same dude as up in the mountains but copping a different slant on my ass for sure."

"Same dude—you sure?".

"One and the same, I'm sure of it, Harry."

"Cool, Cam. I gotta split for a few days. Your dad's gonna get you and I'll be by on Sunday, maybe Monday night. You be good till then?"

"Down, Harry."

* * *

Turned out to be a quiet night on the Harry Mickey Shorts front. Tom was off with some buds looking at a camping site they were thinking of buying, which did seem odd at a time like this. I had long since stopped trying to figure out Tom's motivations. They worked fine for him, so why mess with what worked.

Crissy, much to my surprise, had signed up for an art class and was off for her 'pre-class' evaluation. It might be for the best since we wouldn't have to discuss my weekend getaway if I could avoid her tomorrow. An "I'm off for the weekend with your mom, but it's strictly business," line was destined to fail miserably.

End result, packed some stuff for the trip, a few cool ones and a TV diner, and some games on the tube. The glamorous life of a world class private detective stuck in da sticks of Pennsylvania. Don't get no better than this, now does it.

Chapter 41

The following day was spent doing what I knew deep in my P.I. soul would bring results and possibly some face time with people I hadn't met yet—*follow the money*. That 'I got a sniff' feeling was in the air and I was on the trail.

"Hey, Joe, where would I find old production reports and stuff like that?" I asked Joe Stoner sometime around mid-morning.

"Why, Harry?"

"Just tracking some trends I haven't found yet but might be there," I answered.

"Ask Larry to show you, okay? And Harry, let's not waste a lot of time looking at old numbers when we have deadlines to put the current ones together," Joe said.

"Okay, Joe, I'll try not to. I'm just trying to be thorough and not miss anything. I do something wrong?" I asked.

"Harry, I'm swamped and Larry is swamped too. I have people all over my butt on what happened with the results and why," he said. "I'll worry about what happened in the past and you concentrate on your job. Do that and everything will be great. Got it, Harry?" he said.

"Got it, Joe."

For some reason, the air was getting very chilly when Joe and I were in the same room. I put it off to the pressure getting to him, and went off to find Larry, who just happened to have left the building to get some historical files from the warehouse a little while before. I let it go and played with the information I had on hand for the rest of the morning.

* * *

"Harry, Mister Collins would like to see you," Mary Ann said.

"Now?" I asked her.

"I think so. His assistant called a minute ago and requested it."

"Okay, Mary Ann. Can you call up there and tell her I'm on my way?" I asked.

"Will do, Harry."

Off I went to attempt to see the prez for the second time. Perhaps my luck would be better this time around.

* * *

"Don't say it, I know who you are. I called for you, didn't I?" Ms. Ice Cube said before I could open my mouth. "Sit," she commanded.

I did, but only for a few minutes.

"Go on in, he's ready," she said. How she knew it without a phone call or anything else was mind-boggling.

"Good morning, Mister Collins," I said as I walked into his kingdom.

"Good morning my ass," he said. "We're puking money and nobody can tell me what in the ever loving hell is going on. Is that good, Shorts? Is it I ask you?" he asked.

First impression, if I was a betting man, I'd bet the ranch Collins doesn't know why the company is in the dumper. Also, I'd bet everything I had left he has no clue who or what is behind it and it surely isn't him. First glances can be wrong, but this one looked pretty good.

"Puking money is bad, about as bad as shitting money," I agreed. "Doesn't mean the morning can't be a good one, especially when compared to bad ones," I continued.

"You're a New York guy, aren't you, Shorts?"

"Yeah, grew up in Queens. Woodside to be exact. Been on Long Island recently when I stay put for more than a few days," I answered.

"I grew up in Rego Park, right off Queens Boulevard," he said. "My dad still lives there and I get back to see him now and again, whenever this walking disaster of a company will let me. I go away for a few days, the fan gets turned on and shit covers the walls."

"Unplug the fan," I said

He thought for a few seconds, got it, laughed.

"Or paint all the walls brown," I finished.

"You're a funny guy, Shorts. Enough business, let's talk important stuff—baseball. Where you been, where you at?" he asked.

"Played minors after high school, managed to screw it up bad enough to get tossed. Kept at it in different places around the country at the semi-pro level. As I think you know, the Schooners was a long shot I parlayed into some fun and revisited glory days. Did my thing, got out before I screwed things up again. Now, I'm just trying to make a buck and see the wonders of this here U.S.A."

"This is no wonderland in case you haven't figured that out yet. I might be able to use a guy like you, New York street guy and all. You wanna put the equipment back on and help get my team whipped into shape for the coming season? The idiots I have for coaches need help with the catchers and pitchers, plus it means a trip to Florida for some fun and sun. Interested?" he asked.

"Let me get this straight. You offering me a job to work for the Harrisburg Senators as a coach?" I said.

"At least through spring training for starters," he said. "I hear you do good things with young players, especially inexperienced pitchers and catchers."

"I think I'll take you up on that offer, but give me the weekend to mull it over if I can. Monday morning I'll give you the definite answer. Okay?' I asked.

"Good enough. Now scram, I gotta try and plug some more leaks in this sinking tug," he said.

"I'm gone, and thanks," I, a Harrisburg Senator to be, said.

Chapter 42

Friday afternoon, three o'clock, time to blow town. I took the elevator to the parking garage on the lower level and a waiting stretch limousine. After managing to evade Crissy for the whole day, I wasn't going to chance the main floor and reception area.

"Sorry I'm late," the GC said as she hopped into the back seat. "Something I couldn't avoid."

"That's cool," I said. "It's Stoli, but it will do," I continued as I showed her the libation I had whipped together while I waited.

"It is good to see you are capable of making yourself comfortable, Shorts. That may come in handy before the weekend is over," she said.

"Paul, Capital City Airport, the Trundle plane," she told the driver.

"Capital City Airport?" I asked.

"Just big enough for the Trundle jet, plus it bypasses the formality and complications of bigger airports. It's like a Teterboro, only more private," she informed me.

"Something refreshing for the road?" I asked.

"I think I'll wait until we are on the plane to get refreshed," she replied. She then proceeded to open up a folder and immerse herself in some work.

"All work and no play…" I let hang in the air.

No response from the GC, no recognition I even said anything, save a tiny tap of her finger on the papers she was studying.

* * *

The limo tooled into Capital City and proceeded to a private area behind some hangers. As I was to find out, corporate jets taxied to this reserved area to allow the executives to drive right up to the planes and board without interruption. How they managed it in today's aviation security environment, I don't know. Didn't care either. I just jumped out of the limo and scooted up the stairs, perfectly positioned behind the 'legs to die for' that belonged to the GC.

"Mister Shorts, it is a true pleasure to welcome you back aboard," Greg, or G Man number 2 said.

"The G Men, how the hell have you two been? It's been way too long," I said.

I had coined the term based on their names during my first tour of duty with them.

"I see you have made the acquaintance of Mister Trundle's private crew, Mister Shorts," Ms. Metzger commented. She is one sharp lady to be sure.

"Prior business dealings allowed me to enjoy the comfort of Mister Trundle's hospitality which included the pleasure of flying on his plane."

Just as I finished, the phone in the arm of her chair rang and she answered it. She spoke for about thirty seconds and concluded with "... we are just about to take off and I will have the boys call you when we get close. Dinner would be great, even with Shorts along."

With that, the plane completed taxiing and took off down the runway. Before long, Greg brought a tall glass of something for Metzger, which I later learned was Rum and Tonic, and an Absolut and Tonic for me. I've said it before, and I hope I will have the opportunity to say it many times again, this be flying.

"Mister Trundle sends his regards. Now listen carefully, Shorts. Do I have your attention? Good. This is my cocktail, which I intend on enjoying in peace. These are the headphones that will deliver soothing music to my ears, which I will also enjoy, eyes closed, in peace. Do you get the picture, Shorts?"

"Got it. I'll slug down this drink and probably have a few more while I listen to the sounds that echo within my own personal music chamber. I'm at peace with my inner self."

Her to her headphones, me to my blow-your-doors-off music chamber, we relaxed in peace.

* * *

"Mister Shorts, Harry. Harry, are you awake?" I heard from somewhere off in the distance. It was actually George, the pilot.

"Shorts, wake up," Metzger said.

I was now awake and didn't know why. I also didn't know I had been asleep and had no idea where I was when I woke up. Not to worry, this wasn't the first time it had happened and I could say with absolute confidence it wouldn't be the last.

"Yeah, what's up?" I said to everyone who was causing my awakedness.

"The guys brought some snacks to tide us over until dinner. There is a bottle of Magic Hat for you as well," Metzger informed me.

"Cool," I said. "Where are we?"

"Crossing the Texas border, I think," she replied. "If it's about a five, five and a half hour trip, we should be there at about six o'clock. I'm going in the back to take a nap. If you nod off again, I'll get you up a bit before we land so you can clean up."

"Thanks, I said. "And if you have any trouble sleeping, let me know."

"Shorts, eat your snack and drink your beer. It's the most fun you're going to have on this flight," she said, and then she wandered off to the cabin in the rear of the plane.

The snacks were good, beer tasty, but the nap, or lack thereof, would have been preferred.

Chapter 43

Another limo was waiting for us when we landed. The so-called airport had appeared out of nowhere, and that's exactly where it was located. Nowhere, Mexico. Executive landing strip with a small hut and one gas pump. Nothing and nobody else around to ask questions—obvious accommodations for the rich and famous.

"Ms. Metzger, it is a pleasure to see you again. Please, step inside the car, the boys will see to your luggage. Yours too, Mister Shorts. Please make yourselves comfortable and we will be off in a minute. Mister Trundle is most anxious to see you both," the driver said, obviously having made Ms. Metzger's acquaintance previously.

"Brandy is with Mister Trundle anytime he is in Mexico, anywhere in Mexico. This car is also there at all times to alleviate any potential problems. It is a very well constructed machine for obvious reasons," the GC said.

"Brandy?" I asked.

"He would kill you in a heartbeat to protect Mister Trundle and never think twice about it," she said.

"Brandy it is then," I said.

We traveled for about thirty minutes seeing very few people along the way. The first sighting of other humans was the entrance to a Club Med we passed about halfway to our destination. Nice place if you wanted to get lost for a while.

"We're here, Ms. Metzger," Brandy announced as we pulled into a compound worthy of a jungle warlord. A crew of armed guards at the front gate plus several more walking the grounds as we pulled up to the main house. Or mansion, to be more precise. Three stories of stone and pillars built to withstand an armed invasion.

Metzger was out of the car before I knew it like a kid with a fistful of nickels heading for the candy store. The reason was standing on the front steps, one M. Randle Trundle. A big hug and a kiss on the cheek like they had known each other forever.

"Harry, come in please. It is good to see you again," Randy said as I walked up to join them.

"Mister Trundle, Randle, it has been a short while, but far too long," I said, and I meant it.

"Brandy, will you have someone attend to the luggage, please?" Randy said. "I will be in the study with my guests."

"Yes sir, Mister Trundle. Right away," Brandy replied.

"Come, come, both of you. Let's get you inside and a cold drink to welcome you to my home-away-from-home. Harry, I think you will enjoy your stay here," Randy said.

"I'm sure I will," I said, no doubt in my mind.

We sat and talked for what seemed like hours, but in actuality it was barely an hour. The GC was in her glory and I realized I had missed being around Randy. I let them do most of the talking and watched in amazement how at ease the GC was with a man of Randy's wealth and power. He wasn't Mister M. Randle Trundle, kingpin of the corporate world; he was the man who had reshaped her life and cared for her deeply. Even a dumb P.I. like me could see that.

"OK, let me make a call while the two of you go on up and get ready for dinner. Brandy will show you to your rooms and we will dine in thirty minutes," he said.

* * *

Dinner was magnificent in its simplicity and indescribable taste. A chicken dish with a mustard bread crumb coating cooked in a wine sauce was out of this world; green beans almondine and garlic mashed potatoes followed by a seven layer strawberry short cake that completed the feast. Better than sex is only an expression, but unless the GC is in the cards and she tops the world, this meal may be there.

"That was terrific," the GC said to Randy. "Brandy has truly outdone himself again."

"Brandy was responsible for this meal?" I asked. "Does he do windows, too?"

"He is quite an accomplished chef as evidenced by that delicious meal," Randy replied. "As for the windows, he does whatever is necessary."

"Let's go out on the patio for a brandy, the alcoholic variety," Randy said with a laugh.

We all had a good laugh with that one as we followed our host outside through the french doors. Across the patio was an Olympic size pool with a diving platform and cabana with stocked bar. We bellied up as

Brandy poured three healthy snifters of brandy, the alcoholic variety—I had to say it.

"You look radiant, Madeline. I trust Mechanicsburg and your current position are treating you well, all things being considered?" Randy said.

"I do wish you would call me Maddy, Randle. And yes, I am quite content, all things being considered," she replied.

"Harry, if you might amuse yourself on the putting green across from the pool, I would appreciate a few minutes alone with Ms. Metzger," Randy threw in my direction.

"I live for putting greens," I said with a smile, then moseyed on over to the putting green I must have missed on my earlier visual survey of the grounds.

Chapter 44

"You have been practicing," Randy said when he came over to the putting green an hour later.

"Passes the time when you are away from home. No matter where you stay, there is a rug and a glass. I'm thinking of updating my card to include, 'Have Putter, Will Travel,'" I said.

"Very clever, Harry," he said. "Come, let's talk."

We walked back to the cabana with no GC in sight.

"As you have learned, I have known Madeline for a very long time and she and I have become very close. She is an amazing woman for whom I have great personal admiration and for whom I care deeply. She and her daughter are family and always will be."

Brandy appeared from nowhere with two more brandies, then was gone just as quickly.

"There is some information you need to know that should prove to be useful in your current endeavors. Jock Woodburn is an old friend of mine. We have done many deals together in the past and have butted heads just as many times. I was dismayed when he joined forces with Ralph Windel, whom I don't particularly care for. He is a very good businessman when he keeps his head, a dangerous one when he doesn't. Anyone who has dealings with him should consider him in the same way. Do not underestimate him, nor should you turn your back on him. Am I making myself clear, Harry?" he finished.

"Crystal clear, Randle," I replied.

"Lastly, do not underestimate the situation you find yourself in at this time. While I don't profess to know all the details of your current assignment, what I do know leads me to believe the people you seek are playing for keeps. My help is always available, anything, anytime," he said.

"Thank you, and should I need any assistance I know you would be there," I told him.

"Good. I will be leaving after breakfast very early tomorrow morning to continue on to the Far East. Enjoy the rest of your time here; the facilities and Brandy are at your disposal. There are people in this world who are very important to me and I would not want them to be hurt. I know you are sensitive to that, Harry, and I trust that will always matter to you.

"And before I forget, Ms. Simmons sends her best wishes and apologizes for her inability to join us."

"I would have enjoyed seeing her immensely," I replied.

* * *

The feeling something was missing hit me when I woke up the following morning. Mister M. Randle Trundle commanded his surroundings wherever he went and I knew he was already gone. Time's a wasting and there were facilities to enjoy. I got myself together, donned a bathing suit, and headed on down for some breakfast.

Brandy was sitting at the dining room table reading the morning newspaper. I couldn't imagine how he got today's newspaper in this remote location but Randy probably had a lot to do with it.

"Morning," I said as I entered the room.

"Good morning, Mister Shorts. What would you like for breakfast? Ms. Metzger has already eaten and is out by the pool."

"Eggs over easy, bacon and white toast," I said. "Coffee and orange juice would be great if you have. And call me Harry, please," I continued.

"Coming right up, Harry. Here is the morning paper to enjoy while I prepare your breakfast."

And prepare he did. Eggs over easy were perfect, bacon slightly fatty and strawberry jam for the toast. Freshly squeezed OJ and a hazelnut coffee topped it all off. Plus, a copy of the New York Times to remind me there was another world out there somewhere. Brandy was fast becoming a Harry Mickey Shorts fav.

Breakfast completed, my tummy filled and satisfied, I headed out to join my favorite General Counsel of a small town insurance company. The fact she was the only one I currently knew didn't influence my opinion one bit.

"Morning, Ms. Metzger," I called out as I strolled over to the chaise lounge she occupied. As I got closer, I realized the sun was shining down on a whole lot of the GC's body, as were my eyes that didn't dare blink. Luckily the 'Holy Shit, look at that' didn't come out of my mouth and stayed in my head.

"Good morning, Shorts," she responded without looking up, oblivious to my P.I. visual inspection techniques.

"Been in the water or are you afraid your suit might shrink ever so slightly causing it to disappear altogether?" I asked, not to mention envisioned.

At that she looked up, thought for a second, then shook her head and looked back down at the papers in her lap.

Being ignored is something you get used to, warranted or not. A good private investigator blends into the surroundings and people don't give him, or her, a second thought. The GC was following suit allowing me to blend into a chaise lounge and investigate the insides of my eyelids, otherwise known as a nap.

* * *

The first splash of water was barely enough to cause a slight twitch of the foot. The second was like a tsunami that washed over my body and instantly jolted me awake.

"What the hell?" is what I believe I said.

"Suit's still intact, didn't shrink a bit," the GC said when I realized where the water had come from. She was hanging onto the side of the pool, a mischievous smile on her face, obviously quite pleased with herself.

"You felt the need to nearly drown me to tell me that?" I asked.

"Just a small amount compared to what's left in the pool. I didn't want to spend the entire morning here alone and you would have become 'lobster man' before long. I saved you the pain and embarrassment, Shorts," she said.

"You been whiling long?" I asked.

"Awhiling," she responded.

Clever little GC, isn't she?

I proceeded to perform a perfectly dreadful Greg Louganis from the board causing some of the remaining water to remove itself from the pool. I think it was the dive but the water could have been scared and run away.

"Very graceful dive, Shorts. I take it water sports aren't your forte" she said.

"That would be correct, your GCness," I responded. "What was your first clue?"

"A decent diver doesn't enter the water face and chest first in case you weren't aware," she said.

"Point taken," I replied.

We frolicked in the pool for a while ending up at the shallow end. She swam laps and dove; I frolicked and tried to look good. Mostly I looked at her. Damn, she looked good enough to…

"Race you up and back, Shorts. As you don't seem to excel at the sport, I'll spot you half a length to start."

"Know a sure bet when you see one, I can see. What shall we wager on this one-sided race?" I asked.

"Let's just swim and we'll see how we finish," she said.

One, two, three and off I went. Metzger waited the required half length of the pool, or at least I assumed she did, then did her fish thing. She was resting against the side of the pool when I finally reached the wall.

"Guess I end up on top," was all she said as she jumped out of the pool and walked away. I didn't know what she meant at the time, but man, what a walk.

Chapter 45

The three S's taken care of—shit, shower and shave for those who don't know—I headed down for lunch. My hope was my man Brandy would whip up something scrumdy to appease my growing hunger. At least he could cure the food hunger, I figured.

"Ms. Metzger, a pleasure to see you again. Have you had lunch yet?" I asked, polite in my shame at having gotten whipped in the pool.

"No, Shorts, and not because I was waiting for you. Brandy is off restocking the supplies and hasn't returned as of yet. My laziness has won out over my hunger so far," she said.

"I can wait," I lied. "What have we got planned for the rest of the day?" I asked.

"We, Shorts?" she replied.

"Yes, we, Metzger," was my retort.

"We, meaning I, have some work to get finished this afternoon that will require approximately an hour to an hour and a half. After that, we, meaning I, had no definite plan in place for the remainder of the day."

"We, meaning I, have exactly the same plan in place for today, minus the work to get finished this afternoon that will require approximately an hour to an hour and a half," I said.

Saved by the Brandy who arrived at that very instant. I helped him bring in the provisions and we, meaning we, decided what sounded good for lunch, which turned out to be delicious. Chicken salad is chicken salad, unless Brandy does his magic and transforms it into something you have never tasted nor imagined before; a Waldorf salad as a side accompaniment, followed by mini éclairs and a desert wine that blossomed in our mouths. We were beyond satisfied with our mid-day feast.

Metzger went off to do her work thing and I went out to the pool to digest and vegetate for a bit. We, yes the combined we, decided to meet at the tennis court I had found beyond the putting green for a set or two later in the afternoon. If the GC was as good on the court as she was in the pool, Harry's ass was in for another sound whipping. I could play some, but I wasn't great by any stretch of anyone's imagination.

* * *

Brandy was feeding me some balls as a warm up when this vision in violet tennis togs that fit like a glove appeared. She had on a sleeveless top and a skirt that barely covered her ass to go with the never-ending legs and tiny violet pompoms on the back of her socks. Even Brandy stopped serving balls to steal a glance at the GC in all her tennis splendor. Talent or no talent, I was done.

"What the well dressed GC's are wearing these days?" I asked after having regained my composure slightly.

"It is what this one wears, Shorts," she replied, obviously as composed as can be.

Brandy excused himself and we proceeded to smack some balls around. It was obvious this wasn't her first foray onto a tennis court. There wasn't the fluidity of her swimming stroke, but her tennis stroke got the job done.

"Ready, Ms. Metzger?" I asked.

"Your serve, Shorts. I don't want you whining about it later," she said.

"If you insist," I replied, and the game was on.

* * *

The match was played somewhere in Mexico by two opponents of similar ability and competitive drive. Three grueling sets came down to a final point, the scores standing at: 6-4, 4-6 and 5-4 (40-30), Shorts to serve.

"The gentleman from New York will serve at match point," came the announcement from the Imaginary Chair Umpire (ICU). The tension was thick throughout the imaginary crowd.

Shorts bends down and ties his shoelace, stealing a glance at his opponent. Steely determination is etched on her face, fire in her eyes. Perspiration covers her body, her outfit now stuck to her like a second skin accentuating every part of her.

"Match point I believe, Ms. Metzger," Shorts says, averting his eyes to avoid the deadly 'redwood' dilemma.

"For now, Shorts," Ms. Metzger replies confidently.

"Play will resume, Mister Shorts," demands the ICU.

The ball is tossed upward and the *thwack* of racket on fuzzy ball punctuates the deafening silence. A perfectly placed serve, deep and up the middle, renders the opponent defenseless, match point seemingly belonging to Shorts. But wait, as Shorts moves to the net to receive congratulations from his conquest, a conference between Ms. Metzger and the ICU sends Ms. Metzger back to the baseline.

"Net cord, first serve," Shorts hears in imaginary disbelief.

Ever the gracious sportsman, Shorts retreats to the baseline, ready to duplicate the prior stroke. His next serve is not nearly as effective and Metzger hits a backhand down the line. Shorts gets to it and goes cross court, expertly anticipated by his opponent who fires back a blistering return. Shorts runs it down and throws up a defensive lob that hits the base line, the resulting overhead by Metzger weak and short. Shorts rushes the net and whistles a backhand to the corner, Metzger poorly out of position by now. A high return, a deft drop shot by Shorts safely over the net, Metzger was powerless to run it down.

"Game, Set & Match to the gentleman from New York," announces the aforementioned chair.

As they meet at the net, Shorts is gracious in victory, Metzger complimentary in defeat. As they head back to the main house, over the thunderous applause of the imaginary crowd, Shorts can be heard saying, "I guess we both get to end up on top."

Chapter 46

Cocktails on the patio before dinner seemed like a perfect time for a discussion on the real reason for this trip. A little R&R in a Mexican hideaway was a nice idea but could not be the only reason.

"So, Ms. Metzger, what is the real scoop on this little trip of ours? Randy loves my butt and you are the prodigal child, but your hour with him was more than catch-up, I would have to guess," I started.

"Shorts, why does everything have to have another meaning?" she asks.

"He gave me some important information and it was critical to do it where nobody would be the wiser. It also involved your company to a large degree. You spent an hour with him in the same setting, an hour that could have occurred anywhere if it was just catch-up time," I said in reply

"I'm going to explain this in terms even you can understand, Shorts. The General Counsel has ultimate responsibility for the legal, regulatory and compliance issues of a company. Any irregularities must be reported to the appropriate parties at their earliest evidence. That responsibility extends from internal entities, like the Board of Directors, to all outside agencies or bodies. The General Counsel is the watchdog and legal guardian of the company's assets, its reputation and its employees. Failure to fulfill any fiduciary, legal or moral responsibility is inexcusable."

She stopped to sip her drink and collect her thoughts.

"I take my position very seriously and all that it entails. Randle is well aware of MechInsCo's current situation and is concerned. He is concerned for the company and for me, personally. Our discussions revolved around both."

"And me?" I asked.

"You, Shorts? He is concerned for you and whatever you are currently involved in, as you know. He is concerned for me as well. It seems he knows you and your proclivity for the ladies, both younger and older. Good fatherly advice is always welcome and appreciated," she said.

"Heavy. Perhaps I should mind my business and let you tend to yours. Whatever business of MechInsCo might involve both of us, if any, can wait for now. Presently, another drink would seem to be the business at hand for both of us, one I think I can handle without causing too much additional trouble," I said.

"Trouble. You trouble, Shorts?"

I ignored the GC and got us each another Gimlet from Brandy, perfectly created, as one would expect.

"I failed to tell you how lovely you look this evening, Ms. Metzger," I said as I gave her the drink.

She had on a fairly plain dress, a powder blue I think you would call it. Medium cut in front that showed just enough cleavage, slightly above the knee revealing an appropriate amount of thigh when she sat.

"Shorts, compliments are always nice, but they shouldn't be used with ulterior motives as their genesis."

"Hey, Metzger, can't a guy say a lady looks good without it meaning something else?" I said. I hoped I sounded properly indignant and hurt.

"Finish your drink, Shorts, I'm starved. And by the way, you are looking rather good yourself this evening."

* * *

Brandy did it again. The dinner was served just aside the cabana overlooking the pool. Two waiters in full penguin attire served, Brandy explaining each course as it was presented. Garden salad with a light raspberry vinaigrette dressing, calamari appetizer with an amazing lime based sauce, followed by a tangerine sorbet to cleanse our palates. The rack of lamb was out of this world topped only by cherries jubilee for dessert. Man, this guy was good.

We chatted throughout the entire meal, staying away from business, Crissy and us. The 'us' wasn't a matter to be discussed as of yet and perhaps wouldn't be at any time. Business was and needed to be brought out into the open sooner or later.

"Metzger, I have to ask some questions and you can choose to answer or not. One way or the other, I have to give it a try," I said as our after dinner drinks were served.

"You can ask. I'll decide whether to answer as we go," she replied.

"Fair enough," I said. "How much you know about me and why I am at MechInsCo doesn't really matter. What you know about its present condition and how it got there does matter, to me and to you. I would guess that is part of why we are here."

"Go on," she said.

"It would be very helpful if I had some historical perspective, what the company was like before the New York invasion, the people that ran it, and how the change might have had an impact on the current financial troubles. Any insights you might have would be invaluable."

She thought for a bit and then continued to say nothing.

"Metzger, anything would be good."

"Shorts, I'm thinking. Shut up, okay," she said.

She thought for almost a minute, then continued to say nothing. Finally she spoke.

"Frangelica, I like the taste. It's different but somehow similar to an after dinner drink I've had before. Have Brandy refill the glasses and I'll be waiting in the hot tub."

With that, she got up and headed off into the darkness toward the hot tub. One small problem I could think of that might pertain to her statement—we weren't dressed for a dip in the hot tub. In fact, I didn't even know there was a hot tub and if I asked Brandy about the hot tub, he probably would deduce the same lack of appropriate attire dilemma. Doing the gentlemanly thing and all that, I guessed I should not ask. I got our drinks and followed the GC into the darkness.

Chapter 47

With two fine cut crystal glasses in hand refilled with the same poison, I started in the general direction Metzger had traveled. The powers of a finely trained private investigator are enhanced by the obvious clue. The discarded shoes were my first indication I was headed in the right direction. The dress was another; motivating me to continue on the path I was presently traveling. The hot tub, illuminated only by moonlight, and directly in front of me, was the clincher.

"Comfy, Metzger?" I asked.

"Quite, Shorts," she replied.

The jets were creating a frothy swirl that allowed the GC's current state of dress, or undress, to remain a mystery. When I offered her the refill, she stood to accept her drink, and with Harry Mickey Shorts being a finely trained private investigator as we have discussed, the mystery was solved. Also, having been in tight situations before, it enabled me to hold onto both glasses as I took in the moonlit beauty and striking nakedness of the General Counsel of MechInsCo. It also enabled me to hand the GC her drink, doff my clothes, and hop in the hot tub before the words, "Jesus H. Christ, Metzger?" passed my lips.

"I didn't know his last name was Metzger," she smirked.

Speechless. Harry Mickey Shorts had been rendered speechless by the GC of a nowhere USA insurance company. A knock your socks off drop-dead gorgeous one, though.

"Okay, wise gal, let's talk while we luxuriate in this hell-hole of a paradise," I said.

"Okay, Harry, let's. You ask and I'll decide if I will answer. Fair enough?"

"Fair enough. Just stay below the water line so I can concentrate at least a little bit."

"I'll try, Harry," she said.

"What can you tell me about the New York yahoos I can't already see on the surface?"

"There isn't much I know about them that isn't visible. Brought in to make us 'little time insurance folk' a big-time company and make the venture capitalists a great deal of money. On the surface Collins reeks of asshole and the other guys are New York all the way."

"Do they all follow Collins' lead or are they assholes all by themselves? I haven't met one I like yet," I said.

"They can stand on their own merits—each and every one of them."

"What about the turnaround on the financial side? Any thoughts on why the bottom line turned bright red?" I asked.

"I can't opine on that issue, Harry. I have no facts or proof to back up anything I may believe, so I'll pass."

"But, you have a theory?" I tried.

"Which of the four letters in 'pass' didn't you get, Harry?"

"Now that you mention it, if I had my choice, I'd get a piece of the last three," I said.

She thought on that one for a few seconds, smiled, then had a long, deep sip of her drink.

"All four together I understand," I continued. "Let me try it another way. What is your role in the financial side of the company and who do you get your info from?" I asked.

"I get results and attend board meetings, hear the management spew, same as the rest of the senior management team. As for anything extra, I'm not one of them, Harry. Outsiders are exactly that, outsiders. We are considered part of the old regime that lost its power and we don't matter anymore. There's a new sheriff in town, deputies included, and he and his posse are running things their way."

"Would make it tough to coexist, I'd think," I said.

"Some days are worse than others, Harry. And as for my contacts, they shall remain nameless for now. Rest assured, I do have them, Harry, and they are very loyal and very well informed."

"One more question. Stoner and his people seem to be in the pan on the burner, just trying to avoid the flames. They all copasetic?"

"What you see is what you get, Harry, at least most of the time."

With that, the GC finished her drink, placed it on the tile surrounding the hot tub, and smiled that smile that would sink a navy. She rose and stood for an instant, an instant that seemed like an eternity, with the moon over her shoulder, just long enough to refresh my memory. Stirring what stirs, also.

"That will be all for now, Harry" she said.

I was rendered speechless as I watched her step out of the tub and head for the main house, clothes temporarily forgotten, her French braid swaying back and forth across that beautiful three letter part of pass. When she got to the French doors I was able to take a breath again.

Chapter 48

To say the least, it had been quite a day. A drink in the study sounded like a perfect end to the day and, after showering and throwing on some comfy duds, it was where I headed.

"May I bring you something to enjoy by the fire, Harry?" Brandy inquired. How he appears out of thin air was amazing.

"Yes, I believe I would enjoy a Peppermint Schnapps on the rocks if you have, Brandy," I replied.

"Very good, make yourself comfortable and I'll be right back," he said.

I had made some notes when I returned to my room, post hot tub excursion, and was mentally reviewing them when Brandy brought my libation.

"Thanks, Brandy. Why don't you call it a night and let me fend for myself from here on in. You've already done more than enough today," I told him.

"If you need anything at all, just call. If not, breakfast will be available any time after six tomorrow morning. Good night, Harry," Brandy said as he went off on his merry way.

* * *

Drink in hand, bottle and ice at the ready, relaxation was taking over my body. I hadn't learned anything new today about MechInsCo or the key players but had gotten the heads up again from Randy to watch my back. The GC was equally unhelpful in the information area, but I did learn how delightful she looked in the moonlight. The fact she was naked as a jaybird only served to enhance the experience immensely. Problem was, I hadn't gotten any closer to understanding what the hell was going on at MechInsCo, who the real bad guys were, how they were doing whatever it was they were doing, and why.

"Comfy, Harry?" Metzger asked as she entered the study.

"Quite, Metzger," I replied, sure I had heard that exchange before.

"What are you offering?" she asked.

I looked at her, a vision in a baby blue jumpsuit, the perfect amount of cleavage to behold. I thought hard while weighing my options, then offered a duplicate of what I was having.

"That would be lovely for starters," she said. "It's been a long time since I enjoyed a good Peppermint Schnapps."

I disregarded the 'for starters' comment, for now, and made sure we were both comfortable before the fire. It wasn't cold but the fire seemed perfect.

"Have a good day, Metzger?" I asked.

"A very nice day, Harry. Thanks for asking. You?"

"More than I could have asked for or expected," I replied. "The hot tub was quite a pleasant surprise and very relaxing."

"I like to enjoy a dip in the tub after dinner when I am here. It serves to relax me and it is something I don't have the opportunity to do back in Pennsylvania. Having company was pleasing as well," she added.

"The pleasure was all mine, Metzger. All mine," I said with a smile.

"It's good to give your eyes and imagination a good workout periodically, Harry. I trust they were both working overtime, weren't they?" she asked.

"Double time and a half," I said. "Your stroll back to the house was worth the price of admission all by itself."

"You never know what lies ahead, Harry. You probably forgot to add the tax and tip and you may need to make amends before the night is over."

Hard to disregard that one the ever-wary P.I. thought to himself.

"Crissy know where you are, Harry?"

"No, she doesn't," I said. "I was very careful to split without seeing her and having to explain why I'd be gone for the weekend and where I'd be."

"Good. Let's keep this little trip between us grownups, if you don't mind," she said.

"P.I.'s are sworn to secrecy while they are on a case, Metzger. They never divulge the aspects of an investigation, unless extreme torture renders them utterly helpless."

"We'll see about that, Harry. We'll see," she said.

Drink in hand, the GC rose and started for the door that led to the upstairs quarters. Sleeping quarters to be exact.

"Bring the bottle and ice bucket, Harry. It's time for a little duo detecting that will most certainly bring some immediate and interesting results. Let's hope you are as good as I think you are, Harry."

Metzger turned and was gone with Harry Mickey Shorts, private investigator on the prowl, right behind her.

Chapter 49

Bottle and ice bucket in tow as instructed by the General Counsel of the company I now worked for, I stopped in my room to brush my teeth and slip into something a bit more comfortable. Cliché you say, kiddo. It also happened to be a bit easier to doff as the situation might warrant.

One thing posed a tiny problem. I didn't know which room the GC was staying in and there were too many rooms to choose from. Seemed like a typical Harry Mickey Shorts QAS. How do you find someone when the possibilities are identical and too many to overcome in a short period of time? Reduce the possibilities. Get vocal!

I stepped into the hallway and yelled, "Hey, Metzger!"

A door opened and Metzger poked her head out into the hallway. Problem solved and investigation ready to commence.

* * *

Metzger had taken the opportunity to get into something a bit more comfy as well. I made the assumption it was more comfy due to the fact, as I entered her room, her outfit consisted of a baby blue teddy that required very little imagination and less material to construct.

"Metzger."

"Shorts."

"Drink?" I asked.

"A short one for now," she replied.

"As short as the teddy you're wearing?" I asked.

"Definitely shorter than the redwood in your shorts," she answered.

I poured, we drank, then all hell broke loose and the fun began. The 'get comfy' idea we both employed proved to be well worth the effort. My T-Shirt and shorts, all I happened to have on, hit the floor in a jiff. Sans teddy, Metzger was a sight to behold. Legs that didn't quit, an ass to thank heaven for, and nipples that seemed to grow without stop atop breasts that begged to be caressed and more. Harry Mickey Shorts was ready, willing and able.

The aggressive, driving needs of the gymnastic daughter were contrasted by the careful, longing needs of the mother. Wild passion was replaced by experienced longevity, take and be taken through giving and receiving. It was as if it was meant to be and each and every move choreographed to make the two become one. What was probably not much more than an hour seemed to last all night. The GC's comment from the pool proved to be accurate, she ended up on top. Spent and satisfied, together we slept.

* * *

The sensation of opening your eyes and thinking, 'Where the hell am I, and what did I do last night?' is never good. But, the realization of where you are, and what you did, can at times be totally awesome. When I woke up the following morning, it was awesome time, baby. Best of all, Metzger was still lying next to me, sound asleep in all her GC splendor.

How to wake the sleeping beauty is often half the fun. I gave this one some thought and, since it was still very early, decided to go with the slow and easy version. The slightest brush of tongue on the tip of an ear lobe, a wisp of breath on bare breast, followed by a single fingernail drawn gently along the length of the spine. Wakeful stirring in the subject before you, you carefully cup a hand over an ample breast and nibble playfully on the same ear. The silent moan that ensues signals the subject is now ready for advanced awakening techniques, the further stroking of hardening nipples advancing the process appropriately.

"Morning, Metzger," I said.

What sounded like, "Morning to you, too," came out in a cooing sound.

"I would assume you slept well?" I asked.

"Oh, quite well," she said, now sounding slightly more with it.

"It's fairly early," I said. "We could go down for some breakfast and get a head start on the day, or we could find out if we're just as good together in the morning. Your call, Metzger," I offered.

A playful smile crossed her face as she said, "Let's improvise and use part of your statement, me getting a 'head start' while you 'go down' and then we can 'get together.'

"How about we just get it on?" I said and we proceeded to do just that. We laughed and played, her doing a little of this and me a little of that, an hour of delightful foreplay leading to a thunderous climax. Sheer joy and naughty fun all rolled into one. And, oh yeah, this time Shorts ended up on top.

Chapter 50

"Morning, Brandy," I said as I strolled into the dining room. The shower situation proved to be a little lengthier than planned when the GC entered the picture. The operative word there being 'entered' as it turned out.

"Morning, Sir," Brandy replied. "How would a grand breakfast that includes all our specialties sound?"

"Just what the doctor ordered, Brandy. You are the man."

"Will Ms. Metzger be joining you for breakfast?" he asked. Funny how his face looked slightly different when he asked the question.

"I believe she will be down shortly," I answered.

He should only know we'd already been down, up, and down again this morning.

Metzger entered the room at that very moment, a healthy glow to go with her unmistakable beauty.

"Brandy," she said in his direction.

"You are looking especially wonderful this morning, Ms. Metzger. Breakfast will be served shortly."

"Morning, Shorts," she said in my direction.

"Morning, Metzger," I replied in hers.

The make believe niceties out of the way, we each grabbed a piece of the 'I don't know how it gets here' newspaper. It kept us busy until Brandy arrived with the breakfast feast. Victoria, the sometimes assistant, helped him unload the goodies.

"Will there be anything else either of you might need at this moment?" Brandy asked.

"I think we're fine," I said. Metzger nodded in agreement.

"That being the case, Victoria and I will run out and do a few errands before lunch time arrives. The plane will be available anytime after two," he said.

"Thank you, Brandy," the GC said. "We will be ready to leave at one forty-five if that is okay with you?" she asked.

"That will be fine, Ms. Metzger. You will find fresh towels and iced tea in the cabana if you wish to make use of the pool before you depart. Lunch will be ready any time after noon," he said.

"Excellent suggestion, perhaps we will, Brandy. And maybe a dip in the hot tub as well," she said, glancing in my direction.

* * *

Breakfast was all Brandy said it would be. Tummies filled, we went up to our rooms to pack for the trip home and don our swim attire for a final frolic by the pool. The weekend felt like it had just started and it was already almost done, a memory or two to take back squeezed in between.

No sight of Metzger when I got down to the pool area, so I lay down on one of the lounge chairs, closed my eyes, and enjoyed the warmth of the sun. It felt great, until my serenity was interrupted by a bucket of cold water that came crashing down on my entire body. The old 'GC sneak attack' caught the napping P.I. off guard.

"Yo!" I yelled as Metzger loped across the deck and dove for cover in the pool.

Regaining his composure, the cool, calm and collected P.I. makes his way to the pool edge and executes a devastating 'cannonball' into the middle of the pool. From beneath the surface, he spots the suspect attempting a getaway by climbing out of the pool. His laser fast reflexes allow him to reach the suspect in time and grasp the suspect by the bikini bottom. To his dismay, or perhaps not, the suspect leaves the pool by wriggling out of the bikini bottom and takes refuge in the adjacent hot tub. In hot pursuit, he confronts the suspect at hot tub edge, evidence in hand.

"Lose something, Metzger?" I said, bikini bottom held out before me.

"Nothing I believe I will need in the immediate future, Shorts."

I looked.

She looked back.

"This may require closer scrutiny," I said as I stepped into the hot tub, somewhat surprised to find the matching bikini top floating on the water's surface. Not wanting to feel overdressed, I lost my suit, pronto.

The jet streams provided an extra exhilaration to the following activities, which culminated with a whoop, a holler and a pair of 'ahs'. It was truly a treat to have found a lady as beautiful, intelligent and unbelievably adventurous as the GC. Mother and daughter, so different, yet so the same.

"Time to mosey on up and prepare to leave our little hideaway," I said after we had been resting arm in arm for a while.

"Shorts, it was quite an entertaining weekend, but let's remember who and what we are when we return to MechInsCo. Plus, there is Crissy to think about," she said.

"Madame GC, your position at MechInsCo warrants the utmost respect and I, Harry Mickey Shorts, will be sure to give both you and the position its due."

"Why do I even bother, Shorts," she said in mock disgust.

"Here's why," I replied, and I proceeded to show her why in ways that convinced her one hundred percent.

* * *

Properly attired, we headed back to the house to make preparations for our return trip to Pennsylvania. We chatted casually about people in the office—the good, the bad and the ugly—and in the midst of the conversation Metzger offhandedly said "…maybe Stoner remains a bit off since he still hasn't gotten over what happened to his uncle." We were entering the house and ran into Brandy who indicated lunch would be ready momentarily. We went right upstairs, the GC's comments about Stoner and everyone else locked in my brain for future use.

Chapter 51

"How is he, Tom?" is how I started the conversation when Tom opened his door later that night.

"Cam's asleep now and seems to be healing pretty good considering what they did to him," he replied. "Take your coat off and sit yourself. I'll get us a couple beers to talk with."

I didn't think he meant we would use the beers to talk, but that's Tom. He just likes having a few cool ones, especially when he's about to get down with something heavy. Cam and what happened to him was real heavy.

"The doc says he's gonna be fine, the wrist will heal no problem. He did suggest Cam stay outta the way of swinging baseball bats for a while. He's a funny guy, that doc."

"Yeah, a real scream," I agreed. "Cam say anything else that might help us understand who did this? Any of your good buds know anything? I know you know you shouldn't be asking, but I also know you did. It's who you are, Tom. Anything either way?"

"I didn't ask Cam no more, he didn't say no more. Real quiet right about now is what he is. He'll come out, but gotta be Cam's time to come out his way. And I ain't saying I been askin' around, Harry, but if I was, there ain't no new guys staying anywhere around these parts, or hanging anywhere neither. If they are New York guys, they come and they go when they done what they come to do."

"Well, if you had asked, that would be good info to have. Would save a bunch of wasted time looking for something, or someone, who ain't there to find."

"Yeah, I thought so, Harry," Tom said.

"Let's kick back, drink some suds, talk about old times. Okay, Tom? This bullshit can save for another day," I said.

"Cheers, Harry," Tom said.

"Cheers, Tom. To better times," I replied.

* * *

Monday morning was as cold as a witch's tit, in a brass bra, in a blizzard, on the North Pole. Yeah, that cold. But not nearly as cold as the reception I got from the receptionist at MechInsCo when I walked in the front door.

"Well, Mister Shorts, nice to see you again," Crissy said, never looking up from her console.

"Good morning, Crissy. Sorry I missed you this weekend. I had an emergency come up late Friday and I had to split. I thought I'd be back earlier, but it dragged on. Being with a Metzger is where I wanted to be."

A good doobie never lies!

"Whatever, go away," she said as she picked up the phone and turned her back to me.

Harry Mickey Shorts can take a hint. Off I went, shunned by the younger half of the mother/daughter combination I was presently making merry with. Yeah, I gotta be nuts for sure.

* * *

I proceeded upstairs and headed to the accounting department to begin my work week. Figured it would be good to check the current climate up there, so I stopped by Stoner's office.

"Morning, Mary Ann. How was your weekend?" I asked. "And how is Joe doing this morning? Any catastrophes yet?"

"Morning, Harry. I'm good, Joe's good, the department is good. So far, no eruptions to deal with."

"Still early, kiddo," I said. She laughed, and it was good to hear somebody laugh in this joint for a change.

"Come in, Harry," came a voice from Joe's office.

"Hey, Joe," I said as I sat in one of the chairs in front of his desk.

"Harry, I have to go down to Baltimore for a few days, business stuff, and I'm gonna need your reports when I get back. Any problem with that happening, Harry?"

"Joe, with what you have asked me to do so far, that should be a piece of cake. Anything special you looking for?" I asked.

"No, just do what I asked and nothing more. Got that, Harry?" he said.

"I got you, Joe. I can follow directions with the best of them."

"You didn't before, so make sure you do now," Joe said like he meant it.

"Yes sir, boss," I said and promptly left Stoner's office. Don't get what or who's chewing on his ass, but he best cease and desist chewing on mine.

* * *

The rest of the day was spent doing boring busy work, in a boring office cubicle, looking for something that wasn't boring and would shed some light on the case. My focus remained on 'following the money' without throwing suspicion my way. I'm sure somebody was already watching me. There had to be an angle I hadn't caught yet, a method of playing 'slight-of-hand' with the funds that seemed commonplace and acceptable. Sounds good, but what the hell was it.

Sufficient progress on the reports I had been asked to produce meant I could snoop around a little at the end of the day. I made copies of the premium ledgers and reinsurance transaction reports to study later that night. No reason to go in that direction, no reason not to. Just another rock to lift that hadn't been lifted yet. It was also time to introduce myself to Greg Boalman, the reinsurance guy at MechInsCo, and see where he stood in the scheme of things.

First things first—Crissy. I proceeded to rectify the situation by heading for the front desk.

Chapter 52

"Excuse me, is Crissy here?" I asked the security guard I found sitting at the front reception desk.

"Not here," he responded.

"Yeah, I noticed," I said. "Is she gone for the day?"

"Not here, don't know," the wizard expounded.

"Thanks, and save the words. You may need them to actually carry on a conversation some day," I said as I walked away.

Crissy either left early or was purposely evading me to punish me for my weekend disappearing act. How flighty they are when still young. And all because I was traipsing around Mexico with her mom.

Go figure.

My plans for the evening dashed before they even got started, I decided to go to Plan B. Harry Mickey Shorts' Plan B—when in doubt, drink heavily. Since I needed a drinking buddy, and I was sure my good friend Tom needed a night out, I decided to call him to join me for a few. Cam would have to rest up all by himself for a bit.

"Tom, Harry. My elbow's a tad stiff and my throat's a tad dry. Time to bend the old elbow and lubricate the vocal cords," I told him.

"Harry, I could use a bit of a good time. Just what the doc ordered, I think," he said.

"I'll be by in ten minutes. Be out front and bring your wooden leg with ya—you may need it tonight."

"I'll be curbside when ya get here," he said and hung up.

Growler's was out of the picture, a potential Crissy sighting too much of a possibility. Plus, with everything that has happened, Tom could probably use a little excitement in his life right about now. A Shorts QAS seems to have popped up. What might get Tom's engine revved up some? Some T&A should do the trick. Hooters here we come!

* * *

Hooters wasn't overly crowded when we got there, so we grabbed a spot back in the corner. Served two purposes—gave us some privacy and we got to look at all the T&A in the place. An old detective trick that comes in handy now and again.

"Tom, can you handle a little business talk?" I asked. "I'm spinning my wheels in the mud and getting nowhere fast."

"Sure, Harry. Do me some good to use my brain for a bit."

"Thanks, Tom. Maybe you'll see something I'm not. The New York guys they brought into MechInsCo are clearly running the show, but they're all pissed off at the world and making everyone else suffer for it. The local people are taking the heat and don't necessarily like it. Some actually got fired and the rest live with that fear all the time. Results continue to go downhill and money goes bye-bye faster than they can bring it in the door. And me, I can't find any evidence of who's doing what, if somebody is actually doing something."

Tom had been listening to me and checking out the tall blond with the big tits with equal intent. He thought a minute more, took a hit on his beer, then said, "Maybe ain't nothing to find, Harry. Just maybe the New York yahoos are fuck-ups and can't run an insurance company worth a damn," he said.

"Yeah, I thought of that, Tom. But the company made money before, and these guys are using their contacts to bring in mucho business. They were successful in New York, no reason to think they shouldn't be successful here."

"Harry, you know things don't make no sense sometimes, then they makes all the sense in the world. If it's there to find, you'll find it. Rock after rock, you know the drill. Keep liftin' the rocks and one of these times the clue you need will be there," Tom said.

"Maybe I just needed you to remind me, Tom. Thanks," I said.

"No problem, Harry. Now, can I enjoy my beer and these fine young ladies you brought me here to look at?"

"Admire away, Tom. Admire away."

Chapter 53

Reports and numbers talk to you if you understand the language. If you don't happen to speak the lingo fluently, like me, it's nothing but gibberish sometimes. Later that night, I grabbed the info I brought home and spent time looking at the numbers and reports individually, combined together, and in bits and pieces. Sorry to say, nothing jumped out at me. Here's what I saw:

The company did achieve its goal of growing its premium base—already knew that.

The reinsurance sent out to other companies also grew just as fast, or faster—already knew that.

The old reinsurance companies they did business with didn't grow that much when compared to the overall premium growth—new info.

Two new reinsurance deals were put in place since the New York guys came to town. One was a Captive that had average results, the second another Captive that seemed to be very profitable with a ton of premium going their way and minimal losses.

This second Captive was called UNK RE, and it was real odd—it was buried in a reinsurance transaction that sent money from a standard reinsurance treaty to a second company—a retrocede arrangement as it's called. Okay, enough insurance mumbo-jumbo for now.

What this all meant, I couldn't tell you. All I got from the two hours of mind-numbing number staring was more questions but, considering where I was before that, it was something to follow. Why all that premium and very little losses? And why give away the business if it was that good? And why would the reinsurance company give it away if there were very few losses? All questions I didn't have answers to, but would have to get some sooner rather than later. I also needed to find out who made those decisions.

* * *

"Well, well, well, if it isn't Shorts, the elusive accounting clerk," greeted me as I entered MechInsCo the following morning. "I'm amazed you could find the place two days in a row."

"Morning to you too, Crissy," I started. "And for your information, it is only for the privilege of a glimpse of your gorgeous face I come back at all. Well, that and a paycheck, of course," I continued.

A smile, an, "Up yours, Shorts," and my day was made.

"Mister Shorts." A familiar voice broke the mood. I turned to see mama Metzger, in all her GC splendor, heading toward the cafeteria for her morning yogurt and coffee, French braid in full swing. That ain't all that was swinging either.

"Gotta go, Crissy. A drink soon?" I asked which didn't even get an answer. The Metzger ladies were gonna drive Shorts crazy.

Chapter 54

Getting to see Greg Boalman, the reinsurance guy at MechInsCo, proved to be pretty simple. I called, he said come on over, I went.

"Thanks for seeing me, Mister Boalman," I started.

"Hey, it's Greg, okay. You're Harry, right?"

"Yeah, Harry's good."

"What can I do for you, Harry? You're kinda new here if I remember correctly," he said.

"I am," I answered. "Just trying to meet people here and somebody mentioned your name. I'm over in accounting and I figured since I was working on premium and loss stuff, I'd stop by, say hello, and get the lay of the reinsurance land here."

"Good deal, Harry. My door is always open," he said.

It was time to figure out if he was a player in the game or not. As long as I was there, I might as well take a shot.

"I was working on a few reports for Joe Stoner, my boss, and I noticed the increase in reinsurance the company has ceded over the last two years. Rumors going around linked the poor results to some bad decisions in underwriting, plus the revised reinsurance position as well. I wasn't here and wouldn't have any way to know if it was true. Hard to see just looking at numbers and sticking them in reports," I said dumbly.

"Standard reinsurance decisions in a market that's tough to make an underwriting profit in," Greg said. "You write more business, you cede more business. Nothing on my side of the house is causing the problems here," he said with conviction.

"Hey, Greg, I'm just saying hi and telling you what somebody said. My mistake, I'm sorry. I didn't mean to imply anything about anything. I'll buy you a beer to cool things, okay?"

"Sure, Harry, didn't mean to jump on you. A beer sometime would be great," he said as the phone rang. Saved by the bell I guess. I waved and headed out as he picked up the receiver.

Standard reinsurance in a standard market. Maybe I know less about the insurance business than I thought.

Chapter 55

For the next several weeks, things went along without much to jump up and down about. Work was nothing more than doing reports and trying not to generate any undue suspicion while I looked for clues, any clues. To be honest, I was beginning to think there wasn't anything to be found.

The lady front was equally as cool, with Crissy in Europe to meet with her master and the GC doing her corporate thing, avoiding one Harry Mickey Shorts. I knew there wouldn't be a great deal of contact with mama Metzger, but a wee bit would have been nice. Lots of fish in the sea, but no reason to complicate things any further by making it a trio.

Cam was healing great and Tom was starting to feel better, both about himself and things in general. The guilt bugaboo was starting to wear off and he was actually starting to talk about taking on some new work. Talk is cheap and I didn't think he would actually do it this soon. Tom's a stubborn old bastard and doesn't forgive and forget very easily.

All things being equal, nada going on, until…

* * *

"Mister Shorts, Mister Collins would like to see you," Mary Ann told me as I rounded the corner to my cubicle one morning.

"Now?" I asked, already knowing the response I would get.

"She didn't say," is what Mary Ann said, just as expected.

"Call her and tell her I'm on my way up," I told Mary Ann. The she being the Ice Queen who would have called for Collins.

I hightailed it up to the third floor to see what the Prez wanted with me. The last time he and I spoke we talked about his Harrisburg Senators team and the possibility of me helping out. If it wasn't that, I had no idea.

"Mister Shorts, you may go right in. Mister Collins has been waiting for you," came with a 'Where the hell were you' stare.

So, I went in.

"Shorts, sit down. I don't have much time, so listen good. Pitchers and catchers reported early to Florida and I need someone to help get them ready. You know the league and I don't have anyone else to put any trust in. The management staff is almost all new with minimal Double A experience. Interested?" he asked.

"Would you like me to leave this afternoon or tomorrow morning, Mister Collins?" I asked.

"Good answer, Shorts. Take the rest of today to clean stuff up here and get your ticket from my assistant. You leave at eight a.m. tomorrow morning. Report to the manager, Jake somebody, when you get there. I want a full evaluation of the guys down there, who to keep and who to flush. A week tops. Got it?"

"Got it," I said. "And thanks, Mister Collins. I'll get you a complete analysis of the talent and be back in a week."

"Oh, yeah," Collins said. "Couple of my partners are down there pissing away our money. Take them out and show them a good time while you're down there. Don't let them screw up the team or get me in trouble. Can you handle that, Shorts?" he asked.

"Can do, Mister Collins. You can consider it done," I said.

"Good, now scram." That meant end of conversation in executiveese. I scrammed.

* * *

The boss says get your butt down to Florida, you get your butt down to Florida. Definitely falls under the category of 'Bitch of a job, but somebody has to do it.' Would have preferred to have private jet transportation like in my last excursion, but I'll make do with the first class seat Collins got for me.

I cleaned up what I was working on for Joe Stoner and put in a few requests for some additional information. Seemed in line with what I had been working on and shouldn't raise any flags, but in actuality it wasn't. This info would help me follow up on the conversation with Boalman and clarify some reinsurance angles that needed clarifying. Maybe it was something, maybe nothing, but worth throwing against the wall to see if any of it would stick. Ya just never know.

Chapter 56

Said my 'See yas' to the MechInsCo crew at the end of the day which pissed off Crissy, amused her moms, and worried Stoner. Crissy suggested I do something that should be physically impossible for males to do. Her mom the GC said, "Don't hurt yourself fooling around with that kid's game," and Joe Stoner wanted to know who was gonna do my work while I was gone. I think he was also pissed I was doing something directly for the president. Collectively, everyone was annoyed I was going to be doing it in Florida.

* * *

"Tom, it's Harry. How are ya, man?"

"Harry, haven't heard from ya in a while. I'm okay, been worse I guess," he replied.

This was starting to be a pattern and concerned me more than a bit. Tom's life wasn't getting back to normal and there wasn't anything special happening to jump-start a 'get better quick.' Not normally the 'life of the party,' but nothing that resembled this before either. The ups and downs were troubling.

"Tom, how's Cam? You guys wanna get some food and a few beers tonight?" I asked.

"He's on the mend, Harry, but not here right now. He and some buds are down to the pool hall; probably good for him to get out for some fun right about now."

"Everything all right, Tom?"

"Yeah, don't you worry 'bout me none, Harry. We'll be fine come spring when Cam gets all healed up and this business gets over with," he said.

"You wanna get some grub, Tom?"

"No, you go on by yourself. I got some work to do around here that needs gettin' done."

"Suit yourself, Tom. By the way, I'm going down to Florida for about a week. Some case work, some sun and fun. Take care of yourself and Cam. I'll call you when I get back. Call my cell phone if you need me. Okay, Tom?"

"Sure, Harry. You enjoy yourself and I'll see ya when I see ya."

I gave some thought to taking Tom and Cam with me to Florida, but Tom would want to stick his nose in where it wouldn't belong, and Cam is Cam. Best leave well enough alone and concentrate on what I have to get done down in Florida. Tom's situation does bear watching, though.

* * *

I would have to say I was flat out shocked when I answered my phone that night and heard, "Shorts, I was wondering if I could see you before you leave for Florida?"

"Why sure, Ms. Metzger. It would be a true pleasure," I replied when the surprise wore off and I regained my bearings.

"There's a small bar in Visaggio's Restaurant on Wertzville Road off Route One Fourteen . Meet me there in an hour, Harry, if that's okay?" she said.

"I'll find it," I said, "and an hour is just fine."

"Good," was all I heard before the dial tone came through the receiver. What the hell does the GC want and why now? Beats the hell out of me. Head on over to Vissagio's and find out. Correctamundo—a Harry Mickey Shorts QAS has just entered and left the building!

Chapter 57

An hour later I found myself in a cozy little bar in an upscale Italian Restaurant (for Mechanicsburg, PA) that just happened to have a small motel attached to the restaurant. As I have said so many times before—one never know, do one.

The GC arrived ten minutes after me and bellied up on the stool next to me.

"I'll have what he's having," she said to the bartender before she even said word one to me.

"Absolut Gimlet for the lady," Ned the bartender said to no-one and anyone that was listening.

"Been waiting long?" the GC inquired.

"My whole life," I replied.

Thought, recognition, smile.

"Tonight, Harry, tonight."

"Not long," I replied as Ned placed her drink on the bar in front of her.

"Is here good, or do you want to get a table in the back?" I asked.

"Have you been here before?" the GC asked.

"No," I replied, "but I cased the joint when I came in to see what was up."

She shook her head and said, "Here is fine, Harry."

"So, what's up? Why the urgency? Where's the braid?" I asked.

"I just wanted to confirm a few things for my own understanding, relay a few assurances for your own understanding, and I didn't want either to wait for a week. The braid takes a break every so often when you least expect it."

Interesting I thought to myself, then said, "Interesting," to the GC. Every so often I actually listen to myself.

"Go on," I continued.

"You are subject number one, Harry. An individual with your background and been-there done-that attitude doesn't show up at MechInsCo in Mechanicsburg, PA out of the blue. A friend of a friend does a favor without any explanation needed or given, you get a job, but there's a hidden agenda. I'd bet the rent the poor results of the company have something to do with it. Look all you want, Harry, but remember these are big boys playing for big stakes."

A sip of her drink followed by a deep breath.

"I am subject number two, Harry. Whatever it is you are looking for, if you are actually looking for something, it won't involve me in any way. I am squeaky clean from head to toe, top to bottom, six ways to Sunday. Get the picture, Harry. MechInsCo is very important to me and my career and I wouldn't do anything, not ever, to hurt or jeopardize either one."

A deep breath followed by a sip of her drink.

"Do you understand, Harry?" she asked.

A sip of my drink followed by a deep breath.

"I gotcha, GC," I replied.

"We are subject number three, Harry. Our short time spent together in Mexico affected me more than I would have thought, or expected. Realizing this will be short lived, I seem to have a need to cram as much as I possibly can of Harry Mickey Shorts into my life for as long as I possibly can. The traveling saleswoman registered in Room Seven will be expecting you in ten minutes. And by the way, bring your 'A' game, you're gonna need it."

She got up, tossed the remainder of her drink, and left.

Ten minutes later, 'A' game at the ready, Harry Mickey Shorts left the bar for pleasures known and only imagined.

Chapter 58

"Squirt, how you doing?" I asked my little one since he was the one who answered the phone.

"Good, big guy. Why the call?" he asked.

"I gotta go down to Florida for a week or so and won't be able to make our Saturday soiree this month. Can I get a pass till next month and we will do something special?"

"No," Max said.

"No?" I repeated.

"No, you don't have to do anything special next month. Just seeing you is good enough all by itself," he said.

That little SOB knows exactly what buttons to push.

"Thanks, little one. I'm gonna be around some minor league baseball areas while in Florida and could pick up a trinket or two if you want."

"Yankees," he said.

"Yankees?" I repeated.

"Anything having to do with the greatest of all ball teams would be cool, you know that. A fitted hat would be way cool," he said.

"A fitted Yankee hat it is," I said. "Size eight and a half to fit that inflated head of yours would be in order I would guess." I laughed.

"Very amusing funny guy; you are truly a wit—dim, half, etc." He laughed.

"Tell your sister I said hi and put your mother on, punk! I'll see ya when I get back," I told him.

* * *

"Harry?" the ex said as she came on the line.

"Yeah, it's me, Sherry. How are you doing?" I asked.

"I'm fine, Harry, and it's nice of you to ask. Not too many people ask me that these days," she said.

"Well, I'll have to do it more often I guess. The kids okay?"

"They are fine, Harry. Did I hear you won't be coming up for your Saturday with the kids?" she asked.

"I have to go down to Florida for a week and just found out yesterday.

I'm leaving in a bit and wanted to get to them before I left. Will it be a problem?" I inquired.

"Shouldn't be, Harry. I didn't have any firm plans and I can take them out to Roosevelt Field Mall to get some spring clothes. Briande will love it; Max will bitch and moan and then buy a ton of stuff. Thanks for calling to let me know, Harry."

"Least I can do, Sherry. Buy something for yourself while you're out there," I said. "I probably owe you for some whateverday I missed," I said.

"I appreciate that. Let's have a drink when you get back into town."

"We'll do that. It's been a while and we should talk more often."

"I'd like that, Harry," she said as she rang off.

Have things changed? Don't know for sure, but sounds that way. Have a drink and find out for sure. QAS: ex-wife version.

Chapter 59

The big bird was in the sky and I was on my way to baseball land, spring training minor league style. Déjà vu all over again—again!

Having spent a major portion of last season with the Bayport Schooners of the Double A Eastern League, I have a very good understanding of what happens early on in Florida. The veterans come into camp looking to get into 'game shape,' while the youngsters are trying to impress from the get-go. Compound that with the changes involving the Harrisburg Senators parent club, which will make even the vets showcase a little 'lookee-me' attitude, and it could be an interesting week of baseball. One thing was for certain, there was a bundle of fun to be had.

Baseball scouting for Prez man Collins wouldn't be as much fun as playing for the Schooners, but the Florida weather and a little bit of ball was better than MechInsCo any day. When we landed I went directly to my hotel to drop my gear and rinse the airplane off. It was still early so I figured I'd see what was happening at the baseball complex. Plenty of time for food and fun later on.

* * *

"Hey, man, I'm Harry Mickey Shorts, and I'm looking for the head guy around here," I said to the first person I ran into at the complex.

"Who, and what do you want?" the fine gentleman responded in a most helpful manner. He never looked at me.

"I'm actually looking for Jake Talton, the Senator's manager. But I'll take anyone who can direct me to him if you can't," I said.

"Talton, I think I seen him before. Don't know where he is now, but you can try the coach's room over by the batting cages. Yeah, try there, Mick," he said without looking up.

"You've been very helpful and I hope you find whatever you lost," I told him as I walked away.

He finally looked up but had no idea what I was talking about.

* * *

"One of you guys Talton?" I asked as I entered a small building that had the look of a coach's room.

"I'm Talton," said the tallest of the three guys seated around a table in the middle of the room. The walls where covered with baseball stuff including statistics, schedules, and everything else you could imagine.

"I'm Harry Mickey Shorts," I told him and the other two guys. "Collins sent me down to lend a hand for a week or so."

"Fuck you very much for last year, Shorts," stogie man said.

"Why you are quite welcome," I replied. "Third base coach if I remember, and I enjoyed it immensely I might add," I said with a wide smile.

"Come on in, Shorts," Talton said. "This is Birdie, my bench coach, and I see you already know Gar."

"Birdie," I said as I shook his hand. "And yes, Gar had the pleasure of being on the back end of a royal ass kicking last year courtesy of the Bayport Schooners. I was happy to contribute to his dismay."

"Ass kicking, dick stomping, all over massage with a sledge hammer was more like it," Gar said. "Good to see you're on our side this time."

You know the tune so feel free to sing along with me. "Here a gloat, there a gloat, everywhere a gloat gloat."

"Ah shucks, you're makin' me blush here, Gar," I got out before cracking up.

"Funny, Shorts. Grab a seat and let us tell you what we have to work with this year," Talton said.

The next few hours whizzed by giving me a very good understanding of what I would be looking at on the field. What's in their heads and hearts I'd have to get for myself, on the field and when the sun goes down. The evening work was a bitch, in and out of bars and who knows what else, but taking one for the team was never a problem for me. Sacrifice is my second middle name.

* * *

No rhyme or reason on how the Harry Mickey Shorts mind works, but I got to thinking as I headed back to my hotel room. Who's threatening Tom and scaring his buddies? Who's beating on Cam's ass in a serious way? And who's filling their piggy bank with MechInsCo pennies? All very good questions on the front end of a classic Harry Mickey Shorts QAS. Unfortunately, I don't have any answers and no clue on how to develop solutions—so, this QAS is nothing more than a Q.

For now—Play Ball!

Chapter 60

The logical choice for that night's activities was an easy does it glide into getting to know some of the players. A laid back grab a burger and beer place would let me meet them up front and spend a little time with as many as I could. Unfortunately, it turns out the boys had been working their asses off for a week and tomorrow morning was their first free morning so far.

The possibility of my plan coming off, in any language—Fat Fuckin' Chance! The vets remembered me right off from last year and welcomed me along for the ride. The newbies didn't care—they were going out and a chance to spend time with a guy who was on a winner sounded cool.

Jugs was the establishment's name and the ladies' claim to fame. Typical topless joint with multitudes of T&A everywhere, lap dances for the asking, and babes for the taking. Beer, shots and cigars were flowing freely. We started early and the boys kept on chugging for all they were worth. Food didn't seem to be one of the options for the evening as all available room was needed for the liquid refreshments being consumed. I exhibited unusual restraint and was actually reasonably sober when the fan was turned on. Good thing I was, since things went from honky-dory to potentially very ugly real fast.

It turned out to be college fraternity night-out at the local meat market including a bunch of football jocks looking for some fun and frivolity. The major attraction on this particular evening was 'Miss Luscious' and her bountiful bazooms. She was a blonde bombshell with a body to die for and enough bills stashed in her G-String to support the entire state of Florida for a month. She also was the source of the current upheaval.

"Get lost…" from the frat boys started the fracas, and "Go see your dorm mommy…" from my group kept the fires burning. An all out donnybrook was about to occur when I jumped into the middle of it to protect my ass from Collins' wrath and probably the players well being. Football players in Florida tend to be somewhere between big and bigger. A belly full of suds and a burning desire to claim the fair maiden's jugs for themselves completed the circle.

"You," I said to the kid with the biggest mouth. "Here's what we are gonna do to put an end to this. You and I go outside and get it on one-on-one. You get to take the first poke at me and then I proceed to beat the living snot out of your dumb-ass college-boy head. And I will do it, don't make any mistake about that."

He looked at me real mean like. I looked at him with a knowing smile.

"Or," I continued, "my boys, who get paid to play baseball and be this stupid, buy your guys a beer and we all play nice for the rest of the evening. There seems to be a more than ample supply of tits to go around for all to enjoy."

He looked like he was thinking it over, but I couldn't tell for sure.

"Pick one, Einstein," I said.

Perhaps it was the thought I might actually be able to beat the living snot out of his dumb-ass college-boy head or the realization he was three sheets to the wind. He finally smiled and yelled, "Beers all around on big mouth here," as he proceeded to point at me. Beers plural it turned out to be and my guys made plans to meet up next Saturday night for another round of "Jugs for Fun" with their new found football buddies.

Me, I saved my ass to party on another day. And, oh yeah, while the kid I selected happened to be bigger than me, he also happened to be the smallest guy in the group.

Chapter 61

A message indicating breakfast the following morning with Collins' broker partners from New York was waiting for me when I got back to my hotel. I had continued to be on fairly good behavior just in case, so the 8:30 am meeting time wouldn't cause me too much dismay. The boys were another story and I'm not even sure they'd be in by that time.

A 7:30 wake-up call, the three S's in the books, I strolled down to the lobby to catch the Three Brokerteers as they arrived. No real reason, just habit. I like to size people up and get a feel for them before I actually meet them. Works for me, kiddo, so I keep on doing it.

* * *

Tall and skinny, medium and non-descript, and short and cocky. It wasn't hanging out, he just looked cocky. Three guys about as different as they could be but each one carrying himself like he could sell you the shorts you were wearing.

"Morning guys, I'm Harry Mickey Shorts," I said after the appropriate amount of sneak-a-peek look-see time.

"Yeah, let's eat," Mister Cocky replied. Obviously a man of few words and unquestionable social graces.

As we walked over to the hotel restaurant entrance, tall-boy introduced himself as Billy Johnstone, medium-man said he was Kevin Dunnston, and short stuff kept on walking. Practice must make perfect in the area of broker social skills. I should probably explain what a broker is for the continued un-insurance-educated of our group. We will call it Insurance 101B.

Everyone has dealt with and knows what an insurance agent is—that's the guy/gal who sells you your auto insurance policy, your homeowners policy or a life insurance policy. They either work directly for one company or are considered independent agents and they represent multiple insurance companies. They work mainly in the area of 'personal lines' insurance.

A broker, as in the three dudes I was presently in charge of squiring around, works mostly in the world of commercial insurance. Workers compensation, general liability, property coverages are examples of insurance that businesses would need to protect themselves from potential losses. A broker attempts to convince a business they can get them the best coverages, at the best prices, from the best insurance company in the world.

Now, there are some very reputable insurance brokers out there who work for excellent brokerage houses and strive to provide the best service for their clients. Of course, there is also an equal share of low life, scum-sucking, butt-wipe peddlers of the brokerage trade who cannot be trusted as far as you can spit into the wind. It's a cut-throat business in a very competitive day-to-day environment where only the strong survive and flourish. Takes all kinds and we'll just have to wait and see where my current companions fit in.

* * *

Now that your insurance education has been properly supplemented, we can get back to the Three Brokerteers. If you didn't quite get the explanation given above, don't sweat it, kiddo. There's lots of people who work in insurance who don't understand it either. I'll cover you as we go along if I think there's something you need to know.

"So, Mister Harry Mickey Shorts, just who are you, and what're you doing here, and why should we give a rat's ass?" was the start of our conversation once we were seated.

You guessed it, Mister Congeniality at his best.

"I'm sorry, I didn't catch your name as we were walking over here," I replied.

"You didn't catch jack-shit cuz I didn't say jack-shit," came back.

"Okay, Mister Jack Shit, or perhaps I should call you Mister John Shit to be formal. Which would you prefer?" I asked with an absolute straight face.

"Someunafucking bitch," he said. "I ain't never had nobody come back at me with that one before. You a wise ass or just quick on your feet?"

"Both," I said.

He laughed, the other two laughed, I laughed, we all laughed, and we were on our way.

"Let's eat. We have a tee time at ten and I can't wait to beat your asses for all you're worth. That includes you, Harry Mickey Shorts, if you got the balls," Jack said.

"Jack," I said, "not only do I have balls, I got clubs too."

"Someunafucking bitch," he said. "I may get to be liking you after all."

Chapter 62

We finished breakfast and made plans to meet in the lobby at 9:15. Seems we had a tee time at the most prestigious private club in the area; one that requires God, or his/her right hand man to secure you a tee time if you aren't a member.

Clubs secured in the back of the limo, we were on our way.

"Harry, you haven't answered the boss' original questions," came from tall man Billy as soon as we had gotten settled in the car.

The word boss caught me off guard. It came out without a trace of hesitancy on Big Billy's part, so I figured he was well aware of his place in life and was very comfortable being his mouthpiece when needed.

"Mister Collins asked me to come down and take a look at his players and give him my opinion. I've played some ball in the past," I answered.

"Coaches can do that," Billy Boy said.

"True. He just wants an independent pair of eyes to see what they can see and match it up to the coach's reports."

"Harry, that's probably a bullshit line, but a good enough one on short notice. I'll give you that one," Mister Jack Shit the boss man said.

"And what about us?" Kev asked.

"Boss man, Billy boy and you are along for the ride so far," I answered.

"Someunafucking bitch," the boss man laughed. "I'm liking you more and more every time you open that smart mouth of yours."

"So we are all on the same page, here's the deal," Jack Shit said. "Collins got his nuts in a wringer when he and his 'partners' couldn't make a payment date on the Senators deal, so he came to me. Not exactly chump change mind you, but something we could help him out with. We get to hang around and play baseball guys 'till he tenders payment back to us. No payment, we get twenty-five percent of the club. Short, sweet and simple. Clock is currently ticking."

"Interesting story," I said.

"Yeah, real interesting story from both sides. We bail his ass out and get ten points for a short term loan. He keeps his team and gets to continue playing big man in town if he pays up. He comes up short one more time and we get an 'interest' of a different kind."

"Seems his nuts are still in a wringer if you ask me," I said.

"Don't recall asking you, Harry. But yeah, Collins ain't in the best position in this little ball game," boss man replied. "Plus, he don't have the nut and his company's in a bad way, too."

"We're here, boss," Billy said.

"Let's play some golf and have some fun," boss man said.

Chapter 63

We got it together and headed out to the first tee. I was thinking about what short-stuff said about Collins and it bothered me. The company is in the dumper and bleeding greenbacks hand over fist. Collins and his partners are also in the dumper with the Senators deal and Jack Shit makes the comment, 'He don't have the nut and his company's in a bad way, too.' So, where is MechInsCo's money going and if it isn't Collins, who's got it?

I rode with Kevin the chatterbox. From what I could gather, the boss never lost. Also, from overhearing some guy say hello to the boss man by the putting green, his name was actually Ralph Vasimalo. I liked Jack Shit better.

"You any good at the game, Harry?" Ralphy boy asked.

"I'm very good at playing the game," I replied. "Golf, that's another story."

He thought about that one, looked at Billy and Kevin, and then smiled at me.

"Screw the handicap crap, let's play some Wolf. You good with that, Harry," he asked.

"Yeah, I'm good with that, Ralph," I replied.

He thought about that one, looked at Billy and Kevin, and then smiled at me.

"Ten bucks a hole? Too steep for your blood, Harry?"

"I may have to crack open my piggy bank, but I'll play," I replied.

Wolf, for the uneducated golfers in the crowd, is a partnership game, but not all the time. First guy tees off and has the option to select his partner for that hole. When the next player hits, he says yes or no after he sees his drive. If he says no, the next player hits. Same option, yes or no. If no again, the last player hits his drive. Again, same option. If he doesn't like the fact it was hooked into the woods, he can choose to play alone against the other three players—be a Lone Wolf. His score times three has to be better than the sum of the other three players for that hole.

Ralph stepped up to the tee and prepared to tee off first.

"Anyone mind if I play first?" he asked.

His two butt-boys shook their heads. I looked at Ralph and said, "As long as you are already there, go ahead and smack away."

He did and the game was on.

Over the years, I have learned the art of keeping mediocre or even bad players in the game till the end, and letting worse players win when I had to. Billy and Kev fit the first group and Ralph fit both. And unless I was mistaken, Billy and Kevin were learned members of the 'let the boss win' school of thinking. The things one is subjected to for the good of the cause. What is it they say, take one for the team?

Fifteen holes done and me and Ralphy boy were tied with five winning holes each. Kev and Billy each had three winning holes to the good on their side. They were tanking at all the right times which was very often considering the way boss man hit the little round ball. He played Star Trek Golf—he visited places on the course where no man had ever been before. Plus, he had this habit of conveniently 'finding' his ball in a very opportune location when it seemed to be heading deep in the woods. Just lucky I guess.

"Hanging in there pretty well, Shorts," Ralph said as we got to the sixteenth tee. "Just like Collins, you'll fold when the big money hits the board."

The boys looked at me like they already knew what was coming.

"How's about we go twenty dollars a hole from here on in?" he said.

The boys nodded before he even finished getting the words out of his mouth. A bit of been-there done-that I'm sure.

"Sure," I said.

"Great," Ralph said. "I'm up."

He wasn't, but the boys didn't say a word.

I had to empty the tank and proceeded over to the trees as Ralph walked up and teed up his ball.

Chapter 64

The sixteenth was a slight dog-leg left with trees along the right side and a pond on the left. His drive was hit a mile high and headed for the trees but luckily it wasn't hit far enough to get there and stayed in the rough. I went next and popped one down the right side about 210 yards out.

"Not a bad drive," Ralph said, "but I think I'll pass."

Billy hit one short and left and Ralph laughingly told him his dog turd shot wasn't even worth commenting on. Kevin took out an iron and put one short and in the middle of the fairway. Safe play, especially when the boss could be in trouble.

"Does your husband play golf, wussy girl?" Ralph said. "I think I'll wolf-it on this hole if you boys don't mind."

They didn't and I had no choice but to play along as well.

He clearly wanted to win the three points for the hole and take a commanding lead in the match. I had the feeling he and the boys had been in this position before and Ralphy usually prevailed.

The advance caddy was standing by Ralph's ball when we got there and it had an amazingly good lie. While the boys hacked it around on their way to the green, Ralph took out a long iron and, even with his great lie, proceeded to squirt one down the fairway. Slamming his club first into the ground and then against the side of the cart completed his turn.

My ball was in perfect position with approximately 170 yards to the pin. The boys had managed to get to the green and where sitting about 15 feet from the hole on opposite sides of the pin.

"Going for the pin, Harry?" Ralph asked as I addressed my ball. And just in case you were wondering, I didn't say, "Hello ball."

"Why not," I replied. "I comes to play and I means to do it."

"No good smart ass," he said just loud enough for me to hear.

For most mortal golfers, the sound of Ralph coughing just as they got to the top of their backswing would have caused their shot to end up who knows where, but not anyplace good. Harry Mickey Shorts never even heard him and flew it to within eight feet of the cup, turned and tipped his cap.

Ralph shook his head as he took off in the cart towards his ball, leaving me and the caddy to follow behind.

His next shot found the very front of the green leaving him a good forty feet from the hole. Having watched him putt all day, that wasn't an ideal place for him to be. Kev said he was there in three strokes and Billy in four, one more than Ralph. Me, I was there in two, looking at a birdie.

"You're up there Ralphy boy," I said.

He glared. He lined up his putt and gave it a rip, straight on line, but five feet short. He had picked up his ball and called every putt within five feet good since we started. As he bent down to pick up his ball, I said "You are going to mark that, aren't you?"

"What did you say?" he asked in surprise.

"You are going to mark that, aren't you?" I repeated.

Billy and Kevin were inspecting their spiked shoes when Ralph looked over at them.

"That one's an inch outside of the acceptable limit," I said.

That seemed to amuse the boys who turned so the boss couldn't see them smiling.

"Marking and lying four," he said in a huff.

Kev went next and two putted for a five. Billy whacked his first putt five feet past the hole and missed the one coming back for a seven. He worked real hard to get to seven after starting out in reasonable shape off the tee. You're welcome boss he didn't say. That totaled twelve and I was lying two.

"You make and that would be fifteen when you multiply your five times three. We lie fourteen combined and I'd have to make my putt to tie," I said to Ralph.

"So you can multiply and add. More than I can say for that dumb-ass whiny-faced Collins who doesn't have two nickels to rub together, plus a company going down the dumper, and no clue why. Cry baby would piss his draws standing over this putt," he spouted.

Interesting way to talk about his so called partner.

"Care to go first and put the pressure on me?" I asked.

"Sure, why not," he said. He then proceeded to walk up and drop the putt for a fifteen total on the hole. You would have thought he had just won the Masters the way he danced around the green leaving large gouges in his wake.

"Gonna have to pony up big time today, boys," he said.

"Hey, Ralph, mind if I putt just for the hell of it," I said.

"Go ahead, Shorts. You haven't made jack all day," he replied with confidence.

When you push and pull putts all day to keep a crappy player in the hunt, you have to visualize your normal stroke to get back in the groove. Having the same line as Billy helped and it was right edge all the way into the cup.

I lined up my putt and then looked directly at Ralph and smiled. He was looking right at me. While we played stare down I proceeded to stroke my putt without ever looking down.

Ralph looked over at the ball just in time to see it fall into the hole.

"Someunafucking bitch" he said as he broke his putter over his knee. He got in his cart and drove back toward the clubhouse.

"I believe the match is over," Billy said and then he and Kevin fell on the ground laughing hysterically.

Chapter 65

Harry Mickey Shorts, cracker-jack private investigator and broker baby-sitter extraordinaire, had done stepped in it again. Sinking that putt on sixteen had pissed Ralph off so much, he took off for New York that afternoon, boys in tow. I'm sure Collins will be ever so pleased with the fine job I had done.

* * *

With one of my two assigned tasks now off the boards, I turned my attention back to the Harrisburg Senators baseball team. If I'm lucky, I can piss off the entire franchise and they will leave Florida and head back to Harrisburg, leaving me with a few days of R&R in Florida.

I got to the clubhouse early and caught the manager and his coaches planning the day's activities. Seeing as I had instructions to survey the talent, I had every intention of integrating myself with the team's management staff and lending a hand with the training routine.

"Morning guys," I said with a smile.

"Shorts," came the reply from the only coach that looked up.

"I was wondering if I could be of some help as long as I'm here," I said.

The manager Talton looked up from his clip board, said "No thanks," and looked back down at his board.

"Must be something I can do to help," I tried again. Our last meeting had been a pretty good get together and I thought they were open to my help.

"Listen, Harry, the big guy from up north caught wind of the guys' late night romp at Jugs. He read me and my coaches the riot act over the phone and told me to 'Get some control' or he would find somebody who could. I know you helped, but I gotta close ranks for now."

"Sure, man," I said. "I'll just hang around the sidelines and watch and observe. If you need anything, all you have to do is ask," I said.

"Sorry man, but thanks for the offer, Harry," Talton said.

"No skin off my back, skip. I get to hang in the sun and watch some baseball during the day, try and keep up with the boys and save your asses at night."

"Some tough life," Birdie quipped.

* * *

I hung with the plan for three days and saw all I needed to see. The best of last year's squad was up with the Triple A team and the new arrivals were painfully raw. Scouting talent is an art and I was better than average at it. Getting a report together for Collins would be simple with the most glaring needs in the catching and middle infield departments. Last year's team was weak in the same areas, so I was guessing their minor league system had no help throughout the entire lower leagues.

My evening activities weren't nearly as interesting as my first night. I hung with some of the players and continued to get a feel for the 'team vibe' that would carry them into the season. A few cool ones was a heavy night; word from on high has a way of curtailing one's night crawling when you are trying to make your way up the ladder. Didn't faze me when I was in the same spot, but I pissed away a great opportunity doing it.

The Bayport Schooners were coming in to scrimmage the Senators the following day, so I thought I'd catch one game before I headed back north. My bud Richie, the new assistant GM, would be with them and I wanted to spend a few minutes with him and Coach Curran. You know, rehash old times. Plus, why go back to the cold up north when you can stay where it's sunny and warm.

Chapter 66

"Harry, it's good to see you again. You look good," was how Richie greeted me when he got off the bus the following morning.

"How you doing?" I asked him.

"Harry, this is as you would say—way cool. The job's great and the team looks good. I'm working hard, but I'm loving every minute of it. Plus, Coach Curran and Mister Trundle are giving me major authority and the room to do my own thing."

He was smiling from ear to ear.

"That's great, Richie. You deserve every bit of it," I said.

"Stop by the locker room before the game, okay, Harry? Rusty's with us to get a few innings in and he would love to see you," he said as he grabbed his gear.

"I'd like that. Lemma take care of business and I'll be by."

"Good deal. See you later," he said.

I made sure I was cool with the Senators coaching staff and told them I'd send them a copy of my report so they wouldn't be back doored by Collins. Said my good byes to the players and told them I'd see them back in Harrisburg. I meant it, too. Maybe Collins would let me do some stuff once the season got started. It's hard to find an accounting clerk who can coach catchers on the side.

Packed and checked out, I headed over to the field complex to check on the Schooners. Turns out I knew about a dozen of them, a few left over from last year's team and some of the younger guys who came up for a cup of coffee during the season. And of course, Rusty and Coach Curran.

"Rusty, how are ya, man?" I said as I grabbed his hand and threw a half a hug on him.

"Harry, you old turd. It's great to see ya," he said.

"The wing okay?" I asked.

"Couldn't be better," he said. "They want me to throw every four days and we had off today. So, here I am."

"Schooner time—like déjà vu all over again," I said with a laugh.

"You know it, Harry. Wanna catch a few innings today?" he smiled.

"In a flash, Jack," I said. "If only…"

"Well, well, well," came a voice from behind me that I knew and loved.

"The Coach," I said with a bow of respect.

"You're not on the squad and can't sneak your way into the lineup, so cut the bowing crap," Coach Curran said. "It's real good to see you again, Harry."

"Tough as ever," I said. "Real good to see you too, Coach,"

"Come by and see me before you go. Okay, Harry?"

"You bet, Coach."

At that moment Richie came into the room and called out to get everyone's attention.

"Listen up, guys. Some of you have been here before and know the Schooners have a tradition that occurs about this time every year. The past two years, the GM gave his 'da bushes' speech to the delight of one and all. Unfortunately for him, very fortunately for us, he is not in a position to do so this year. Therefore, much to his surprise I'm sure, I'm going to call upon the reigning 'Master of da bushes' to deliver this year's inspirational speech to the troops."

Richie looked at me and smiled.

"I give you my friend, Harry Mickey Shorts."

Whoops and hollers all around as I got my ass pushed into the center of the room. What I was gonna say, I had no idea. Richie was gonna owe me big time for this little stunt.

"Your Assistant General Manager has caught me off guard here and shall pay dearly for it in the near future. But, as long as I have the floor, I'll say a few things. A lot of you players come from big cities and have played with all star teams that travel to the big venues for high caliber tournaments. Bayport it ain't, and you're gonna have to get used to it. Plus, if you get sent down a notch, you're gonna play in some towns small enough you'll blow through 'em if you close your eyes. That's right, out in 'da sticks' is where you'll find yourself."

I let that settle in for a minute while I tried to figure out what I was gonna say next.

"You also gotta use da sticks to win games. Pitching is the key, but you can't win if you can't score runs. Have fun and go up there each at bat hacking all the way—let da sticks do the talking for you. Swing 'em like you mean it."

The players were getting into it now, and a couple "You tell it Harry's" could be heard. I was on a roll and knew where I was going and how to finish with a bang.

"Baseball is all about hard work and *fun*! You may be living in da sticks, playing in da sticks and swinging da sticks, but you gotta love every minute of it. Now, contrary to the advice in speeches given in the past and the same stern advice doled out, I am here to tell you otherwise. You only get to be young once. When the game is over and you kicked some serious ass, head out on the town and find yourselves some sweeties. Then, following in the footsteps of yours truly, the *Master of da bushes*, unleash da sticks in your pants and ride 'em till the cows come home."

With that, I turned and left to the thunderous sounds of Harry! Harry! Harry!

Chapter 67

It's Monday morning and I'm sitting in George's Restaurant across from the building, having breakfast, thinking "this ain't Florida—not even close." But, then again, most of the country ain't Florida, so Mechanicsburg, PA is in good company.

I'd still rather be in Florida.

* * *

Upon my return to my little hole of an apartment, there was a message from Joe Stoner telling me to meet him for breakfast on Monday morning. That's the reason I was at George's, but we don't really 'know' why.

"Morning, Harry. Sorry I'm late," Joe said as he breezed in and sat down.

"Morning," I answered to be sociable. "What's up?"

"Same old shit, same old town, same old job, same old piss on me—different day," he said as he picked up a menu.

Buns, who just so happens to be my favorite waitress, came over as I was about to say, "Makes my sorry ass feel a whole lot better after listening to you."

It's Buns 'cause she has the cutest buns in the world, knows it, and shakes them every chance she gets for anyone who'll take notice.

I noticed.

"Three egg omelet with everything you can throw in it, sausage and double bacon, rye toast, coffee and a big OJ," Joe said to Buns.

"Sure thing, Joe," she said, and then did her thing as she strolled away.

How the hell does a skinny guy like Joe eat all that food and stay that skinny, I thought.

"How the hell does a skinny guy like you eat all that food and stay a skinny guy?" I said to him.

"Who knows," he said. "The wife looks at food and gains ten pounds. Me, just lucky I guess," he said.

"How was Florida?" he asked.

"Warm," I said.

"Real funny, Harry. I meant—whad'ya do?"

"Got some sun, played some golf, watched some ball and drank some suds. How was your week, about the same?" I asked.

"All peachy-creamy, same as yours," he said.

"Peachy-creamy?" I said.

"Yeah, just peachy-creamy. The whole world wants something yesterday and Phillips is all over my butt wanting to know how we keep losing all this money. You wanna know what—screw him if he thinks he can do it better."

Buns brought Joe's order at that very moment and gave him a nasty scowl. Me, I got a great big smile just for being me and a whole lotta show time as she went back up the aisle.

"If you're done bitching and moaning, what do you want from me?" I asked.

"The reports I asked you to finish before you left. They're on your desk and I need them fixed by the end of the day," Joe said.

"Fixed?" I said. "They were just what I was told to do by you and were on your desk before I left," I said.

"The request, Harry, was to compile the numbers and dump them into a spreadsheet on a gross basis. That's exactly what I asked you to do. Nobody told you to go off on your own and pull all the reinsurance stuff you did and crowd up the report with gross and net numbers. Take the reinsurance out and leave reinsurance alone, Harry. Last time I'm gonna tell you."

"Sure, Joe. I just thought it would be better with the additional information," I told him.

"Don't think, Harry. Just do what you're told and you won't get your ass or my ass scalded."

With that, he got up and stormed out of George's.

No reason for both of us to be hasty and wasteful. I sat for a while, enjoyed the rest of his bacon and toast and my favorite buns.

Chapter 68

When I got to the office, my day proceeded to scoot downhill even further. You go away for a week of fun and sun, life's starting to look up, people find a way to piss on your parade.

Crissy gave me the cold shoulder when she saw me. Though it is a delightful shoulder even when encumbered by clothes and coldness, I didn't need an attitude from her right about now.

"Morning doll face," I tried.

"I hope you enjoyed yourself in Florida, Shorts. We froze our asses off while you frolicked in the sun doing who knows what to I don't care who," she said with that mean face she puts on.

I thought it best to keep my mouth shut, so I did.

"Collins wants you; now get lost," was how I was dismissed.

Dismissed, I left and headed for my cubicle and whatever else the day had in store for me.

* * *

My plan for the morning had been to fire up Word on my computer and put together a report for Collins. After giving it some additional thought, I had come to the same conclusions on the Senators—the most glaring needs were in the catching and middle infield departments. I would emphasize last year's team had been weak in the same areas and adding players from the organization's lower minor league teams had produced no help.

I had planned on doing it, so I went ahead and did it.

Finished dotting the i's and crossing the t's in the report, I picked up the phone to call Collins' office to see when he might be available. Never got a chance to make the call.

"Harry," Joe's assistant Mary Ann whispered.

"Yes, Mary Ann," I said as I turned to see her. Her face was all red and she looked like she had been thrashed severely. Verbally I presumed.

"Harry, Mister Stoner would like to have his report. He said you were working on it and he wants it right away. He was very insistent he get it right away, Harry. Right away he said," she mumbled on.

"Hey, kiddo, calm down. I'll go see him myself. Okay?" I told her.

"That would be good, Harry. I don't like to go near him when he gets like this, using the 'f' word and some others I don't even want to think about."

She was gone before I could ask if he was in his office.

I saved the report for Collins once more and took a shot Joe would be in his office. What the hell, a little more urination on my already pissed upon parade couldn't do any more damage.

"You looking for me, Joe?" I said as I knocked on his door.

"Looking for you? Yeah, I'm looking for you. Where's my report? They are killing me."

"They?" I said.

"The third floor, that's who. You got the report done? You better have the report done," he raged.

"It's Phillips, isn't it? That the CFO's name?" I asked.

"Yeah, Dom is getting his balls broken, so he puts mine in a vice. Assholes should have stayed in New York and we wouldn't be in the mess we're in. We were going just fine without 'em."

"Hey, Joe. I'll get you the report right after lunch. Doesn't say much, though, without the reinsurance stuff. I wanted to get back with Boalman and look at some stuff," I told him.

"Harry, listen up," Joe said. "Leave Boalman and your fascination with reinsurance alone, like I told you. You hear me?"

"Yeah, I hear you. I gotta go see Collins and then I'll do your report."

As I left his office, I could hear him saying under his breath, "Fuck Collins, fuck Phillips, fuck 'em all."

* * *

"Mister Collins will see you now," the Ice Queen informed me. I had only waited twenty minutes—not bad.

"What'd you do to Vasimalo? He called me every name in the book and made up a few I never heard before to boot. I told you to take care of them and don't let them screw up my team," he fumed in words.

"Mister Collins, I did what you said. We ate, we drank, and we played golf. I carried him all day and sank one putt on sixteen to halve the hole. He freaked and split. The other two guys—Billy and Kevin—they got a pretty good laugh out of it," I said.

"Freaked. He freaked on me for ten minutes. You know what, screw him and his money. Gimme the report and I'll call you if I need anything. Maybe help out with the catchers when they get back up here, or something. Company's tanking and my ass is grass. Windel's all over me, my guys don't know crap, and the money's pouring out the door. I can't think about that asshole or baseball right now."

"Okay, Mister Collins, just let me know if you need anything else."

I left and was glad to be doing it.

* * *

The rest of the day consisted of me finishing Joe's report, giving the report to him, listening to him bitch again, and then doing nothing. You have to work at doing nothing while looking like you're real busy in case somebody comes by. I've practiced plenty, so I'm a master at it. Makes me a Double Master I guess.

Chapter 69

"Tom, I hate to say it, but I'm confused," I told him as we sat in his living room.

"What have you got, Harry?" he asked.

"Bubkiss is what I got, Tom. I got so much bubkiss even my beer is empty."

"I may not be able to do much anymore, Harry, but at least I can fix that," Tom said. He headed to the kitchen to get some more refreshments.

I sat there looking at my empty bottle of Rolling Rock.

* * *

"Harry, after hearing that, I agree. You got bubkiss; no, you got less than bubkiss," Tom said.

Unfortunately, he was dead on.

"The money keeps going down the toilet and nothing points to nothing. Collins is half again crazy 'cuz the New York guys are all over his ass. The New York guys are bullshit 'cuz Collins doesn't seem to know shit from Shinola. Stoner is all over your ass 'cuz the CFO Phillips is stickin' a heavy dose of gimme up his ass. Right so far?" Tom asked.

"Dead on, Tom," I responded.

"You're doin' what I'd be doin' and be in the same place, Harry. Worse thing is we both know it's there to be found and probably gonna drive you nuts when you figure it out."

"So, what next?" I asked Tom.

"More of the same is all I can think of," Tom said. "I got Cam up to my brother's place for a while to get him out of the way. I can help out if you think I can do some good."

"No, I appreciate you wanting to get back in the hunt, Tom. But, the guys that did Cam may catch wind and no telling what may happen. No, I need you in the background for now, doing just what you're doing. Help me think, and plan, and protect you and Cam till we get a handle on who the northern crew is," I told him.

"All right, Harry. You got any ideas in that thick skull of yours might lead you somewhere?" Tom asked.

"Three things, Tom. First priority is I'm gonna get Crissy back on track and hopefully in the sack. If I can't figure out anything about this case, least I can do is have some fun looking and feeling stupid."

"Worse things could be your top priority," Tom said smiling.

Good to see Tom smile for a change.

"Second, gotta get momma Metzger back in play. She's been around too long not to know more that can help. GC or no GC, I need her to open up and shed some light on this confusing mess."

Figured Tom didn't need to know every which way I wanted momma M back in play, so I left it at that.

"And third, when in doubt, follow the money. I know I can crack this baby wide open if I can sniff just one smidge of 'Here I am' that will show me the way to go. I've been smelling it for too long, Tom. It's there for the taking, I know it is. I've been all around it, every which way but loose. I just gotta hound dog it down."

"Anything at all I can do, Harry?" Tom asked.

"Yeah, maybe there is, Tom," I said. "Review everything you've done on the case from the get-go and write down anything you can think of. Don't assume anything is stupid or unimportant. Small facts may be what gives us a direction to follow. Also, be there when I need ya, and get me another beer before I go dry."

Chapter 70

My P.I. instincts came in very handy in this instance. I kept copies of every piece of information I looked at since I started looking into the MechInsCo case. Copies of reports and the source data often provide a wealth of insight into what's important in situations like this. If there was something to be found, I'd find it in the details, if my guess was right. Or, I'd go blind, or crazy, or both.

But, first things first.

* * *

"Crissy, my darling sweetie-pie," I said as I sauntered up to the front desk the following morning. A tad hung over, but nothing life threatening.

"Shorts," was all she replied.

"You are looking ravishing this morning, as you do every morning I might add."

"What do you want?" she asked.

"Want? Why nothing in particular," I replied with my best Harry Mickey Shorts smile.

"Don't waste the smile, Shorts. When you're out of the doghouse I'll let you know. Till then, scram," she said.

"Then I presume drinks after work and a Hershey Bears game would be somewhat iffy as we speak?" I inquired.

"Iffy? Iffy? Who…who…" she stumbled.

"You're repeating yourself, but your imitation of an owl was great," I said.

"Beat it, Shorts," she finally said in utter exasperation.

"I'll call you later to decide on the time," I said as I walked away.

One never knows.

* * *

"Harry Mickey Shorts to see Ms. Metzger," I said to Candy.

She looked up and didn't say anything.

"Cat got your tongue?" I asked with every intention of pissing her off.

She continued to look up and still didn't say anything. Sanity returned and she said, "You don't have an appointment, Shorts."

"Correctamundo. So, can I see her now?"

"No, you absolutely cannot see the General Counsel without an appointment," she said, obviously regaining her pain-in-the-ass approach to life.

"How about if we call her plain Ms. Metzger. Can I see her then?" I asked.

"The General Counsel isn't plain anything," she defended defiantly.

"Oh, let him in," came from the GC's doorway.

I believe the sound Candy made as I passed was something in the area of "Huh."

"What?" is all she said as she sat down behind her desk.

"Long day, week, month, year...?" I asked

"All of the above," was her reply.

Too bad, I thought.

"What do you want, Harry? I have a lot of work to do."

A move up the food chain—Harry, not Shorts.

"I need some information, and you would seem to be a logical source to tap," I said.

"Tap?" she said.

"New York word. I can't help myself, sometimes it just comes out."

"Okay, let's 'tap' then," she teased.

"I'm gonna name some people and you say the first thing that comes to mind. Don't think real hard, just toss it out there. I'll follow up with questions as necessary. Okay?" I said.

"Fine, but not now. I'm busy. Lunch on me?" she asked.

"I'd do anything on you, sweetie-pie," I said with the HMS smile in full bloom.

A shake of her head in disgust, but there was the tiniest of smiles to go along with the head shake.

"Why did I get myself into this?" she asked herself.

"Just couldn't help yourself, I think. Don't let it get you down, though. It happens to the best of them sooner or later."

"Harry, go away. Now! Find my place at noon and you can ask your questions and maybe I'll feed you."

She picked up a report and started to read—a get out sign for sure.

P.I.'s know when to scoot while the getting is still good—I scooted.

Mother-daughter 'sweetie-pie' in the same morning in case you missed it. This situation could get to be trouble if I don't watch myself.

Chapter 71

Doing as I was told, I spent the rest of the morning putting Joe's report together in exactly the way he wanted. Didn't tell ya nothing and would have been much more informative and useful my way. But, he be the man, and I be the do-dat.

The whole case was puzzling and I didn't think it should be this tough. There's nothing obvious going on, and the people who should be able to figure out why the company's tanking are running around like chickens with their heads cut off. Somebody's bullshitting everyone else and doing a damn good job of it. Or, the business on the books sucks, the executives suck, the insurance industry sucks, and the company just plain…got the picture.

If I only had a clue.

* * *

Finding the GC's place was a piece of cake. I could have used all my P.I. skills and know-how to dope it out. Or, I could do what I did and look in the phone book. Easy works more often than you would think.

Where to park and not take the chance of being seen was something else I had to worry about. The old HoneyBee kinda stands out if I didn't mention it before. Metzger's place was off Green Ridge Road, just past 81 up Rt.114. I wound my way up to her house and around the side to where I was pretty sure I would find the garage. Chanced the garage door would be open, and as it turned out, the GC and I were on the same wavelength. Or, she forgot to close the garage door. You pick for a change, but my choice would be brilliant minds and all that.

"You wanna eat first, talk first, or do both at the same time," the GC asked as I walked into the kitchen.

Nice place I thought. Not real big from the outside, but roomy once you got in the door. The kitchen/breakfast area was adequate and the family room had a fireplace and good size to it. Place to spend some time, I thought. Maybe if I was a good boy I'd get to see the rest of the house.

"Well?" she said.

"Let's eat and talk," I told her.

"Good. Sit down, eat and talk. I'll get the milk."

On the table was a jar of peanut butter—Skippy with nuts of course, Smuckers strawberry jam and potato bread—lightly toasted. A bag of Wise BBQ chips was open and the crumbs on the table clearly showed she had already started without me. Pretty brazen of her.

"You really know how to put out a spread," I commented.

"If you don't like what's there, I could offer you something else. I won't, but I could," she said as she started with the peanut butter.

"PB and Smuckers is just fine. Queens, New York delicacy at its bestest," I said.

"Town?" she asked.

"Woodside," I told her.

"I have a cousin in Sunnyside I think it is," she said.

"Hop and a skip from Woodside," I responded.

"Here's the peanut butter—make your sandwich and let's talk."

Good amount of peanut butter on one slice of bread, a little less jam on the other, and a bunch of chips on the PB. Slap them together and you have a dynamite sandwich. The chips in the sandwich surprised the GC a bit, but she threw a few on hers and loved it. You learn something new every day—try it, you'll like it.

Metzger got up to answer the phone while I enjoyed the finer things in life—a delicious peanut butter and jam sandwich and a good view of the GC's finely shaped butt.

Chapter 72

"Ask," she said as she sat back down at the table.

"Okay, here goes. Collins," I started off.

"Comes across as an obnoxious bully, but his bark is worse than his bite. The New York 'thing' that executives from the big city think will intimidate every last poor soul from the sticks—that's his tool."

"Tool?" I asked slightly askance.

"Concentrate, Harry," she said.

"Okay."

"Behind closed doors he is a pretty good businessman who actually had the company going in the right direction when he first came down here. We were putting premium on the books and diversifying our blend of business, both geographically and by product lines."

"That's a different picture than what I've seen and been told," I said.

"The old timers hated him from the start and still do. Even when he did good things he got no credit from them. Attitude and how you treat people is important in this part of the country," she said.

"So I hear," I agreed.

"Anyway, he's confused by what has happened and a little, no, a lot scared. He can't figure out where the money is going and why MechInsCo is going broke. Windel is breathing down his neck more and more and the Insurance Department wants more information all the time. Enough?"

"Plenty," I said. "Let's try Phillips."

"Phillips," she repeated. "Phillips tries to fancy himself to be in the outward Collins mold—New York asshole. Unfortunately, he's doing a very good job of it. Pisses off anyone and everyone, cares not one iota. Also, unfortunately, he's not very good at dealing with adversity. When things were going good, he was riding high, touting the profits to the old executive staff still hanging on. When things starting going south, he didn't have a clue how to put a game plan in place."

"The troops rally around him?" I asked.

"The troops, the old MechInsCo troops that is, smiled behind his back. Not in words, but in deeds, they told him to stick it."

Two down. Maybe Millwood from HR would evoke a little better response.

"Millwood is a problem. Collins' butt boy who doesn't have any outward balls if you ask me. His assistant, Nancy Cross, she's cool and a good source of information. According to her, he was a very strong executive while they were in New York. Played by the book he knows very well, and didn't back down when something needed to be done. Got out of the gate strong here and the people liked him, but lost his edge when things soured. Now, Collins tells him to jump and he says where and how high."

"What happened?" I asked.

"From what Nancy says, the pressure of employee complaints plus Collins and his boys' defiance got to him. He's afraid of getting fired and won't stand up to the big guys."

"Not a pretty picture so far," I said.

"Crumbling companies usually have plenty of pooh piled up inside, Harry."

"I hear ya on that one. Joe Stoner?" I threw out.

"First job out of high school was at MechInsCo. His uncle gave him the job and paid for him to go to night school at HACC—the local community college. Took him seven years, but he got an accounting degree by the skin of his teeth. That's how he got to where he is now, and where he will stay until he retires, or the company folds, whichever comes first."

"His uncle still around?" I asked.

"Ah, no," she said. "He left just before the New York invasion."

"Joe any good at what he does, or was he ever good at what he does? And, what's in Baltimore?"

"Tries real hard and his people love him. Takes him a lot longer to do things, but they get done. Barb getting fired riled him and the rest of the old timers real bad. Hurt him, too. She was very valuable to him and did most of the heavy lifting in the department. We don't have a Baltimore office, but Joe has family there."

The GC looked at her watch and then back at me. She went over to the fridge and got out two pieces of chocolate cream pie, minus the cream, and a can of whipped cream.

"One more if you don't mind—Boalman."

"Fairly new. I don't know much about him or his background. He and

Joe work a lot together and I'm pretty sure he is the main reinsurance resource we have."

Pie gone, question time also obviously over, Metzger got up and headed for the hallway off the family room. She stopped when she got to the doorway.

"It's twelve-thirty and I have a two o'clock conference call. Grab the whipped cream and hustle your buns in here—play time has begun."

A trained private investigator, a can of whipped cream and a General Counsel with a vivid imagination—you better believe play time had begun.

Chapter 73

"Late lunch, Shorts?"

That's what greeted me as I swung around the corner past the reception area. No chance Crissy would be off doing whatever she does when she's off doing it.

"Yeah," I said. "Had to work on some stuff for Stoner and it took me past my normal lunch time," I lied.

"Whatever," she shrugged.

I was about to keep on truckin' when I heard her "ah-hum" me. I hate being "ah-humed."

"Yes, Crissy? Did you want something else?"

"I'm having dinner with my mom tonight, so I can't see you after work," she said.

"Oh, man that's too bad. I was looking forward to getting together and heading over to the Hershey Bears game."

I purposely left it open ended.

"Not tonight, Shorts. I don't know what it is, but mom has been acting real happy lately. She went by a little while ago and asked me to dinner tonight. I think maybe she met someone," she said.

"That's interesting. I'll catch you tomorrow," I said as I walked away.

No "ah-hum" followed me, and luckily no mention that I looked newly scrubbed, smelling of girlie soap and shampoo. And perhaps the apple of some mommy's eye.

What hath Harry Mickey Shorts gotten himself into this time!

* * *

Feeling slightly tired and overly rejuvenated from my lunchtime conversation and recreational activities with the GC, but bummed by my conversation with Crissy, I began the task of re-following the money. I tried it once before, but not with the appropriate vigor required to do the job right. I didn't have a clue what I was looking for last time and the results showed—a half-hearted attempt. Still haven't an inkling what, where, when or how, but I'm gonna attack it hard this time.

Two minutes into my rededicated effort—the phone rang.

"Harry Shorts—can I help you?"

"It's Tom."

Nada else. Tom drives me crazy when he does that. Calls ya, says "It's Tom," then he doesn't say another word.

"Hi, Tom. What's up?" I said as you always have to do to get him to continue the conversation or tell you what the hell he wants. Tom doesn't just call to say hi. When he calls—there's a reason.

"I followed up on the stuff you asked me to do. Got the info if you have time now," he said.

"Now's good, Tom. What do you have?" I asked.

"I tracked down all of the execs who left MechInsCo when the New York crew came to town. The two we figured retired, both did; both moved to Arizona and don't bother nobody. The finance guy, Danny something, he took up with his brothers and opened a restaurant in Hershey. Making good money from what I hear tell. Mead moved to Maryland and sails his big boat most of the time. That's it—nothing much, Harry."

"Who's Mead," I asked.

"Mead's the ex-president, Harry. You never knew that?" he asked.

"I actually never heard his name and nobody's ever mentioned it since I got here," I told him.

"Well, it's Mead, Tad Mead. People still talk about him now and again. Barber shop and around. Talk ya into almost anything, he could. Real gift of the gab," Tom said. "Loved that company, too. People say it hurt him real bad when they told him to leave. He just picked up and went away without another word."

"Well, thanks Tom. You did good work, but I expected you to. I'll look into the Mead thing a little more. Maybe I'll ask Metzger what she knows of him, both when he was here and after he left, if I get a chance."

"Okay, Harry. See ya soon?" he asked.

"Yeah, Tom. I'll stop over in a few days."

"Cam's being Cam and I had to let him come on home. Maybe you can come to dinner this weekend."

"I'd like that a lot, Tom. Say hi to Cam and I'll see ya soon," I told him as I hung up the phone.

Not much to go on, but I wasn't counting on much when Tom and I discussed him looking up the ex-MechInsCo guys. Maybe something to the Mead thing, probably not. One more thread to follow. You got it, kiddo—one never knows.

Chapter 74

"You got kids, you know," was what I heard when I answered the phone that night. I had just gotten in the door and ran for the phone.

"Max, my favorite squirt of a son," I said.

"Squirt's getting bigger, but you wouldn't know that, would you?" he said.

"You got me there, Max. I've been tied up with this case and haven't been thinking about the other things in my life enough."

"Yeah, well, it's getting close to our Saturday time and you better not try and tell me and Bri you aren't coming," he said rather assertively.

"Wouldn't think of it," I said. "You guys cook up something good for this go-round?" I asked.

"It's a week from Saturday," he said, "and don't make plans for Sunday, either."

"Sunday?" I asked.

"Yeah, it's the day that follows Saturday. You know it. You used to miss most of it sleeping off one of your beauties, then watch football or some other sports event on TV all afternoon."

"Ancient history my little man."

"Not that ancient if you listen to mom," he said.

"Let's not spoil a perfectly good phone call, okay?"

"Okay. Saturday and Sunday. Plan on it," he said and hung up.

* * *

I woke the following morning to the Coffee and Amy show on WTPA—93.5 FM on your Harrisburg radio dial. Not exactly Imus of old, but listenable. Coffee was reminiscing about how he would whine when Jammer was late for work and Jammer would make another lame excuse for being late, and how the ever lovely Amy would laugh at the two of them. Amy's a real hottie, by the way, as illustrated by photos once posted on another station's web site.

There was a minor dull ache in the general area of my head. I had spent many hours the prior night sorting through all the information I had accumulated since I started at MechInsCo. In nice neat piles were five years of policy and premium information, five years of claims payments and claims expenses with the corresponding reserve change data to go along with both, and five years of general operating expenses. I still had to sort through the mess of brokerage commissions being paid out and the reinsurance ceded premiums going out with corresponding ceding commissions coming in from the stuff I had pulled together.

Unfortunately for my brain, I had kept myself going by consuming a fairly large quantity of Magic Hat with an Absolut and Tonic thrown in for good measure. If I forgot to tell you earlier, Magic Hat has definitely replaced St. Paulie Girl as the beverage of choice for Harry Mickey Shorts.

So, I had all this stuff sorted and squirreled away in my apartment. While I was going through it, I had hoped something would catch my eye and I'd have a brilliant breakthrough in the case. One of those 'aha' moments that happen now and again. No 'aha', not this time, hopefully sometime soon.

Tired and hung over—I headed for work.

Chapter 75

The executives have reserved parking spots right outside the front door, plus spots in the underground parking garage in the basement of the building. Nice weather, you park outside and hop right in and out of the building. Very convenient. Weather's bad, you park inside and never have to battle the elements like the rest of the common folk who work in the same place you do. It's called executive perks, I believe. Perks meaning—I got it, you don't.

Anyway, as I was about to enter MechInsCo after parking in my non-perk parking spot, the GC was getting out of her car. Yeah, in her perk parking spot. I'll leave it alone now.

"Morning, Ms. GC," I said.

Her mind must have been somewhere else far away—my voice seemed to startle her.

"Oh, morning, Shorts."

"How was dinner?" I asked.

"It was good. Crissy and I don't spend enough time together and we needed to talk about Europe," she offered.

"She still planning on going in the fall? Work with da master?" I asked.

"Yes," she said rather shortly.

We had gotten to the entrance to the building and I wanted to ask her about Mead before she got away. So, I did. I'm good like that.

"Metzger, one more name if you've got a second?"

"Name?" she puzzled.

"Yeah, a name like yesterday."

"Oh, yeah, yesterday," she said and smiled.

"Mead," I asked.

"Mead," she repeated almost in a whisper. "That would require a bit more time. Call Candy and get a few minutes this afternoon."

With that, she whisked away and I was left standing by the front door. And yes, Crissy had watched the whole exchange.

* * *

"Morning, Mary Ann," I said to Joe's assistant as I entered the accounting department. "Joe in?" I asked her.

"He's running a little late," she said. "I'll tell him you were looking for him when he gets in."

"Thanks, kiddo. No biggie, just checking in," I told her.

Situated myself in my cubicle, fired up the P.C. to check the sports scores from the night before, then went about doing boring accounting spreadsheets. Necessary, but boring. The morning seemed to drag on until around 10:30 when Candy called.

"I believe you were supposed to call me to set up an appointment with Ms. Metzger, Mister Shorts," she huffed.

"Oh, yeah, I was. Slipped my mind with all the critical company business I'm dealing with here," I told her.

"Yeah," she said. "Ms. Metzger said to let you know you could come at two pm. You can have five minutes."

Five whole minutes, I thought.

"That would fit my schedule perfectly. Please tell Ms. Metzger I would be more than happy to come at two in her office. Five minutes isn't much time, but I'll try my best."

"It will have to do, Shorts. Ms. Metzger is a very busy person," she said and hung up.

Not knowing what was up, Candy didn't catch the double meaning. I'm sure you all did as you know the situation. If not, you're slipping, so go back and look for the double meaning. If you don't see it, I'm sure it will come up later.

Chapter 76

Crissy wasn't at the front desk when I cruised by heading for lunch. That meant I was flying solo for lunch and decided to try a place everyone talked about but I hadn't been to yet—the Spot, in downtown Harrisburg. Supposed to have the best hot-dogs. Being from New York, and one who loves the dirty water dogs (gotta be Sabrett) with a little mustard and onions from the cart vendors in New York City, the Spot had a lot to live up to in the eyes of HMS.

If you've never had one, next time you are in New York, stop by one of the Umbrella Clubs—all vendor carts have umbrellas and, as I am wont to do, I nicknamed them Umbrella Clubs. Have yourself two with mustard and onions and enjoy. Add some kraut and you have an 'arm bender'—another gem of mine. Tell 'em Harry sent you; won't mean didly but what the hell.

Not bad at all is how I'd rate the Spot dogs. I'll take an Umbrella Club dog any day, but in a pinch, Spot dogs will fit the bill quite nicely.

* * *

Took my time heading back to MechInsCo and stopped at Dicks Sporting Goods on Carlisle Pike. If Collins follows through and wants me to help out with the Senators when they get back into town, I'd need some gear. I could pick up some when I go back to New York to see the kids, but I'm sure I'll need more. Being prepared like a good washed-up ball player/private eye should be.

After screwing around at my desk for a bit, I headed up to the GC's office for my 2:00 pm meeting. Had to remember to talk fast since I only had five minutes or Candy would be all over me like white on rice, like holy on the Pope, like stink on...

"Good afternoon, Ms. Candy. Harry Mickey Shorts for his 2:00 pm appointment with Ms. Metzger, General Counsel for MechInsCo, as instructed."

"You never give up, do you Shorts," she said. "Wait here while I see if Ms. Metzger is ready for you."

Have to admit, Candy girl was looking mighty appetizing today. While I do have my standards, needs be needs and one never knows when they may have to be lowered should the situation become desperate. Convincing Candy would be a whole other story.

Being the nosy guy I am, I was trying to read the papers on Candy's desk while she announced my coming to the GC. I'm not bad at upside down reading but it does take time. Candy girl was too quick and I couldn't get anything useful.

"Go on in, Shorts," she said upon her return.

On in I went.

"GC, as I only have five minutes, let's dispense with the chit chat and get to Mead," I started.

"Okay, Harry. Mead was the president here at MechInsCo for nineteen years. Practically built the business from a nothing local player to a respectable regional carrier. Grew the staff, a family oriented atmosphere from day one, and was loved and respected by everyone. Wrote good business, gave people the authority to do their jobs, and made money—plain and simple. Would still be at the helm if it wasn't for the greed of the new owners."

"I gather you liked him?" I asked.

"He treated me fairly, had integrity and a belief in the business and the people. I owe him a lot," she said.

"How did he leave MechInsCo?" I asked.

"He left with his head high and a hell of a party that people still talk about now and again."

"Know what he's up to now? Do you keep in contact with him, or is there anyone else you know that does?"

"Christmas card is about it. He put the company behind him when he left and spends his time on his boat; the only contact I've heard of is relatives who visit him fairly regularly," she said.

"Relatives?" I asked as Candy popped her head in the door.

"Ms. Metzger, Mister Collins wants you right now and from what I heard it sounds urgent," she told her.

"Okay, Candy. Tell him I'm on my way," she told her. "Gotta go, Harry. I guess you actually only had five minutes after all," she said as she proceeded to get up from behind her desk and head for the door.

Something was better than nothing but it wasn't exactly what I was hoping for. There was more I needed on Mead, something I couldn't put my finger on yet. I sensed the GC could be the person to provide the info. I'll have to follow up with Metzger on the topic of Mead another time.

Chapter 77

The rest of the week was more of the same and amounted to the same end result—nothing. During the day I did what I was told like a good little accounting clerk. At night I wore my eyeballs to death looking over all the MechInsCo information and data I had accumulated and squirreled away in my bachelor's pad. I still had the Harry Mickey Shorts feeling it was right there in front of me and I was seeing it, but not seeing it. It's a P.I. thing.

Crissy was still avoiding me and her moms took off right after talking to Collins. That translates into all work and no play making Harry a very ornery and horny boy.

I sometimes have to remind myself Crissy is only in her early twenties and does what people of the female persuasion at that age do. It's been a while since I've been involved with that portion of the persuasion.

I also have to remind myself the GC is in a whole different class and age bracket altogether—one the likes of a P.I. shit bum like me don't usually get the chance to delve into. High class is what I'm referring to and her early history notwithstanding, Metzger was definitely one who belonged.

Twenty-early-something or thirty-middle-something? Too tough to decide and not ready to give up either one. Play both hands at the same time and ride it till the wheels come off one, or both. A Harry Mickey Shorts QAS that had the makings of a damn good time or ultimate disaster.

* * *

The dinner Tom put together on Saturday night turned out to be a welcome-home shindig for Cam. A few of Cam's buds came by and Tom had a couple of his buddies from way back along for the ride as well. Some people woulda felt like an outsider crashing a family get together; but me, I'm always comfortable anywhere I go, and Tom always makes me feel like I belong.

"You ain't you're normal self tonight, Harry," Tom said about an hour into the night.

"I'm cool, Tom," I told him.

"Well, get yourself another Rock and come on over and talk with the boys. They're riding my ass good for no reason and I need some of that New York bullshit you're so good at flinging around to save my ass," he said.

I looked at him.

"Ah, Harry, just break some balls and you'll get into it and have yourself some fun too. These boys can take it and give it back just as hard. They ain't gonna let some city slicker come into their town and get the best of them. Especially in my house and me tellin' them what a master you are at it. They ready to whip your sorry ass, boy," he challenged.

"Well, if you put it that way, Tom, I may just have to show the town folk what it is to have their asses roasted extra well done—city boy style."

He laughed, I laughed, and the bullshit tossing began.

* * *

There are times in everyone's life when you are absolutely floored by a turn of events. This night was one of those times. We started throwing zingers and they came fast and furious. All of us, including Tom, were bobbing and weaving to avoid the verbal jabs and hooks, occasionally throwing a few roundhouse winners till we just laughed ourselves silly. Shit-kicking back-woods this and big-city sky scraper that.

I loved every minute of it and would have declared it a draw if we were keeping score. Tom practically split a gut he laughed so hard. Even Cam and his buds got into the act and kept up for a while.

The surprising part came when we pissed on each other's music. I was doing the country-warbler cry-me-a river serenade and they did the can't-understand-a-word rap crap. One of Cam's dude's did a Vanilla Ice white-boy rap bit that had us all rolling.

The weirdest thing happened when one of Tom's friends mentioned Harry Chapin, a personal fave of mine. My dad was into him and Harry Neilson, the guy who did the music for Midnight Cowboy. That's how I got turned on to both of them.

Bosco was his name, Tom's friend that is. I never found out why. He was on his way into the Harry Chapin concert on Long Island when he found out Harry had died in a car accident earlier that day. My mom and dad were at the same place and my dad told me the same story many years later. "Shit happens," he said, "and sometimes shit really sucks."

Bosco agreed.

"Harry was a real storyteller, could keep you listening for hours," Bosco said. "Specially liked that Mister Tanner song he did with Big John Wallace 'bout the tailor."

I knew the one and it was one of my favorites too.

We talked about Bowie from his Ziggy Stardust days, and Jethro Tull, and Emerson Lake and Palmer—all the old masters today's young kids missed. Max knows—I taught him well.

We lifted our beers and toasted Harry, then somebody farted and we got back to pissing on each other until we were all good and drunk.

Takes all kinds, and obviously all kinds loved Mister Chapin. Still do.

Chapter 78

Bingity-bingity, bangity-bangity. That's what was happening in my head when I woke up the next morning. After fifteen seconds of, "Where the hell am I," I realized I was on Tom's couch in the basement of his house. Pass out drunk and who knows where you might end up. Trust me; I've landed in worse places, much worse. At least I was alone which wasn't always the case in the past.

"Morning there, Sport," Tom said as he got to the bottom of the stairs.

"Yeah," was all I could get out.

"Coffee or a little hair of the dog?" he asked. "I already done the hair and I'm on to the coffee now."

"What time is it?" I asked.

"'Bout nine I guess. Been outside for a time and didn't check before I came down to fetch ya," he said.

"Nine in the morning? We couldn't have crashed before two or three and you've been up how long?" I asked.

The bingity-bingity, bangity-bangity was getting louder.

"Couple hours," Tom replied. "And it was two-thirty or so when we shut 'er down."

"Coffee and gimme some aspirins if you got 'em."

"Right there on the table. Figured you'd need 'em when you woke up," he said.

"What's that noise?" I asked.

"Raining like a mother out there since about seven. The boys were headed up to the races and left a bit after six. Needed to fill up the coolers at Bosco's place and wanted to get there early 'fore the crowds got there."

"Yeah, whatever," I said. "Some guys get to have all the fun."

* * *

By ten I was semi cleaned up and feeling almost human. Tom had a plate of eggs, bacon and toast ready for me and I dove in with surprising gusto. Tested the stomach with a few mouthfuls and determined it was worth a go. The four aspirins and three cups of coffee helped the situation.

Bingity-bingity, bangity-bangity was starting to lower its intensity to a dull roar now.

"Thanks, Tom, this tastes great. You eat?" I asked.

"Oh, yeah. Me and the boys ate before they left. Had to be hospitable, but I gotta admit even I was a tad wobbly when I first opened my eyes. Damn good time, though," he said.

"A hell of a night," I agreed. "Cam okay?"

"Suppose so. He and his bunch left about one and he was staying over at Ben's. That's the Vanilla Ice kid so you know."

"Pretty funny kid," I said.

"Yeah, he's a good kid. His mom raised him since he was little when his dad went out for cigarettes and never came back. You heard that story a million times but this kid actually had it happen to him and his mom," Tom said.

I just shook my head and started back on my eggs.

* * *

By the time I left Tom's at noon I was feeling almost half decent. Not great, but good enough to motivate on home. As the fog in my head cleared, I kept thinking Bosco said something else that was important but it wasn't there for me to grab onto. I think it had something to do with some guys he saw recently that he knew from when he lived up in New York, but I couldn't be sure.

It would come back to me later and prove to be important.

Chapter 79

I was sitting on the spacious 4x6 balcony that juts off my living room enjoying one of the girls—St. Paulie variety as I was Magic Hat-less at the moment. A three mile run late in the afternoon burned off the rest of the alcoholic fuzz from the night before and I was beginning to think about my next moves.

The temperature was beginning to inch up to let us know spring was coming soon. A light breeze was cooling me down and I was feeling pretty good right about then. A cool breeze…a cool brew…not a single clue…

That was then. The phone has a way of changing things quickly.

"Hello," I said when I answered it.

"Harry, its Tom. I just got a call. Some guy on the phone and 'Leave it alone' was all he said before I heard a click and he was gone."

"Tom, don't move. I'll be right there," I told him.

I had all I could do to suppress the urge to slam the phone until it turned into little pieces. Slam it like I was slamming the face of a coward who hides behind a phone instead of running his act face to face.

The phone rang again and I jerked it off the hook.

"What?" I yelled into the receiver.

"I do have a way of getting your blood boiling, don't I, Harry?" Metzger said.

Calm down, get it together, everything's cool.

"Sorry, Metzger. You caught me at a rather troubled moment. You back?" I asked.

"No, Harry, I'm not. I only called because I ran out on you before we could finish our conversation and I felt bad about it. I'll be gone until Wednesday and didn't want to let it lay until then," she said.

"No problem," I answered. "Big time GC doesn't have to apologize to the lowly accounting clerks of the world," I said.

"Harry, big time GC's are no better than the clerks of the world when it comes to common decency and treating other people like human beings. Especially clerks that have caught this particular GC's fancy at the moment," she continued.

"Ah, shucks," I said.

She laughed.

"Thanks, Metzger. I know you didn't have to call and I appreciate it. I'm looking forward to seeing you when you get back. We can finish our conversation and then maybe try and find something to make us stop conversing," I said.

"That would be nice, Harry. Dinner Wednesday night when I get back, perhaps? There's a black tie affair at the downtown Hilton I have to attend and I'm staying there overnight. I could order some room service afterward and we could talk then."

"The Hilton, pretty lady in evening attire, a late supper—how could a guy refuse an invitation like that?" I said.

"Come prepared, Harry. You never know when a traveling saleslady may materialize and try and sell you something."

With that she hung up and, if I had this one pegged right, I had much to look forward to come Wednesday evening.

That would be then; now I had to deal with Tom.

What could have provoked a call like that and why now? Tom had been off the case for months and there was no reason to tie me to it unless somebody ran his mouth at the wrong time to the wrong people. As far as anyone knows I'm just a family friend who needed a job, an old acquaintance of Tom's from a number of years ago. I don't get it.

Quick shower and I was off to find out—I hoped.

Business called and thoughts of Metzger were out of my mind entirely. Well, maybe not entirely. She's her, I'm me, and you've seen what that combination hath wrought before.

Chapter 80

Sent the HoneyBee to flight and landed at Tom's doorstep at about 6:30 pm. He met me at the door with his usual bottle of Rolling Rock in hand.

"Harry, man, I don't know what's up…I'm worried," Tom said as I plunked down on his couch.

The cooler was situated in the middle of the living room floor loaded with liquid and ice. Tom must have felt we were either gonna hunker down and fight it out from the living room windows or he was real thirsty. Me, I was thirsty, so I grabbed a Rock.

"Tell me again, Tom. Real slow. What did he say, what did he sound like, what could you hear in the background? Young or old, white or black, or maybe something else, smoker's voice, or accent from up north or down south? Something, anything to go on. Clear your head and hear the call—you know how to do it, Tom," I told him.

Tom closed his eyes and you could see him straining to come up with something from the three word message. Only three words, but there could be a wealth of information you could take away from them.

"Neutral and slow. Said the three words like they didn't belong together, like each word was a sentence all by itself. Wanted to make it intimidating without saying it. Wanted me to know he meant business. No accent I can remember and, if I had to guess, I'd say white dude from New York or New Jersey, like that. You know.

"There wasn't any time to catch any background I could hear. It was boom, boom, boom and then click. Clean connection so you would think land line, but the cells are so freakin' good these days you can't tell. Coulda been next door, coulda been in BumfuckEgypt for all I know."

Tom opened his eyes and looked at me. He desperately wanted to produce more, but there just wasn't much to go on.

"Nothin' there, Harry. I can't see or hear anything when I play it over that gives us anything to go on. Just those three words—'Leave it alone.'"

"You done good, Tom. If you are right about the New York/New

Jersey thing, we tie him back to the earlier stuff and probably Cam, too. Now we need to figure out why," I said.

"Why?" Tom repeated.

"Yeah, why?" I said. "Why come back at you now for no reason. If you did something or talked to some guy, now's the time to spill it, Tom. Any reason for them to think you were back on the case and they should try and scare you back off? Anything at all, Tom?" I asked.

"Oh man. Cam," he said.

"Cam what?" I asked.

"Cam hasn't come home yet from last night. He was supposed to call if he wasn't gonna be here for dinner, but I haven't heard from him."

"You call the kid's house yet?" I asked.

"No, I just thought of it right now. He should have called cuz he knew we were gonna eat early tonight. Gonna rain later and I got some steaks to cook up on the grill outside. He shoulda called by now," he said.

"Let's not get our balls all twisted for no reason, Tom. Call the kid's house and check on Cam. I'll have another Rock and you get the phone," I told him.

He had the 'why me' look on his face as he went to the kitchen to get the phone. I did what I said I was gonna do—I grabbed another Rock.

* * *

The detective who answered the phone at Ben's house knew Tom. Vanilla Ice Jr. lived over in Hampden township, so no way I could know him. Tom listened for about thirty seconds without saying a word and then handed me the phone.

"Hello," I said.

"Who's this?" was the response.

For some reason the old line, "I don't know, I can't see ya," entered my head. Luckily it stayed there.

"My name is Harry Shorts, a friend of Tom's. Is Cam okay? Can you tell me what's going on?" I asked.

"This is Detective Mitchell, Marc Mitchell. And no I can't, at least not over the phone. I've known Tom for a long time and he should probably come over here to help us figure this out," he said.

"I'll bring him there right away," I told Detective Mitchell.

I got Tom to focus and we headed on over to see what could be happening knowing it couldn't be anything good.

Chapter 81

"Where's Cam?" Tom shouted when we finally got into the house.

"Tom, over here," Detective Mitchell said as he walked toward us.

Not what I expected to see. Mitchell was probably six foot five and weighed two hundred fifty pounds, easy. Real pounds, too. A man who obviously hit the gym and quite often too. Trailing him was a female detective who couldn't have been more than five two and a hundred ten pounds soaking wet. A good little package though with this cute dimple thing going on.

Talk about your Mutt and Jeff pair.

"Is Cam okay, Marc?" Tom asked.

"Easy, Tom. Come over here and sit down so we can talk," Mitchell said.

"I don't want to sit and I don't want to talk. Where's Cam?" Tom said in an increasingly louder voice. "Where's Cam?"

"Tom, come on over here and let's see what we can find out 'bout what's going on," I said to him. "Let's let the people do their jobs, okay?"

"Harry, what the hell's going on, man?" he said to me as he followed me over to the couch.

"I don't know, Tom, that's what we'll have to find out. One piece at a time—you know the drill. Come on and think," I said.

He calmed down some, then said, "Sure, Harry. You do it, man. I'm all twisted up and can't think," he said.

"You got it, Tom" I told him.

Tom sat back and closed his eyes and I began the process of figuring out what was going on.

* * *

"I'm in the business, same as Tom," I told the two detectives. I had to do it so they would have some clue why Tom was trusting me to do this.

"Good to know," the cute one said.

"Is Cam hurt?" I asked.

"We don't know. Neither Cam nor Ben were here when we arrived," Mitchell started.

Neither—nor I thought to myself.

"An anonymous nine one one call came in directing us to this address. Suggested we get over here right away and don't bother looking around—the front door would be open," he said.

"Any idea who?" I asked.

"None—as anonymous as they get," he replied.

"Sorry, go on," I said.

"We responded, my partner and I, and found the premises quiet at first inspection. No answer to our knocks, so we tested the front door and did indeed find it unlocked. Still no response to our calls upon opening the door, so we entered the premises."

Mitchell looked at his partner for some assurance he was telling it straight—she nodded in agreement.

Hair was dirty blonde, kinda short, with this don't care unruly thing going on. Sexy, I thought.

"No obvious signs of a struggle in the downstairs areas; in fact there was no sign anyone was home at all. With that, we proceeded up to the second floor and began checking the bedrooms. The master bedroom is where we found the situation," he said

"Situation?" I asked.

"Yes," he responded, checked his notes, then continued. "Again, there were no signs of a struggle; everything appeared to be in order. As we entered the room, we found the individual on the bed—Mrs. Sands we came to find out. She was naked, spread-eagled on the four poster bed with her hands and feet tied to the bedposts. She had duck tape over her mouth and a terrified look that scared me to the quick."

He stopped again and took a deep breath. I don't think detectives in Hampden township come across a scene like that too often.

"There was a pillow under her bottom that caused her to be in a rather exposed position. We believe it was intentional, sending a message."

"What message?" I asked.

"She had not been violated at all as far as we can tell, thank God. But, they wanted everyone to know they could have done anything they wanted if they chose to. That, plus the actual message written on her chest in magic marker," he said.

"What did it say?" I asked.

He either didn't hear me or chose to ignore what I said.

"They caught Missus Sands as she was about to leave her house through the garage. They told her they wouldn't hurt her unless she gave them a reason to. Just took her upstairs, took off her clothes, piled them neatly on a chair in the corner, then did the rest," Mitchell continued.

"The message," I repeated.

"Under normal circumstances, I would not be able to divulge that information. Knowing Tom all these years and seeing what we now know from our short investigation, I guess I can."

Again, a look at his partner for assurance.

"Go ahead, Marcus," she said.

Cute voice, too.

"The message written on her chest said, in bold letters, Leave It Alone," Mitchell said.

Stunned, all I could say was, "Holy mother of shit."

Chapter 82

"I suggest you tell me what's going on here, Tom," is how Dell Muoio, the Chief of Police, greeted us when we got to the local police department office.

"Dell, I can't give you all the details, but this was no isolated incident," Tom told him.

"Tom, we go way back, you and me. I can cut you some slack for a time, but push comes to shove and I'm gonna have to have it all—you have to know that," he told us.

"I know," was all Tom said.

We had convinced Detective Mitchell to take Tom and me over to the local police station where Tom would feel a bit more at ease telling his side of the story. His honchos wanted to put the cabash on that idea but Tom clamed up and wouldn't say Jack to anyone in Hampden. They finally agreed as long as their guys, including cutie pie, got to go along for the ride and be in on the discussions.

"I'm gonna lay it out for you, Tom," Dell said. "We have an innocent civilian who just got the scare of her life and may never be the same. These guys were professionals, Tom, guys who knew what they were doing. If you are involved in something that pertains to this case, I have to know."

"What did she tell them, Chief?" I asked.

"Shorts, is it? Don't ask me any questions. I'll tell Tom what I want Tom to know and you can hear it 'cuz he says so. Other than that, shut up."

"Yes sir, Chief," I replied. I shut up as instructed, but listened real good.

"What did she tell them?" Tom said.

Good question, I thought.

"Not much and, under the circumstances, it was more than you could expect after what happened to her. Mitchell and his Chief told me the kids had just left via the front door and she went out the garage about ten minutes later. Two guys grabbed her and you can figure out what happened from there. The only other piece of information you haven't been told is she heard one of the guys say, 'Make sure it's the same message,' when they wrote it on her chest."

"Is she gonna be okay?" Tom asked.

"Scared the living piss out of her; but yeah, physically, she's gonna be okay," the Chief answered. "Can't tell what something like this will do to her head as time passes."

Tom just looked at him.

"Anything you wanna tell me, Tom?" the Chief asked.

Tom just looked at him, then at Mitchell and cutie pie, then me and said, "Nope."

* * *

We had gone around in circles for another hour when the Chief let Tom and me leave. He was pissed, Mitchell was pissed, and even cutie pie was kinda pissed by the time we left. We were actually thrown out of the Chief's office with instructions to, "Wise up," and come back when we were ready to help with the investigation.

"What'd ya think, Tom," I asked him in the car on the way back to his place.

"Glad Cam and his friend wasn't hurt. Sorry the lady got messed with 'cuz she's a nice lady and nobody should be messed over like that," is all he said.

"I meant, what are we gonna do?" I asked him.

"Go home, find Cam, and get us a few beers to wash the taste out of our mouths, then figure a way to find 'em and even things up," he said.

"Why'd they do it?" I asked.

"Show me they can do shit like that and tell me they can do shit like that to Cam or anybody else they want, anytime they want," he said.

"But you already knew that from the cabin stunt and the first time they worked Cam over. Why do it again? What happened to make them do something now?" I asked.

"Harry, knowing you as I do, I don't think it could happen, but maybe they caught on to you, or maybe Cam said something stupid...I just don't know, Harry," he said.

"We'll figure it out, Tom," I told him.

"We had better, Harry. I liked that lady and she's been good to Cam. Ya can't just go around playing with people's lives for no good reason. Somebody's gonna have to pay for what they done to her—and pay real hard," Tom said.

Knowing Tom, he meant every word of it. The poor bastards who did this were in deep doodoo now!

Chapter 83

When I find myself confused and don't know what to do, the best thing for me to do is nothing. I was definitely confused by this latest turn of events and decided to let it lie for a day and occupy my time with something else. Something that takes total concentration and stimulates both my mind and body.

What's that you say? No, it does not involve a bed and a creature of the opposite sex. But, now that you mention it, I may give that one a try some time in the future.

No, it's an all out ball pounding marathon.

Skipped out of work early and I started by heading over to Bumble Bee West in my HoneyBee. It's a driving range and miniature golf combination with an identical set-up over on the East Shore a bit down Linglestown Road from Blue Ridge Country Club. I'd like to but I haven't played that course since nobody has invited a shit-bum like me to play there. But I hear the head pro Pete is a good guy and does a real nice job.

Two large buckets of balls, my golf bag, and the score card from Bethpage Black on Long Island was at the ready. Here's what I do— warm up a bit, then make like I'm on the first tee at Bethpage Black and I hit my drive to start the round. After each shot I mentally calculate where I'd be on the hole and then chose a club to hit the next shot just like I was on the course. Gotta use your imagination quite a bit, but it's the next best thing to being on the course.

Two hours later, I've got the makings of a golf score. Head to the miniature golf layout and play eighteen holes to complement the eighteen I just played on the range. Combine the two together and shazam—an eighteen hole round of golf without stepping on the course.

Don't ask—I hit the ball like crap and putted like a blind monkey.

* * *

Back in the HoneyBee, I motored over to the Sports Emporium off Interstate 81 and headed for the batting cage. An hour of whacking baseballs from the Iron Mike machine will clear your head for sure. Two to left, two to center, two to right and then you start over again. Caused a few blisters and some mighty sore muscles as well.

The whole time, during golf and b-ball, my subconscious was running the past month or so through the mental wringer to see where I may have screwed up and tipped my hand. Sometimes you come up with the answer, sometimes you don't. Came up empty this time and I don't believe it was me. Maybe I'm missing something, but I just don't think so. I just can't see how I could be the cause of what happened.

It was after eleven by the time I was done and I was whipped. Physically I ached and mentally I was exhausted. Just what the doctor ordered.

The bad guys were still on the loose, one step ahead of the good guys, but tomorrow would be another day.

Chapter 84

By Friday night, I was ready to get out of Dodge for a while. Packed some things and hit the road for New York. Crissy was off with some artsy friends to Baltimore, the GC was gonna be stuck working all weekend, and Tom and Cam were headed to a combination gun show, concert weekend in West Virginia. Beats me, so don't ask. Maybe Tom will get some useful information out of Cam while they're gone. Do them both some good to get away together.

The HoneyBee was tooling along and I had time to think about life in general—and the case in particular. When you're behind the wheel with two hundred miles or so to cover, the mind needs to be occupied somehow. Let's see—the plan called for I-81 to 78, to the New Jersey Turnpike, to this, to that—boring ride at best. There's a miniature village or something on 78, and Pat Garrett's joint, the Crayola factory near Easton and a Golf Museum of some kind in Jersey—you get the picture.

* * *

The message sent through the Sands lady was still throwing me for a loop and making me angrier every second I thought about it. Serious guys doing serious stuff but not bad enough to do permanent damage to anyone. I'm not saying what they did to the lady wouldn't mess up a person pretty bad, but they could have done much worse to her. The mind can be a terrible thing to mess with but when you actually do the physical act, it can scar a person irreparably.

I didn't get it. If there was a pattern to what they were doing, I couldn't see it. Maybe that was the point, there was no pattern. Take Cam up to the mountains and then bust him up later on. Give Tom a warning and then terrify a poor defenseless lady. It's like they want to scare us away but don't want to hurt anyone bad. Real bad guys don't care about anybody or anything. Sometime bad guys do care but hurt who they have to; guys playing bad guys care about what they do and who they do it to. There doesn't seem to be a definite slot where the players we're up against fit.

What and who the hell were we dealing with? Just don't know. Find out before somebody gets busted up for good.

A Harry Mickey Shorts QAS that needs fast work for sure.

* * *

The ride was going great until I got to the New Jersey Turnpike right around the Meadowlands. Unfortunately, I was just in time for the New Jersey Nets basketball game to get out. Bad enough sitting in traffic when leaving a game, I was stuck in traffic from a game I didn't even have the chance to enjoy.

The Nets had been my team for a long time. I've suffered through some very bad periods. Kidd was and still is one of my favorites even in Dallas. He couldn't carry Pete Maravich's jock from what my dad tells me, but he can play some, and the Nets are looking like they won't be anywhere near the top for a while.

After what seemed like forever, I cruised over the George Washington Bridge and across the Cross Bronx Expressway headed for the Throggs Neck Bridge. It was clear sailing at that point and I hit the Cross Island Parkway full speed ahead motoring for Manhasset and my home base.

The town looked quiet for a Friday night when I turned off Northern Boulevard by St. Mary's Church onto Plandome Road. One long block and I hung a right turn onto George Street. Half a block later, I turned up the driveway to my digs.

Home sweet home.

Funny how you can miss a small apartment in a town where you still don't feel you belong when you've only been gone a short time. Well, short time to me, a wandering fool, who thinks a little jaunt of six or seven months is a short walk-about. But you get the picture, kiddos.

* * *

I was hungry. Starved was more like it. It hit me all of a sudden as I was putting away the small amount of stuff I brought with me. Might be because I hadn't had anything to eat since lunch time. In fact, I hadn't had that much to eat then either, so I suppose there was a very good reason I was hungry.

Too tired to hit the town with an early morning and long day ahead, I toasted some bread from the freezer and settled for a peanut butter and jelly sandwich. As I've told you already, the key to a dynamite P&B sandy is putting potato chips, preferably BBQ, inside the sandwich to go with a bunch on the plate as well. Don't say yuck if you've never tried it. Give it a whirl and then we can talk.

Kids in the morning and I'm really looking forward to some good old fashioned 'beat daddy's ass' sanity after what I've been dealing with lately.

Chapter 85

Promptly at 8:45 am the next morning I was in the HoneyBee and on my way to pick up the little darlings. The message on my answering machine said to bring some warm clothes, so I grabbed what I had available and hoped it would keep me from freezing. What the hell was I in for this time?

The kids were waiting by the front door when I pulled up to their house. Knock my socks off, the old wifey-poo was standing there with them, all smiles and waves as they jumped into the car. We will make the assumption it was directed at the kids and couldn't be for me.

Oh yeah, they had a large cooler that weighed a ton, two gym bags filled to the brim and a 'keep the pizza hot from the takeout pizza place' thingy. What was inside I couldn't even imagine.

"Hello there my favorite little munchkins," I said when we were all secured and ready to go.

"Yo, pops," was Max's greeting.

"Daddy," was all Briande said. She grows up a lifetime between every visit. Before you know it I'm gonna be kicking some poor kid's ass for doing what boys and girls do. I did it, she'll do it, and eventually Max will, too.

Max's adventures I'll be able to handle. Briande—gonna be a struggle for me.

* * *

The IHOP was jumping for an early Saturday morning. It's how we start every daddy/kiddie day and today was no different than all the rest. The surprise wasn't the mounds of all kinds of breakfast goodies—as you all know they are required fare for these feasts. What got me was the bowl of strawberries & raspberries requested by Briande and the fact she was actually eating them in place of some of what Max and I were pigging out on. Another one of those 'growing up' things I guess. I'll have to ask Sherry (the ex for those who may have forgotten) what else is happening in her life.

Food consumed, bill paid, the appropriate burps and farts from the disgusting male members of the Shorts contingency having their normal embarrassing effect on the female Shorts member, and we were off.

"So, where to, kiddos?" I inquired.

"Long Island Expressway heading away from the city," Max deadpanned.

"That's it?" I asked.

"For now," he replied.

"Think you can remember how to find your way to the Southern State Parkway?" Briande chimed in. "You know, the one that goes south," she continued using her wise little mouth for no good use.

"I'll find it, missy," I said. "And you better buckle up, 'cause Mister HoneyBee is ready to start buzzing."

"Oh goody," Max said. "Maybe that means we might even hit sixty miles per hour in this marvel of automotive wonderment!"

"I'll give you automotive wonderment you little punk," I answered, and we all laughed that fun laugh shared by a dad and his punk rotten kids.

* * *

Today's secret destination turned out to be the beach—Jones Beach to be precise. It's on the south side of Long Island and has a particular section called the West End. It was there we met up with ten other dads and their kids for the annual 'it ain't warm but we're on the beach anyway' get together. Since my kids' dad wasn't able to participate in the past—I was the missing dad blowing in the wind at the time—this was our initial involvement with IAWBWOTBA.

Before you get deep into April, the beaches on Long Island definitely aren't warm places to be. So, the kids had included in their gear: a cooler with hot dogs and burgers plus soda and a few cool ones for their beloved dad to toss down while hiding in the dunes; three blankets and an extra sweatshirt for each of us; tiny hibachi with charcoal and lighter fluid—for cooking as well as warmth; a frisbee and nerf football for recreation, plus some miscellaneous extras too numerous to mention.

The pizza 'keep-it-hot' thingy had bacon and egg croissants and McDonalds breakfast bagels for everyone. The crowd was whipped into a frenzy when they saw those little babies. I chowed down with gusto until I remembered one little fact—I paid for all of them.

The kicker was the inflatable tent one of the dads was in the process of getting patented. He brought one for each family and made arrangements for his company to come and take them away at the end of our festivities. From six inches square to a four man tent (or four person tent to be politically correct) in thirty seconds all by the simple pull of one cord. It was amazing to see and a valuable resource when the wind started blowing later on.

* * *

The day was an all out blast. Two full-blown football games—one nerf and the other frisbee football. Luckily there were a few dogs along for the ride to retrieve the football and Frisbee from the surf. Max caught the winning touchdown in the nerf game and Briande got to knock her secret sweetie flat on his ass, so the Shorts clan was happy all around. For me, getting to see the kids happy was good enough.

Oh yeah, for informational purposes only, I threw the touchdown pass to Max if you really must know.

Chapter 86

A day at the beach on a good day can knock you on your ass. A day at the beach this time of year with temps in the low 50's and the wind blowing can knock you on your ass and then throw sand on your sorry body to finish the job.

That being said, the kids surprised me by asking me to drop them off at the high school when we got back to Manhasset. Seems the school does this all night thing occasionally; they lock the doors at 10:00 pm and don't open them till 6:00 am. Keeps the renegades off the streets and gives the kids something to do other than boozing, drugs and whatnot.

"You can just stop at home and drop off our stuff. Mom will be there and is expecting you," Max said.

"Oh, yeah," I said.

"Oh, yeah," Max said.

"Oh, yeah," Briande repeated.

Since we all seemed to be in agreement, I dropped them off at school and headed over to see Sherry—my beloved ex.

I had a bad feeling about this one—like I been had by bodies much smaller than mine and, if at all possible, minds much more devious.

* * *

"Harry?" came out as more of a question when Sherry opened the front door in response to my knock.

"In the flesh," I responded.

"Why?" she asked. She must have used up her allotment of words for the day.

"Why not?" I answered mostly to be a pain in the ass.

"Harry!" she said. That was her 'you're pissing me off' Harry.

"Sherry," I said. I used to say that whenever she used her 'you're pissing me off' Harry on me.

Realizing I was standing on the porch all by my lonesome, she asked "Where are the kids?"

"Up at the school," I answered. "Didn't you know they were going to this all night thing they do?"

"No, I obviously didn't," she said. "Well, don't just stand there, bring that stuff into the house," she said as she walked away from the door.

Guess I wasn't going to get any assistance.

"How've you been?" I asked after I had lugged all of it into the house.

"About the same," she answered. "I was just making myself a drink. Want one?"

"Sure," I said after the shock of being offered a drink by my ex-wife in the confines of her home wore off.

"Same?" she asked.

"Same," I answered. She knew I had been drinking Absolute Gimlets since two years before Christ was born.

I took a visual trip around the part of the house I could see and dropped my tired bones onto the couch just as Sherry came back into the room.

Gimlet with crushed ice for me, the usual Black Russian for her.

Crushed ice—a little effort on my behalf?

"The kids had a great day," I told her after taking the time to thank her for the drink and the crushed ice.

"Good, they've been looking forward to today for a long, long time," she replied.

I replayed the day for her as I found myself taking my second visual trip around my immediate surroundings. Sherry had on a pink tank top and it was obvious she wasn't wearing a bra. Average breasts at best when one was being generous, she had oversized nipples that where prominently displayed at the moment. Cut-off shorts, which she tended to cut-off fairly short, showed off her long legs which were tucked under her at the moment. She sat semi facing me which displayed all of her best features in their best light.

"Care for another drink?" she asked when I was done telling her about the day and taking visual inventory.

"Sure, why not," I replied. I was there, might as well enjoy myself.

"Good," she said. "That way you can get an equally good look from behind as well."

She got up, took my empty glass, and put on a show as she went off to the kitchen to refresh our drinks.

After all these years and everything we've been through, she can still straighten the old wand with a wiggle and a walk. Turns out it was obviously the case this time, as Sherry commented, "Nice one," as she handed me my new drink.

"Nice one?" I asked.

"Nice hard-on. Haven't you been getting enough lately?" she asked with a smile that said 'gotcha.'

"Two part answer," I replied. "One, the subject at hand who has caused said 'nice one' was always able to do so quite well; and two, some, but never enough."

She pondered that.

"You?" I continued.

"Two part answer," she replied. "One, the subject at hand with said 'nice one' has always been able to produce a similar effect on me as well; and two, some, but never enough, especially lately."

"It seems we find ourselves, both subjects at hand, in somewhat similar circumstances," I commented, as I nudged slightly closer.

"We do," Sherry said as she nudged herself a whole lot closer.

Soon thereafter, subjects at hand were fully engaged with various objects in hand, mouth, etc. and the usual that follows. And let me tell you, there was a whole lot of unusual that followed as well. From the couch, to the floor, to the bed, and to the floor again—a good time was had by all subjects at hand.

Will wonders never cease, I wondered. And continued to wonder all night long.

* * *

By the way, getting the kids at six was no problem. The only problem was getting out of the house and away from a very horny ex-wife in time to get there.

Chapter 87

It was early afternoon when I rolled into the office to chat with my favorite EBIL. I had caught a few hours sleep and packed up my gear to head back to PA.

"Big Mel, how's your ass these days?" I asked as I entered his office.

"My ass is more tired than a, than a, oh, it's tired," he finally got out.

"Business good at least?" I asked.

"Actually, best month we've had in about a year. Sold three houses I personally brought into the shop and had the buyer on two of them. And no, you can't borrow any money," he replied.

"Way to kick ass, Big Mel," I congratulated him. "That should make the first half of the year all by itself."

"Could be. What brings you in here on a Sunday? See the kids yesterday?" he asked.

"Yeah, I did and it was a blast. Spent the day at Jones Beach then dropped them off at the high school for some all-night whatever they do. Got 'em at six this morning, so I'm dragging kinda low myself."

"See my sister in the midst of all that?" he asked.

"Yeah," I replied after a beat.

"Just yeah," he said.

"Yeah, just yeah," I answered.

He looked at me, thought a sec, and then said 'no shit' to the ceiling. Me, I didn't say a word.

"You have to be shitting me, you hump," he laughed.

"Hey, shit happens you know. And sometimes where, when and with who can surprise the piss out of any mortal man," I said.

We both laughed.

* * *

I screwed around with the case file and had it updated through the past week when Bunny came in. Talk about making your wand stand up at attention.

"Well hi there, Harry. I didn't expect to see you here today," she said with a sly little smile.

"Just dropped in to update some files and say hi to Mel. I'm heading back out of town in a few. You working or just passing through?" I asked.

"Sitting at an open house for the afternoon and I'm late already," she replied.

"Too bad," I hinted.

"Too bad is right," she said as she generously bent down to get nothing important out of the bottom drawer of the strategically placed file cabinet. The short skirt enhanced the experience immensely.

Mel didn't miss taking a peak as well.

"Maybe next time," she giggled as she headed for the front door. She was gone before I could reply.

"Same old Bunny Malone, Big Mel," I said.

"Same old Bunny Malone," he agreed.

"Before I split, what happed with your friend Smooth?" I asked him.

"How'd you hear about that?" he asked in surprise.

"Sherry mentioned she heard something."

Smooth, by the way, was a good bud of Mel's who played college ball in the south somewhere. Kentucky or Wake Forest I think. His jumper was the best around back then and looked 'smooth as silk' everyone said. Hence, Eddie ceased to exist and Smooth was born. Plus, Smooth Henson had a real ring to it.

"Big mouthed sister. Ya can't trust her with dick," he said.

Sometimes you can, I thought, sometimes you can. He should only know.

"He got himself jacked up over something he didn't even do. Hired a guy about a year ago who talked him into hiring his cousin for a nothing job. They turned around and stole a huge chunk from the company and split town leaving Smooth looking not too smooth in the company's eyes."

"What happened?" I asked.

"They found the guys and got back about half the cash. Smooth got his balls in a wringer because he didn't have the proper safeguards in place to protect against something like that. Plus, he didn't even know it happened until a quarterly audit found it later on," he finished.

"His ass get fired?" I asked.

"No, but he had to front a piece 'cuz the cheap-ass owner didn't have enough insurance to cover the loss," Mel said.

"How's Smooth?" I asked.

"Out too big a wad and the wife is threatening to leave him if they lose the house. The daughter is pissed since her wedding got moved from the Plandome Country Club to some hall over in New Hyde Park. Fiancée's family is making a stink and he may pull the plug on the wedding."

"Really," I said.

"Bad situation all around. That sister of mine better shut her big mouth before the whole world knows about it," he fumed.

How apropos of Big Mel to mention his sister's big mouth after last night and how glad I was she wasn't doing what he wanted right about then.

"I gotta split, but tell Smooth I feel for him when you see him."

With that I was gone and on my way back to Central PA to deal with my current predicament. Memories of the day and night with the kids, the night and early part of the day with Sherry, plus a high and a low at Mel's office would keep me busy for the four hour ride back to MechInsCo land.

Chapter 88

I woke to the end of the 7:00 am news on WPAT 93.5 FM—Coffee and Amy show. Amy was now out on maternity leave and Coffee was doing the sports and weather. Liked it better when Amy did it. After seeing pictures of Amy, I'd like anything she did better.

Coffee kicked into this bit they were doing called "Adopt a Writer" after he finished the weather. Some guy wrote a book and got himself published. Problem was he had to do all the marketing and promotion himself and was hounding Coffee to "adopt" him to get Coffee to use his local pull to get an unknown author enough notoriety to sell lots of books. The guy had called himself Mister Persistence and wouldn't give up and was now trying to get Amy to convince Coffee to relent and say yes.

Time will tell on this one—but good for the writer and good for Coffee for having the balls to even think about helping out a struggling first time writer. We need more guys like him, but mostly we need more lookers like Amy.

* * *

"Shorts!" rang through the halls as I entered the MechInsCo building.

"Crissy, my dear," I said as I turned to face her at the reception desk.

Quietly she whispered, "Don't Crissy my dear me, you prick. Where have you been for what seems like forever?"

"Morning, Shorts," the GC said as she swept past the reception area heading toward the elevators.

"Ah, morning my dear or Crissy, my dear—same thing," I told her.

"My ass," she said.

I tried to peak over the reception counter to take a look at her ass as I thought I had been instructed.

"Get back down there," she hissed. "My ass they aren't the same was what I was trying to say."

"I was just doing what I thought I was told to do. And a fine ass it is by the way, my dear," I said as I sprinted for the door to the stairs.

"Shorts!" was all I heard, knowing full well there was more that followed, all of which I didn't want to be subjected to.

* * *

The accounting area was all a flutter when I got there. The little bees were buzzing around Mary Ann's desk with what I assumed was new juicy gossip.

"Morning everyone," I said as I approached her desk. I figured some advance warning was only fair enough.

"Oh, good morning, Harry. We were all just getting our day organized together, that's all," Mary Ann the queen bee lied.

"Yes, that's all," the worker bees agreed as they scattered.

"Your boss in?" I asked her.

"No, he's due in any minute," Mary Ann told me. She was going to make up a story to cover for him, but changed her mind and started at her keyboard instead.

"Joe okay?" I asked Mary Ann.

"He's fine, why wouldn't you think he was fine when he is fine. I mean, ah, he's fine as he is always fine, I mean, ah," I think she said.

"Calm down, kiddo. I was just asking and didn't mean anything by it," I told her. "Do me a favor and let him know I stopped by to see him, okay?"

A nod without looking up and more keyboard typing. Funny thing—there wasn't anything on her desk to be typing from.

* * *

Sitting at my desk in my not so spacious cubicle, I took stock of what I knew up to this point. Didn't take long—I didn't know much and that was my biggest problem. With the amount of time I had spent on this case I should have been much further along.

Why? I don't know. Back to basics.

Another HMS QAS in the books.

Back to basics meant listing what I knew from start to finish. Define the facts, separate the clues from the worthless stuff, pose the questions that need answers and determine the next steps. A plan that has worked before and should work again. Problem was I already did this twice and still couldn't figure out Jack and doing it again wasn't going to get me any further along than I already was.

Oh well, let's play some ball.

Chapter 89

"The president will see you now, Mister Shorts," the Ice Queen informed me.

"Thanks," I said as I went into his office.

"Shorts, sit down and give me a minute," his presidentness said. Unfortunately, he looked like hell and not at all like a commander in charge of his troops.

"Yeah, I heard you. I just said I heard you, didn't I. I'll get the money by the end of the month just like I told you last week," he said and promptly slammed down the phone.

"I'm Paul Collins, President of Mechanicsburg Insurance Company, and I got some small time schmuck of a broker pulling me around by my dick," he said both to me and himself at the same time. "Jesus H. Christ, what a mess."

"Anything I can do to help, Mister Collins," I asked.

"With him, no; but, thanks for asking anyway. Just about every other supposed executive I got here is hiding under their desk hoping I won't stick my head in their office and ask them anything. Supposed executives I bring down here from New York to run a company and they turn into pansies. Pansies I tell ya. You hear me, Shorts—pansies every one of them!" he shouted.

Harry Mickey Shorts—not a pansy in the eyes of a small Central Pennsylvania failing insurance company president. Oh, how I have grown in such a short space of time. Oh, the honor of it all. The glory that will be mine...I'll stop if you insist.

"One thing you can do for me, Shorts," he continued in a more civilized voice.

"Yes sir," I answered.

"The Senators are back in town and I'm still worried about that bunch of coaches I got in charge. Take a week and work with the pitchers, will ya?" he asked. "And gimme the lowdown on this star catcher we just got graced with from the parent club. Nobody asked me if we needed one, but I guess that's what you get the way this particular game is played."

The last comment confused me, but the rest sure didn't.

"I'd be pleased to help out, Mister Collins. I'll head over there first thing tomorrow morning and do the best I can for you and the Senators," I brown-nosed.

"Sure, now get out. And when that prick broker Ralph Vasimalo and his two lackeys show up, don't let 'em know nothing or do nothing. Okay, Shorts?" he said.

"Done, Mister Collins," I answered and proceeded to get the bums rush out the door.

* * *

Got a case I can't make heads nor tails of, an old friend and his son I'm letting down, a mother and daughter tandem that keep me hopping—in and out of bed—and an ex-wife that has come out of nowhere to occupy a larger than expected piece of my thought time.

But, as I have quoted a learned thinker on more than one occasion— "Baseball been berry, berry good to me!"

Chapter 90

The Harrisburg Senators team that came north after spring training in Florida looked pretty good—on paper that is. A good mix of proven talent and hyped youngsters put them at the top of the list to unseat the Bayport Schooners in the Double A Eastern League. That would be the Champion Bayport Schooners who were led the prior season by none other than player-coach extraordinaire, one Harry Mickey Shorts—plus a few others, too.

Collins retained the administrative staff when he purchased the team and I started my day by meeting with the General Manager, Todd Vander Woude. I knew him from the prior season and he is one of the best GM's in all of minor league baseball. Runs the team great and has the fan's interest at the top of his priority list all the time. Good man all the way around.

"Good to see you again, Harry. You here to cause the Senators grief again this season?" he asked as we shook hands outside the club's quarters on City Island.

"Nope. Not this year, Woody. I'm actually on your side this time," I told him. "Collins has asked me to help out with the pitchers for a few days and see how good this new hotshot catcher is," I continued.

"That's good to hear, Harry. The new kid played A ball the end of last year after signing a late contract. Ripped the cover off the ball for a month with them. He's from somewhere in the Dominican Republic and I'm told he can really play. Could be the next real deal passing through Harrisburg on the way to stardom," he said.

"Can he catch?" I asked Woody.

"Nobody saw anything other than the ball flying off his bat every time he came to the plate," he stated.

"We'll see then," I said. "Time I did what I'm not getting paid for," I told him as I started for the clubhouse.

"Stop by and see me later," Woody said. "You can gloat a bit and rehash your championship if you want."

"I'd never do that—well, maybe a little," I laughed. "I'll catch you later, Todd."

* * *

I could hear the coaches meeting in the skipper's office when I walked into the player's portion of the clubhouse. I said hello to the guys I was friendly with from Florida and acquainted myself with the new players. After I left, couple big studs got moved up from A ball at the very end of spring training in Florida and made the Senators club.

One of them was the new catching sensation. He was built like two brick shithouses and was obviously no stranger to the weight room. He proceeded to crush my hand as we shook. He said, "Call me Ozzie."

"Harry Shorts, Ozzie. Pleased to meet ya, man," I volunteered.

"Guys say you a cool dude and all," Ozzie gushed. "Be cool you help me out with my stuff."

I assumed he meant his baseball skills and told him, "No problem, kiddo."

"Kiddo, that's cool and all," he said with one of those big kid grins all over his face.

Let's hope I was gonna find a little more going on upstairs when we hit the field. No Einstein imitation so far, but that's cool and all.

* * *

With their meeting over, the coaches were leaving the manager's office just as I got ready to stick my head in.

"Talton," I said to the top of his head.

"Shorts," he answered without looking up.

"Mind if I come in?" I asked as I sat down in front of his desk.

"Don't seem as I got much choice, do I?" he answered.

Still hadn't looked up from the player charts on his desk.

"So, how they hanging there, Skip?" I tried.

At least that got him to pick his head up and look in my direction, but not without a great deal of effort I might add.

I smiled. Harry Mickey Shorts at his lovable best.

"You think Collins got any clue what's going on with this baseball toy of his?" he asked me.

"Three possibilities," I said. "He recognizes the sheer brilliance I exude just stepping out on the field, he thinks you and your coaches are warmed-over dog shit, or he has no clue at all."

"Allum," Talton expounded with great effort.

"My sentiments exactly," I agreed with slightly less effort.

"If you want, take the new dumb-ass kid and make him a catcher. And that big hick lefty don't know pitching from horseshoes. They're yours for a week—good luck."

His head went down and I got the distinct feeling it wasn't coming back up. Meeting adjourned I decided. Big time P.I.'s can do that you know.

"You got it, Skip," I said.

Chapter 91

The big lefty turned out to be a kid from Kentucky who grew up on a farm. Classic example of six foot six and 235 pounds of walking country bumpkin who goes by the name Jed Furness. Walking and chewing gum at the same time seemed like it would be a major struggle for the kid, and kid he was. God forbid you should ask him to think at the same time. Nineteen years old and only one year removed from high school. What in the hell was this kid doing here?

A 98 mile-per-hour fast ball. That's the reason he jumped from rookie ball last summer and by-passed Single A for the time being. A 98 mile-per-hour fast ball and most of the time not a single clue where it was going.

A 98 mile-per-hour fast ball. That's the reason he's here.

God help the weak and, in this case, Harry Mickey Shorts.

* * *

"Jed," I called over to my new project.

He was sitting on a bench next to the dugout and looked up to see who was calling his name.

"Jed, over here," I called out.

I was at the other end of the dugout with the second half of my project—Ozzie, the so called catcher. At least he was holding a catcher's glove in one hand and a catcher's mask in the other.

Jed got up slowly and ambled on over to where Ozzie and I were standing.

"Jed, I'm Harry Shorts. Coach Talton has asked me to work with you and Ozzie here for a few days. Kinda like preferred treatment for the new kids on the block," I said.

"Ain't they that singing group all the kids are goo-goo over?" he asked.

Puzzled, I looked at him, Ozzie looked at me, I looked at both of them.

"What do you mean, Jed?" I asked him.

"The singing group—The New Kids on the Block," he said.

Even Ozzie shook his head and wondered what space ship kidnapped him and just now dropped him back in our laps.

"Forget it," I said. "Let's head down to the bullpen and do some throwing."

* * *

To put it very mildly, with as much understatement as possible, I had my hands full. My pitching project had arms and legs going in every direction with no sign of bodily coordination at all. It was amazing he could throw the ball at all, never mind at 98 miles-per-hour. But somehow, some way, he could bring it when the ball finally left his hand.

Ozzie was lucky to still be alive and, more importantly, still had the capability of siring offspring sometime in the future. At least I assumed he hadn't sired any little Ozzie Jrs to date.

Couldn't have Jed throwing to Ozzie and getting him killed on the first morning I worked with him.

"Jed, why don't you do your running first and we can do some light throwing later on while we work on your mechanics," I suggested to him.

"Good idea, coach," he said.

Why he thought it was a good idea I didn't know, but it got him out of my hair for the time being.

"Ozzie, come on over here," I told him. "How many games did you catch last year?"

"Well," he hesitated.

"Well, how many?" I asked again.

"I ah, well I ah...I did a lot of DH'ing last year," he finally replied.

"That doesn't answer my question, Ozzie. How many games did you actually catch last year?" I repeated.

"Well, ah, not too many," he said.

"Define 'not too many' in numbers for me, Ozzie," I said to him.

"Maybe about two," he said quietly.

"Two games total," I said in amazement. "Just two total games," I continued.

"No," he said.

"No what?" I asked.

"Not total games," was his answer.

"Not total games or whole games. How many innings?" I asked.

"Well, ah, I mean, um, four," he blurted out.

"Four! Four innings total!" I said.

"Yeah, four innings," he confirmed.

"Fuck me," I said.

"No thanks, Harry," Ozzie replied.

I had to smile at that remark.

Chapter 92

It was two full days later before I started to feel like I was getting somewhere. I started from scratch, and I mean like with a kid who is ten years old and wants to learn how to be a catcher. Ozzie and I drilled basics morning, afternoon and night. He was a quick learner and had some natural instincts. Truth was, Ozzie named catcher as his position when asked, but he had never played any position more than a couple of games a season since grade school.

Why not? He plain assed sucked at it. Designated Hitter. No plainer Harry Mickey Shorts QAS will you ever see.

Coaches threw him behind the plate a few innings a year so they could claim they had the best catcher to play at that level since—fill in the blank. They couldn't play him there more than a few innings by necessity, which was mostly to save his life. Problem was, when I asked him if anyone ever worked with him on his catching, he said, "They told me to stop worrying about catching and keep working on my hitting."

* * *

Jed could run non-stop for days without getting tired. He really was a 'run two miles back and forth to school' kid while growing up in Kentucky. Never stopped running and strong as a mule from working on the family farm. The combination made for one hell of a raw talent.

"What are you thinking when you are out on the mound? What goes through your head?" I asked him on the second day we were together.

"I ain't thinking nothing," he said. "I just throw."

"That's part of the problem," I told him. "You're nothing but a thrower now. Thrower's very rarely make it to the big show. *Pitchers* make it to the show and you have to quit throwing and learn how to be a pitcher."

"You can do that, Harry?" he asked.

"I'll sure as hell try," I assured him.

"What do we do?" Jed asked.

"What kind of music do you like, Jed? You do like music, don't you?" I asked him.

"Well, I sure do, Harry. We got music back home you know."

"What's your favorite?" I asked again.

"I write some songs a little bit, Harry. I kinda like a bit of bluegrass and southern rock all mixed up together. Got me a guitar and I pick it when I can," he said.

"Good. Now here's a little story that might help. Skinny Polish kid I played high school ball with used to get a song in his head when he pitched. Looked like he was off somewhere else, but his rhythm and control and the coordination of his mechanics were all timed to the music going on in his head."

"He any good?" Jed asked.

"He was damn good, Jed. Controlled the game his way and could throw the ball on a dime with four pitches. It was his ball and he let you play with it when he wanted and how he wanted. I told him he sucked, it was the music that did it," I said.

"He a major leaguer, Harry?" Jed asked.

"Nah. He got hurt, worked a while, wrote some books and got famous. Now he sits on the beach writing mystery books, sucking on suds, and banging all the broads he can handle. Bitch of a job, but somebody's gotta do it," I said.

"Wow!" Jed gasped.

"Focus on what I'm saying here, kiddo," I urged Jed.

"Okay, I'm listening, Harry," he replied.

"Point is, Jed, get something going in your head and stop thinking about nothing and let your body follow the rhythm in your head. Slow and smooth, fast and furious, big and bad. Your mind says—you the man and they are just little kids playing your game—then the game will be yours."

Harry paused to let it sink in.

"That's when you'll stop being a thrower and start being a pitcher, and a good one too," I tried to convince him.

"One of my all time favorites is Jessica by the Allman Brothers with Dickie Betts on guitar," Jed said. "I like the Allman Brothers a lot."

"Jed, my man, you couldn't pick a better tune to groove to on the mound or a better band to get off on. I'm all over that sound. Let's get it on, okay?" I asked.

"I'm down," he said, trying to be as cool as possible.

"You sure are. Let's go," I told him with as much conviction as I could muster.

Chapter 93

The sun was shining, life was good, then Jack Shit and his boys showed up. It was my fourth day with the Senators.

I was down in the bullpen working with Jed and Ozzie. Jed was throwing breaking balls in the dirt and Ozzie was blocking them. Both of them had progressed real well and this was adding extras to their game before we showcased their progress to the skipper.

"Well lookie here, boys," Vasimalo said. "You never know where Shorts is gonna show up, do we now?"

I excused myself from Jed and Ozzie and told them to keep working on the same drills we had been working on. "Be right back," I told them.

"Gentlemen," I said as I strolled over to the railing next to the bullpen.

"What the hell you doing here, Shorts?" Jack said. "Don't you do nothin' but hang around ball yards? Or is it the players you're looking to hang around?" he said with a nod and a wink to Billy and Kev.

The boys laughed on cue.

I decided to try the polite route first.

"Mister Collins asked me to help out with the club's pitchers for a few days and I was more than happy to lend a hand," I replied.

"What you doing with that hand to help out?" Jack Shit went on.

The boys seemed to like that one even better.

Since the polite route may not have been the best choice, I went to plan B.

"It's good to see all of you again," I continued. "What brings you down here from New York? Business, or just couldn't stand not seeing the Senators work out?"

"Business meeting in Baltimore last night and looking after my investment today," Vasimalo said. "Don't want anything to happen to them before…"

The pregnant pause hung in the air like a big fat whackame hanging curve ball.

"Before what?" I ventured.

"Before none of your fuckin' business. Not for nothin', Shorts, but you ask a lotta questions for a nobody company jerk-off," he said.

Plan B was a bust. So, as I often do, I went on the attack with Plan C. Collins or no Collins, the man had pissed me off royally.

"Sorry for bothering you with questions I have no business asking, Mister Vasimalo. Let's forget that, okay? I'd love to play another round of golf with you and your boys here, but I told Jed and Ozzie I'd play with them this afternoon when practice is over," I goaded.

"Maybe give you a chance to take a chunk of my money this time around. Too bad you had to leave early last time and couldn't beat me good," I went on.

The butt boys turned their backs so Jack Shit wouldn't see them laughing their asses off.

"One lucky putt was all. One friggin putt for Christ's sake! Tell you what, you wise-ass putz. You bring Mutt and Jeff along with you and me and my boys will kick your asses six ways to Sunday."

"Well…" I started to respond.

"I ain't done yet," he interrupted. "A hundred a man in a scramble. You and your yokels know what a scramble is, don't you?" he asked.

"I think we can figure it out. Location?" I asked.

"Kev here knows some guy over at Blue Ridge Country Club. Find it and be ready to tee off at one o'clock. Don't be late, Shorts," he finished.

"We'll find it," I told him.

Chapter 94

Blue Ridge turned out to be everything I had heard about it, and more. Even though it was real early in the golf year, the fairways were in perfect shape and the greens were true and fast. They must be like polished glass when the heat of the summer kicks in.

Pete, the head pro, personally checked us in and we were off at one on the dot. Kev was the only one who had played there before and he had played the course only once. Put us all on even terms as far as course knowledge went.

True level of play turned out to be a different story.

I very quickly learned the butt boys, Billy and Kev, actually had to struggle quite a bit to let Ralphy boy win when they played. Billy could hit it a mile off the tee and Kev wielded his irons like they were an extension of his arms. Jack Shit was plain Jack Shit along for the ride.

My guess was that more than one set of poor unknowing souls had been snookered by Ralph and his two trained golfing monkeys.

The first hole was a fairly long par four. Billy boomed a drive 275 yards down the middle and Jack started laughing immediately - long and loud.

"Didn't know my man Billy could do that, did you Shorts? Care to give up now and avoid the embarrassment?" he asked.

"Well, now that you mention it, I didn't. But I think we'll give it a go for at least a few holes if you don't mind," I answered.

After Kev and Ralph hit it was our turn in the tee box.

"Jed," I said loud enough for everyone to plainly hear. "Was it your uncle who owned the golf course right next to your daddy's farm in Kentucky?"

"Sure was, Harry. That's how I got to play all the time after my chores were done," he replied.

"And how old were you when you won the Kentucky State Amateur Championship," I continued.

"Was seventeen, Harry. I lost the year before on the last hole to the guy who won like four or five years in a row 'fore that," he said.

"Thanks, Jed. How about I hit first, then you Jed, and we'll have Ozzie bring up the rear. Okay, boys?" I asked them.

We had already decided on the way over, but it sounded good on the tee.

We did as planned and I hit one about 210 down the left side. Not bad, but not good enough when compared to Billy's ball about 65 yards further down the fairway.

"Good one, Shorts," Ralphy boy said. "At least you can see Billy's ball from there, I think."

The three of them had a good laugh after that comment.

Jed went next and hit a high drive that landed about 240 down the middle with very little roll. We were in play now and Ozzie could give it a rip.

"Hey Ozzie," I yelled. "What was your longest drive when you won the long drive contest at the team's tournament in Florida?"

"I think it was three hundred and twelve yards, but I didn't get all of it," he said.

He promptly launched one that took off low and continued to rise as it soared down the fairway. I liked it and said, "Houston, we have liftoff!"

Me and the boys had a little laugh of our own with that comment.

"Someunafucking bitch," was all that came out of Jack Shit's mouth.

* * *

We each won a hole on the front and came to the turn all square. Vasimalo was beside himself and had taken to screaming at Billy and Kev by the seventh hole. He hadn't contributed a single shot, but that didn't seem to matter. They were getting paid for days like today and they were letting the boss-man down in front of a nobody company jerk-off named Harry Mickey Shorts and his b'ball scrubinees—Mutt & Jeff.

We both birdied the long par four 10th and did the same on the 11th, a tricky downhill hole thanks to a bending ten foot putt by yours truly. You could almost see the 'Someunafucking bitch' forming on his lips, but it never came.

The 13th was a long par 3 over a valley with a green sloping so much from back to front it would leave a billy goat a-huffing and a-puffin by the time it got to the top.

Imposing little sucker from the tee.

"I believe your team is up," I said. "Tough looking hole that's got the poopies flowing right outta my ass. Try and relax, now. Don't squeeze that club too tight."

Ralphy boy glared and proceeded to hook one out of bounds to the left. The usual string of profanity followed. Billy let it leak to the right and ended up in the trap above the hole—not the place to be. Laser-iron Kev fired one directly at the hole but way long leaving them a twenty-five foot side-hill down-hill putt. Talk about poopies flowing outta your ass.

"Worthless dickheads," Ralph moaned.

Jed swung, the ball flew like a dart and disappeared into the hole. Hole-in-one and we be up one.

You guessed it—"Someunafucking bitch," Vasimalo screeched loud and long in disbelief.

Chapter 95

It stayed that way until we reached the 18th tee. No chatter from anyone and Jack Shit was seething to the point of exploding.

"Any balls there, Shorts? Double up or one hundred—we win the hole and you owe us one hundred each. You win or we halve the hole and we owe you two hundred each. Got enough balls to lay it all on one hole?" he asked.

"Interesting proposition," I said. "Boys?" I asked Jed and Ozzie.

"I don't mind taking some more of their money," Ozzie said.

"Me neither," Jed echoed. "But how does this sound big guy," he said in Vasimalo's direction. "We all hit but only you and Harry putt. As Harry says, 'You got the brass ones for it' big guy?"

"Brass ones my ass," he almost screamed. "Done your talking… let's hit," he finally said in desperation.

Billy's drive went about 285 down the right side and Ozzie cranked one five yards past him, same side. Kev was able to hit another laser shot right at the pin that stopped four feet below the hole. Easiest putt on the green—slightly up hill with no break at all.

With all the confidence in the world, I proceeded to shank one left into the trees. Not pretty. We had Ozzie hit next and he very gracefully hit a worm-burner fifty yards down the fairway. That left it all up to Jed if we were gonna stay in the hole.

"This ain't no cow pasture, amateur kids game, sonny boy. This here is money in the pocket, grab your balls and play with the big boy's time," Ralph said, obviously trying his best to intimidate Jed.

"Correct, Mister Vasimalo. Except the money's going into my pocket when you walk off the green," he said. He then lofted a beauty to within ten feet of the cup.

"Finish him, Harry," he said to me and started walking down the fairway whistling a fair version of Jessica as he headed for the clubhouse.

"Someunafucking bitch," I heard Ralphy moan as his cart took off toward the green.

* * *

I was ten feet away from the hole which meant I 'was away' in golfese and would normally putt first. Same basic putt for both of us, straight up the hill, mine six feet longer then his.

"Care to make an attempt at sinking yours first?" I asked Vasimalo.

"Shorts, after I sink this putt, you're gonna be shaking so bad you won't be able to hold that tiny little pecker of yours never mind a putter," he said.

Ralphy boy walked up to his putt without even looking at the line. Eyed it up and stroked it home like he was born to putt for dough.

Billy and Kev let out a collective whoop and high-fives were shared all around.

"Time to choke like the loser you are, Shorts," Jack Shit laughed.

As I looked over my putt, Ozzie stepped behind me and said, "After you sink this puppy, I'm gonna make those two butt-sniffin' pukes buy till we're crossed eyed."

I stepped up and got ready to putt.

"Let me see if I have this right," I started. "I get lucky and this putt some how goes in, we win—you lose. That right, Ralphy Boy?"

"Ain't gonna happen, but you got it right, Shorts," he laughed.

He was beet red and seemed to be enraged beyond what you'd expect.

"You're gonna choke like a sorry dog and I'll really enjoy taking your money. On my brother's grave, that whistling hillbilly's gonna pay once I own him and the rest of that sorry excuse for a team...and, and, and, ...and a piece of your ass," he stammered, "and that sorry assed Collins ...and, and that mother-humping no good prick's company in a tailspin..."

He was gesturing like a lunatic by now, making no sense whatsoever, hands and arms making like whirlwinds and spit flying everywhere.

Billy and Kev were trying to calm him down which only enraged him even more.

I'd heard and seen enough of the circus act being performed on the 18th green of Blue Ridge Country Club. I gestured to Ozzie to head for the safety of the clubhouse. Without looking down, eyes still locked on crazy man Vasimalo's eyes, I stroked the putt and started walking toward the clubhouse. Didn't need to look back.

"Someunafucking bitch" echoed down the fairway confirming what I already knew—we were in the money!

Chapter 96

I partied with the boys to celebrate our victory and was halfway to a major league hammering when my cell phone rang. Probably saved my ass from a mother of a hangover and sobered me up instantly. Information that points you to the door and holds answers to questions you haven't been able to figure out can do that.

The Web Dudes are guys I know who work systems in a nowhere insurance company by day and provide information for pay at night. They are the 'information kings' and earn every dime they charge. And trust me, they charge heavy duty dimes. You ask for it and they come up with it—I don't know how and I'm sure I don't want to know.

"Dude, my man," Jaxy the number one Web Dude said as I clicked on.

"Jaxy, my man," I replied. "You got me a line on what we talked about?"

"Hook, line and sinker, dude." His old man owned a fishing charter company off Montauk, Long Island.

"Where?" I asked.

"The usual string," he said.

"Gimme ten to go secure land," I told him.

To stop your frowning—'where' was asking how I should contact him, the 'string' meant the usual phone number (string of numbers) we had set up long ago, and 'secure land' told him I was headed to a pay phone that couldn't be tapped or traced.

We copasetic? Good, let's go on.

* * *

"Gents, I gotta split," I told Ozzie and Jed. Ozzie heard me I think, but Jed never moved a muscle. "Give my boys here a few more and keep the change," I told the barkeep. "Then get them a cab." I wrote down the address just in case and tossed a deuce of twenties on the bar that should have been enough to cover the rest of their evening and then I headed for a phone.

"How's the ex and the kids?" Jaxy asked when we re-hooked up. He met Sherry once and she immediately didn't like him. She was like that sometimes.

"Good, Jaxy. Thanks for asking. How's your squeeze?"

Jaxy always had a main squeeze. Some stayed a day, some a week and one stayed almost six months. Didn't matter when they came and when they left—one appeared the next day every time. I liked Jaxy.

"Two-weeker," he said.

Same old Jaxy.

"Sing me a tune," I told him.

"You got yourself hooked up with Dylan this time, Harry," he said. Jaxy liked to spill using music as his means of delivery. He could have been a song writer or something like that if he wasn't a master information thief. He knows every word to every song from every singer since the early eighties, which is just about the same time he discovered crime surely does pay. The internet just makes his life so much easier.

"They be 'Tangled Up in Blue' while 'Blowin in the Wind,'" he said as he finished giving me the dope I needed to tie certain people to the case and tie them to each other. It had been all there jumbled up in my head, right before my eyes. Facts and figures, figures as facts. Only needed to lay them out in the correct order and trust my instincts.

Follow the money—it never fails. Well, almost never.

"Like always, you the man, Jaxy," I told him.

"Like always, you pay the man," he replied as he hung up.

* * *

I needed some gossip and I needed some sound facts. Much as I hated to double dip in the family fountain back-to-back, a private eye's job is a tough one with ethical dilemmas constantly getting in the way. The only question was—age before beauty or beauty before age. Either way, I win.

Chapter 97

Age before beauty lost out this time.

"Crissy, the most beautiful sight in Central Pennsylvania. No, correction, in all of Pennsylvania," I said when she picked up the phone.

"You drunk, Shorts?" she said. "Don't think you can treat me like crap and ignore me, go out partying, then call me after all this time to get your rocks off when you strike out. And do you know what time it is?" she asked.

"Ah, well…it's…no I don't," I confessed.

"It happens to be…oh hell, I don't know either and I don't really care. Plus, I'm horny as hell. Get your butt over here and you better not be too drunk to make me happy. And you better say you're damn sorry or I'll throw your ass out faster than you can say… you can say…ah just get over here."

"Don't worry sweet cheeks, I'm all about being sorry and ensuring you'll be happy," I said as she hung up on me.

* * *

"Well, what a surprise, its Mister Shorts. That is your name, isn't it? The voice sounds familiar, but it has been awhile," the GC said.

I had called her as soon as I got off the phone with Crissy.

"Yes, it is I," I said

"I?" she said in query.

"Read it in a book and though a little sophistication might score me enough points to get me out of the dog house with such a beautiful and intelligent and wonderful…"

"Shut up, Shorts."

"Okay, if you insist," I replied quietly.

"What do you want and why are you calling me at home at this hour?" she continued.

"Out of curiosity, what time is it?" I asked. Partying has a way of making the clock scurry along so.

"It's almost ten thirty," she said.

Better hurry or I may not be able to make Crissy happy after all.

"Sorry to call so late," I tried. "I'll just keep you a minute."

"If you have something on your mind, Harry, why don't you come on over and we can deal with it in some fashion. Hold on, I have another call," she said.

Time for some Shorts fast thinking, and fast.

When she came back on, I said, "It's quite late and I know you must have your hands full at work. I was going to suggest that perhaps we could get together tomorrow after work. I talked to a friend and I have some questions you might be able to help me with. Plus, maybe a few other things we might be able to help each other with."

"Something a traveling saleswoman might be able to help you with?" she asked.

Instant severe case of dicktus erectus.

"Why, yes. There is something one particular traveling saleswoman is known to have extensive expertise in," I stammered out.

"Good then, Mister Shorts. I believe I should be able to get in touch with that particular traveling saleswoman and arrange to have her meet you in the same place as last time. I'm quite sure she is looking forward to renewing prior relations. Around six-thirty should be good and don't worry about dinner. I'm sure she will have all the nourishment you desire," the GC said.

It was now a raging case of dicktus erectus enormicus.

"Tell her I'm looking forward to going into things a little deeper this time," I teased.

A pause, a catch of breath. The GC at a loss for words. The Harry Mickey Shorts charm working its usual wonders.

My crotch was actually getting in the way of my words about now.

"Mister Shorts, I'm quite sure the traveling saleswoman will be able to take hold of your subject and provide services much deeper and far beyond what you can imagine," she whispered.

Dicktus erectus enormicus erupticus seemed imminent.

"And in closing, Mister Shorts, say hello to Crissy when you get there," she said as she hung up the phone.

Dicktus erectus enormicus deflateicuss.

Chapter 98

"I'm surprised you remembered the phone number, and even more surprised you still remember the address," Crissy said as she answered the door.

When they open the door, say something, then walk away leaving you standing there, it normally isn't a good sign. Chances of rocks being gotten off doesn't follow very often from my past experiences.

"I've been real busy and it hasn't been that long since I've seen you," I said to her back. Real nice back, too, I might add. She had on a Yankees tank top and shorts that showed just the slightest hint of cheek. First right, then left as she walked away. Being left behind wasn't such a bad place to be at that very moment.

She turned and tried to look defiant: hands on hips, stern eyes, mouth set. Evidenced by a pair of very firm nipples assisted by a lack of bra, it was either very cold in her apartment or she wasn't as pissed at me as she was letting on. Hurts the defiant look a bit.

"Crissy, Crissy, Crissy," I started. Helps to reinforce the idea that you haven't forgotten their name. "I'm here now, so let's sit, have a beer and talk. We don't get the chance to talk enough, just you and me."

"Fuck now, talk later, and you better fuck me good and hard, Shorts," she said as she headed for her bedroom shedding what little clothes she had on as she went.

Being smarter than the average P.I., I quickly followed in her footsteps dropping clothes as I went, not wanting to be too far behind when I arrived.

* * *

Having done as I was told, I was pooped. A quick little romp in the hay or a casual afternoon in the sack leaves you satisfied and content with enough energy to have another go at it not too long thereafter. Done properly, fucking good and hard wears your ass out to the point of not now baby, gimme a chance to recuperate a bit. With Crissy, good and hard could lead to all out traction.

"I forgot how good it could be," Crissy said afterward, her head resting on my chest.

Bathed in moonlight, she looked damn good wearing nothing but sweat.

"We'll have to make sure you don't get the chance to forget so often," I said and immediately wondered what the hell that meant.

"You can remind me as often as you want, Shorts," she said, all thoughts of being angry with me seemingly forgotten.

"How about I get us a few brews and we can have that talk you mentioned before. That is, if I managed to perform my manly duties to your satisfaction, my dear?" I tried.

"Maybe close, but you'll have to try again soon if you are going to get it just right," she said.

"Your wish is my command," I answered with a lick and a peck on her left breast. The purring sound in response was a nice touch.

Bare assed, I wandered into the kitchen and grabbed four Bud Lights from the fridge. If drinking light beer is what keeps her ass looking that delectable, more power to the light beer manufacturers, and let's get the word out near and far. Somehow, I think working out and fucking good and hard may have a little bit to do with it as well.

"Here's a cool one to cool you down," I said as I jumped back into bed. The sweat was almost dry but she still looked damn good.

"Thanks, Harry. Now, what was so important you had to call me at this time of night and come over right away? Thinking about it, the coming right away part wasn't half bad." She giggled.

"I wouldn't exactly say it was 'right away'—would you?" I asked.

"No, you got that right, Shorts. Ask your questions."

"Simple. Short and sweet—one question. What was the company like before the new guys came to town?" I said.

"Well, I haven't been there that long, but people talk and I listen. That good enough, Harry?"

"That will do, kiddo" I answered.

"People say it was like family. Everyone worked together, liked each other, and they all made some money. Not a fortune, and I have no idea what a good amount of money is, Harry, but they did okay according to the accounting guys I know."

"Like who?" I prompted.

"Joe for one and Barb before the bastards fired her. I liked Barb," she said.

"What were the execs like, if you know?" I asked.

"Like I said, it was a family place. It didn't matter where you fit in the company, everyone stuck together. The president hired relatives, like Joe, and anyone who had family that happened to be looking for work got a place somewhere in the company. I only met him once, but the entire place would have killed for the president from the way they talk about him," Crissy said.

"Interesting. Anything else you've heard?" I asked.

"It's quiet now. Nobody talks much about the old days any more—it's sad—and the new creeps in charge run around like paranoid freaks. Nobody would dare try and bring in somebody they know under the current circumstances. Joe's cousin was the last one that I know of," she said.

"I didn't know Joe, and it is Joe Stoner we're talking about, had a cousin at MechInsCo?" I said.

"Actually, he's got two. One's down in the basement in systems somewhere, and the other is Greg."

"Greg?" I asked.

"Yeah, Greg Boalman," she replied.

* * *

The entire time we were talking, between sips of her beer, Crissy had held the beer bottle in her left hand while slowly stroking the bottle's neck with her right. Up and down, up and down, fingers wrapped tightly around the neck. When she took about a quarter of the bottle's longneck into her mouth and sucked down the rest of the beer, that was all I could take.

After what seemed like an eternity, bathed in moonlight, we both looked damn good wearing nothing but each other's sweat.

Chapter 99

"Harry, you been scarce, man," Tom said the following morning. We were sitting in a tiny greasy spoon wolfing down eggs, fatty bacon and coffee.

"Yeah, I've been all over the place, Tom," I replied.

"All over 'cept seeing your good bud who got you that great job over to MechInsCo," he said with a smile.

"Up yours, Tom," I said with the same kinda smile.

"That's the nicest thing you said to me in a while, Harry. You must be getting soft," Tom said.

"Alright, enough of that blubber. What's going on," I asked.

"Well, been nosing around here and there like you told me to. Not doing nothing too obvious, but enough to let on I got a bug up my ass and need to get back into the case. Like that, you know, Harry?" he said.

"Yeah, I'm familiar with you with a bug up your ass, Tom. Any takers?" I asked.

"Thought I was whistling up the wrong tree," Tom said. "But yesterday I heard some guys been asking around about me again. Sounds like maybe they the guys we need to have a nice friendly conversation with. Big guy and a skinny partner could be from up north, my buddy says."

"From what we know so far, they could be the dudes," I said.

"One thing, Harry. And you know I don't give no rat's ass about getting into any kinda tussle. I ain't so young, nor near as fast as I used to be. Not quite as tough, neither. And maybe all this bullshit has just plain tuckered me out. I need to get my fair share piece of these suckers, but me on them and I'm afraid my ass gonna be fried real bad," Tom admitted.

"Tom, you can take this to the bank. Nothing is ever gonna happen to you, and nothing is ever gonna happen to Cam again as long as I'm here. Together we are gonna mess these mothers up like they never been messed up before. That, Tom, is my promise to you, to Cam, and to that nice lady they messed with. What they did to that lady for no reason at all is gonna cost them a world of god-awful pain. That I promise you."

"Harry…" Tom started and couldn't finish.

"We discussed how this should go down, Tom. As long as you don't go playing cowboy on me and try and be a hero, we are gonna be fine. And they are gonna be dead meat when we are done with them. Me and you, partner, just like you taught me."

"I'm not worried with you at my back, Harry," Tom said.

"No worry at all, man. Now, you gonna finish that bacon or am I gonna have to feed you like a little kid, too?"

"Thanks, Harry, and by the way, screw you." Tom smiled.

* * *

There were some reports in my in-box when I got to the office that morning. The glow that radiated from the front reception desk could have blinded a blind man. My assumption was Crissy enjoyed her night's activities. Come to think of it, I'd have to say I kinda enjoyed them myself. One shouldn't neglect the needy as I had been doing lately.

The reports were sent up by this nerdy twerp I had the fortune to sit next to one day in the cafeteria. He'd only been with the company a few weeks and hadn't connected with anyone yet. Maybe the fact he looked like a major league twerpy nerd had something to do with it.

Conversation went something like this:

"Hey," I said to him trying to be polite.

"Ah, hey," barely came out of his mouth.

"I'm Harry, Harry Shorts," not wanting to prolong the conversation any longer than necessary by including the Mickey in Harry Mickey Shorts.

"Ah…ah…I'm….ah…," he stammered.

"Hey, ah," I said to try and get real words out of his mouth.

He thought about that for a minute and then smiled.

"It's not ah, is it?" I asked.

"Ah, no, it's Stanley," he finally said.

A Stanley, it figured.

"Hey, Stanley, whata you do?" I asked to try and give him an easy one to answer.

"I work in the basement," he said.

Some kind of janitor I thought, so I said, "Some kind of janitor?"

A quizzical look came over him and then the light bulb came on.

"Oh no, Harry. I work on computers down there. In the IS department. I do programming. I've always done programming. Since

I've been small. Well, I'm really still small, I guess. Ah, short, I mean, but not small like in younger. That kinda small when you're younger."

To end the misery, I stopped him with, "I get it, Stanley. You've been programming since you were a kid."

"Yeah, that's it," he agreed.

Could be a resource here, I thought.

"What are you working on?" I asked him.

"Nothing special right now," he said. "I'm still learning the system, so I'm just fixing up the premium/reinsurance file-sharing databases in the system. I came from an insurance company that used the same kind of shared data protocols and I know that stuff pretty good. Ah, pretty well, I mean," he corrected himself.

"Reinsurance, you know much about reinsurance?" I semi-quizzed.

"Yeah, my dad's been in reinsurance all his career and I've been around it all that time. Kinda know a lot about it, I guess," he admitted.

Does the word '*BINGO*' sound familiar? I now had my source to get what I needed without Joe or anyone else knowing what I was doing. And that, my friends, is how the reports got into my in-box. Reports programmed to my exact specifications, wants and needs, that turned out to be stone-cold golden. Everything I needed to confirm some of my thoughts were there in plain sight.

Who woulda thunk it. Twerpy, nerdo Stanley turns out to be a major player in cracking the case.

Chapter 100

Crissy caught me as I headed out at the end of the day. It was a little late and I should have been in the safe zone—Harry leaves and doesn't have to see Crissy to discuss last night's frivolities and what was going on tonight.

"Hey, kiddo. You're here kinda late tonight," I said when I realized I was caught.

"Doing some stuff on the computer that I have to send to Europe. Mom wants everything done months before it needs to get done to make sure dumb-ass blondie Crissy doesn't forget," she mocked.

"You may be blond, but you're not dumb by any means," I said. "And as for your ass…" I purposely left open-ended.

"My ass for your information, Mister Shorts, will be sitting in this chair for the next hour. "After that, though…" she also left open-ended.

"In an hour or so I'll be deep into something that has been waiting for me to get to for a while. Been neglected and can't wait. Rain check, kiddo" I said.

"In the rain would be fun," she said and then looked down at her screen.

"That it would, that it would indeed," I said as I headed for the back door.

* * *

When I arrived for my appointed rendezvous, there was a little yellow sticky on the door of the motel room at Visaggio's. It read: TRAVELING SALESLADY INSIDE (with da goods) – ENTER AT YOUR OWN RISK!

Having sampled the particular goods of this particular Traveling Saleslady on a previous occasion, I proceeded with plans to enter multiple times before this particular session had come to a conclusion. Risk could go to hell!

"Welcome, sir," the Traveling Saleslady said as I entered the room. "If you happen to be looking for something, I just might have what you're looking for."

Not only was it the sexy way she said it, but the red satin baby-doll she was almost wearing that added a certain something to the presentation.

"While you peruse my goods, perhaps a glass of champagne and a chocolate truffle would be nice," she seemed to purr.

"A glass of champagne and a chocolate truffle while I peruse your goods would be quite nice," I replied. "I'm sure all three will taste splendid and equally as good."

"And be sure to enjoy all of them in heaping quantities for as long as you desire, sir," she finished at about the same time satin kissed carpet.

* * *

Two hours later, the goods were either gone or spent. Heaping quantities of all three were served up and devoured with all the gusto a Traveling Saleslady and her appreciative customer could expect to put forth. And put forth they both did.

"Harry."

"Yes, GC."

"You're going away soon, aren't you?" she asked.

I didn't know what to say.

"Don't get me wrong, Harry. I've known from the beginning this was going to be a whirlwind slam-banger; have fun while it lasts and hope we part with some good memories to think about later on," she continued.

I still didn't know what to say.

"But, it's been a rejuvenation for me. A wake-up call to remind me I'm a woman with a lot to give and the need to start taking. A young stud like you was exactly what I needed to get the motor started and begin rebuilding my life and future."

"Pretty heavy for a Traveling Saleslady," I said.

"Oh, somehow I think the Traveling Saleslady is leaving town for good after tonight. She came, peddled her wares, and sold every one of them, Harry. I don't think I need her around any longer," she said with conviction.

"Madame General Counsel, Maddy, GC—the Traveling Saleslady is history."

We talked for hours and she told me everything she knew about MechInsCo. About the company before and after the New York invasion, about the people who ran MechInsCo during both regimes and how they affected the general population within the company. Who she trusted, who she didn't, and who she suspected of what. She knew her duties as General Counsel and what was required, but she couldn't prove anything. She was counting on one Harry Mickey Shorts to make it right for her, for the company, for the industry.

When we were done talking, I had what I felt were the last few missing pieces to the puzzle. Now, Harry Mickey Shorts was going to make it right. Now, Harry Mickey Shorts was going to lay some hurt on the people who had been doing some bad things for too long.

But first things first. Now, Harry Mickey Shorts was going to make the sky light up and shower down sparkling fireflies of delight. Now, Harry Mickey Shorts was going to make the Traveling Saleslady's final foray in da sticks a sales call to remember. Now, Harry Mickey Shorts was going to make love to the most beautiful woman in the world and make sure she knew she deserved every minute of it.

Now, Harry Mickey Shorts was saying good-bye the best way he knew how.

Chapter 101

"This is Ms. Timmons speaking, may I help you?" was what I heard when I was finally connected.

"You could help me, I could help you, we could surely help each other," I answered.

"Remains to be seen, Harry, remains to be seen," she said, always getting in the last word.

"Good to hear your voice again, Wendy, ah, I mean Ms. Timmons," I teased.

"Ms. Timmons will be fine, Harry," she said trying to sound businesslike.

"I have no doubt either Wendy or Ms. Timmons would be very fine," I said getting the upper hand for the moment.

"Finer than fine wine and frostier than a frosty mug," she one-upped me.

"I give, Ms. Timmons. You win as usual. How's Randy these days?" I asked.

"Extremely busy," she replied. "He has been in Europe all too frequently and has just left London on his way home. He should be in the office tomorrow, but I believe he has allocated the entire day for business having to do with the Schooners," she said.

"Schooners have an exhibition game by some chance?" I queried.

"The possibilities surrounding Mister Trundle's business dealings in all areas are endless as you are acutely aware, Mister Shorts," she answered in officialese.

"What time?" I asked.

"If you are referring to the business meeting Mister Trundle has centered his business dealings around for tomorrow, I do believe that would commence at approximately one oh five pm," she said.

"That's interesting. Any chance I could see him before that; and also, any chance there might be an extra seat at this very important business meeting he will be attending?" I asked with what would have been a straight face if I was looking at Ms. Timmons. Of course that assumes I was looking at her face at all at the time. The interesting facets surrounding Ms. Timmons are also endless I might add.

"Unless I'm mistaken, Mister Trundle will be leaving from the office and will be traveling to his business meeting alone. His scheduled departure time is ten-thirty am and there was some mention of 'tube steaks' on the menu for lunch," she informed me.

"Would it be possible for me to meet Mister Trundle at his place of employment, and I do mean 'his place' literally since he does own the place, and travel with him to this very important meeting?" I asked.

"I'll have to check with him, Mister Shorts. Can I get in touch with you later today at the normal cell phone number?" she asked.

"Ms. Timmons, you can touch me there or any other place your little heart desires to touch me," I tried.

"Mister Shorts, I have no doubt you have been in touch with your inner and outer self more than enough for both of us."

With that she terminated the connection.

Damn that lady.

* * *

I planned on the trip to New York and got everything in order to present the information I had gathered along with my business proposal to Randy. His opinion was very important to me and, knowing Randy, I believed I had an offer he couldn't refuse.

Stanley's reports provided the finishing touches to my research and proved beyond the shadow of a doubt what had been done. It was clever in its simplicity and very skillful in its ability to inflict maximum damage on MechInsCo. The information was there to be found if you looked in just the right places and for just the right combination of factors. Modesty aside—luck was an important factor. I've always said it's better to be lucky than good, but being both helps.

* * *

"Harry, Mister Trundle will see you tomorrow morning in the garage at ten-thirty am sharp. Please don't be late," Ms. Timmons told me when she 'touched' me with a message on my cell later. Even that felt good.

Chapter 102

"I'm on my way to New York right now," I told Tom via cell phone from the car. "I'll take care of business there and be back your way tomorrow morning so we can put the next piece of our plan in motion. Did you get the word out?" I asked him.

"Word's on the street with the main guy I trust in town. He knows how to get it underground and he's the guy I used last time we needed information on the street," Tom said.

"Perfect," I told him. "You still good with our plan? You can't bail on me last minute and Cam has to play his part just the way we discussed it," I both asked and reminded him.

"Harry, if there is one thing you can count on as definite right now it's my ass being there to back up your puny ass. And don't worry about Cam. He's all in on this job and thinks it's gonna be a blast," Tom assured me.

"Puny ass? See ya late tomorrow," I signed off.

* * *

The city, New York City that is, can be a deserted island on some Saturday mornings. Of course, on others, it can be a bear. The bears were in session when I crawled into town on a beautiful April Saturday morning. When you have been living in da sticks of Central Pennsylvania with clean air, no traffic and three cars at a light is a traffic jam—having your car windows open sucking on auto fumes and listening to horns blaring everywhere is pure heaven. Welcome home again Mister Shorts it screamed.

Charlie and I were old pals from my previous adventure working for Mister M. Randle Trundle. He was seated at the wheel of Trundle's *violet* Rolls Royce limousine. He saw the Shorts mobile pulling into the parking garage and got out to meet me.

"Mister Shorts, Harry, good to see ya again. Some people miss ya when you don't come around too often," he said as we shook hands. Like old friends shaking hands.

"Charlie," I said, "you looking good. How are the wife and those grandkids of yours?" I asked, and meant it.

"Good as gold," he replied. "At least the grandkids are," he smiled.

"Good to hear. How's Mister Trundle these days? The start of the new season must have brightened up his spirits. Papers say he has another winner on his hands."

"No matter how good they turn out to be, there's no way they could compare to last year's team, Harry. No way at all," he said.

"The first winner is always the best," I said.

"Not what I meant by that, Harry," Charlie said.

"I know, Charlie, I know," I finished as Randy walked out of the elevator at exactly 10:30 am.

He walked right up to me, took my hand and said, "It's good to see you, Harry. Everything okay in PA-land?"

"Getting there, Randle," I replied. "And who's the youngster you have trailing behind you?" I teased.

"Ms. Timmons has asked to join us for today's game. I can't begin to imagine why, but she might be of some assistance if we happen to get into discussions concerning your trip to Mechanicsburg," he said.

"What's with the get-up, Ms. Timmons?" I asked with the best straight face I could muster.

"For your information, Mister Shorts, I happen to own a complete collection of casual clothes that I do happen to wear when not working," Ms. Timmons said in a lame attempt to explain her outfit for today.

"Ms. Timmons, um Wendy, if I may be so bold as to call you Wendy with you currently garbed in your 'not working' casual clothes. Violet sweater, over a darker violet top, and shorts also of a violet nature would be of and by itself, a bit too much even for an ex-Schooner like myself. But the violet anklets—with little violet pompoms—and sneakers to match, push the outfit over the edge," I said with apparent amusement.

She started to say something but couldn't seem to get any words direct from her brain to that beautiful mouth of hers.

A "Get in the car, Harry," from Randy saved her ass. And we all know her ass, while having been fully covered at all times in this poor little private eye's company, is well worth saving.

Charlie started up the *violet*, not purple, chariot and we were on our way to Bayport, Long Island to watch the Double A Bayport Schooners take on a squad from Erie, PA. Randle must have been feeling particularly pleased with life on this fine morning.

"Charles, did you prepare the refreshments as I asked?" he inquired.

"Sure did, Mister Trundle. In the cooler and basket by Mister Shorts' feet," he replied.

We soon found ourselves sipping on Mimosa's from crystal goblets and nibbling on freshly baked warm croissants with sweet butter and strawberry jam. I shit you not! A small bit of Harry Mickey Shorts must have rubbed off on Randle.

"Randle, I do believe you will never cease to amaze me," I said and meant every word of it.

"And Ms. Timmons, um Wendy, the libations must agree with you as your cheeks are currently sporting a lovely shade of pink that becomes you quite nicely."

She blushed on top of the resident pink of the moment.

I was referring to the cheeks I could see, of course.

Chapter 103

We got to the ballpark fairly early, so Randle went off to meet with Coach Curran, his general manager, and his assistant general manager, Richie. Wendy had a bunch of important looking people I didn't know there to meet her. I went off to see the guys on the field after realizing Ms. Timmons would be working after all. Didn't actually surprise me. Randy was always working even when he pretended to play. By necessity, Ms. Timmons did the same.

I was hoping there would be time for me to talk to Mister Curran, my old coach and friend. Plus a chance to chat with my new friend, Richie, would hopefully come later.

There were a bunch of guys left over from last years' team, plus some who came up from Single A I hadn't met before. I knew a few from the franchise news we got on occasion during the season and one or two who played for other teams and were brought in by Randy to play on the best team money could buy. Double A—Steinbrenner style.

"Harry, you old piece of walking dog turd. Get over here and say hi to the new guys," came from behind me.

Dong, whose nickname was well deserved, played for the Schooners last year and was going to be the ace of this year's staff. He just needs more innings at this level and by mid-season would probably be in the rotation at the Triple A level with his buds from last year's championship team. A championship team whose primary catcher happens to be someone you have gotten to know quite well by now.

"Dong, you still here with the Schooners? I'd of thought they would have smartened up by now and shipped your sorry ass back to the boonies where it belongs. How's it hanging my man?" I laughed.

"Long and strong, just like my arm," he said.

"Good to hear, bud. Who are these worthless excuses for ballplayers you Schooners are trying to push off on the poor fans that pay good money to watch you guys play?" I asked.

"They ain't worthy of being called true Schooners yet, Harry, but I'm working on them. Guys, this here is Harry Mickey Shorts, a washed up, broken down catcher who the pitching staff managed to carry all last year," Dong said. "You'll have to find out who they are, Harry. They haven't earned being called by actual names yet—just yo and hey so far."

With that crack Dong took off so the new guys couldn't inflict bodily harm on his poor-assed body.

Before I could get to know all the new guys' names, somebody yelled for me from the dugout. I didn't have to turn around to know who it was.

"Doc, what are you doing here, man," I asked as we hugged in front of the dugout.

"Harry," was all he said at first.

"I heard you were up in the bigs with that new program they started for the best trainers down in da bushes. Don't tell me they already figured out you ain't worth shit?" I kidded.

"Not yet, still fooling even the best of them, Harry. I heard you were gonna be here today and had to come over and see ya," he said.

I happened to spy Ms. Timmons over Doc's shoulder looking in our direction and smiling. How Doc found out I was gonna be in Bayport was now very obvious. Doc was a key figure in my last case involving the Bayport Schooners and had turned into a good friend as well.

"It is damned good to see ya, Doc," I told him.

We chatted for a while and then he went off to do some work on the pitchers. He was and is very good at his job, and some major league team is gonna get themselves a real good trainer pretty soon. A damn good man, too.

The players had started to head back to the locker room to get ready for today's game. So, I headed up to Randy's box situated behind the first base dugout. Looked like my chance to talk to Coach Curran and Richie would have to wait for now. Maybe after the game if there was time. If not, I'm sure I'll be out to see the Schooners enough during the season after I get back from my glorious adventures in MechInsCo land.

"Enjoy being back on the field," Ms. Timmons asked as she slipped into the seat next to me. It wouldn't be her seat once the game started, but Randy wasn't around, and the usual babe-attraction magnetism of Harry Mickey Shorts must have been working full force.

"Always good to be on a baseball field and have a chance to talk shop with the players. One problem though, they seem to get younger every year," I told her.

"*The Harry Mickey Shorts* couldn't possibly be feeling old, could he?" she asked with some hidden amusement.

"You could find out personally exactly how old Harry Mickey Shorts is feeling any time your little heart desires, Ms. Timmons," was my somewhat defiant response.

"All good things come to he who waits," she whispered as she stood and walked past me.

I must have been admiring her exit far too well and much too long. When I turned around, Randy was sitting in the seat next to me looking in the same direction and smiling.

Chapter 104

God got up one morning and knew there was something lacking in his/her life. Turned to St. Petey, who had just returned from his stint at the pearly gates, and said, "We forgot something, I'm sure of it."

Being God, another miracle was to be cast upon us and we then had it—hot dogs, a cold beer and baseball in the spring.

Randy was in a particularly good mood when he came back from his visit with his baseball people. I figured that out all by myself, what with me being a crackerjack P.I. and all. Plus, Randy said, "Damn fine day for a ballgame and I'm gonna enjoy every minute of it."

We crackerjack P.I.'s are quick to pick up on clues when they are presented.

* * *

Bottom of the fourth and the Schooners are ahead 4-1. The defense looked sharp and Dong was on his game. He had been working on a change-up last year and seemed to have gotten it to where he could use it with confidence. The catcher I had mentored last year was calling a good game and all was right in Schoonerland.

"So, Harry, what was it you wanted to talk to me about?" Randy asked out of the blue between bites of his second dog. "Your project in Mechanicsburg going all right?"

He caught me off guard and I had to put my thoughts together fast. I knew what I wanted to talk to him about, just not at that point in time. So, I thought for a moment.

"Mechanicsburg is finally coming together," I started. "The Web Dudes, I believe I mentioned them to you before, came up with the information I needed, and I found another source by accident. The combination proved to be dynamite. I poured through all the facts and semi-facts I had and I'm fairly sure I can put the whole thing together," I finished.

Randy said nada. Another bite of his hot dog and the last gulp of his beer were all that he gave me to ponder. Nothing else to do, I plodded on.

"Well, now that I have it, and I'm assuming I actually do have all of it, I need to figure out how to unravel it without destroying the company and the innocent people who haven't done anything wrong. Also, what do I do with the bad guys, who aren't all real bad guys, and how do I do it without outing myself?"

Randy remained silent watching Dong strike out the side.

"I can't keep showing up as the guy who solves these cases and still be able to do what I do best. Going undercover won't work very well when everyone knows you're under the covers," I pontificated.

Guy used it in a movie I watched the other day and it sounded like the right word to use—pontificated. Harry Mickey Shorts the pontificator. Has a ring to it.

At least Randy looked at me as he said nada.

"Here's what I have and how I propose to proceed," I said. I told him all of it from start to finish, or almost all of it, leaving out a detail or two concerning the mother/daughter goings-on.

He finally contributed to the conversation.

"And you want what from me, Harry?"

"Well," I continued. I spelled out how and why I was hoping Randy would assist in the final chapter of this nasty escapade. It was a well thought out plan and something I was pretty sure Randy, or Trundle Industries to be more precise, would be interested in. At least the financial components of my final plan, that is. The other part, the get the low-life bastards that did this and make them pay, I believed Randy would revel in its unorthodox finality.

He thought. He had one of his people get us each another hot dog and beer while he proceeded to think some more. When he had finished his dog and had enjoyed a healthy drink of his beer, he responded.

"Ingenious in its simplicity and downright conniving. I would never have guessed he had it in him."

He stopped and I waited.

"Sounds like a good plan, Harry. I'm beginning to like this private investigator assistant stuff. Not as much fun as making bazillions of dollars the old fashion way—being better than the other guy in all ways possible. But, laying low-life scum-buckets to waste has its moments. Is that a correct term, Harry? Low-life scum-buckets."

"Correctamundo, Randy. Low-life scum-buckets they are. I can assume from your enthusiasm you're in?" I asked.

"You are correctamundo. I and all Trundle Industries has to bare are in, Harry," he said with a big grin.

"Correctamundo?" I repeated.

"As you say, I'm down, kiddo."

Chapter 105

The Schooners kicked some serious ass from the fifth inning on and won 11-1 going away. Randy enjoyed the team's victory and told his general manager and coach he'd be back more often from now on. "Works fun, but this is real enjoyment," he said and he meant it.

Coach Curran and I spoke for a few minutes before he had to get back to the locker room and tend to his guys.

"Harry, there's room for you on my coaching staff any day you want to come aboard," he told me. "Good people are hard to find."

We shook hands and he took off for the locker room. Good men are hard to find and I had found one and was proud to call him a friend.

Richie was all smiles when I caught up with him on our way to the car. One look at his face and the way he carried himself, you knew he was where he belonged.

"Harry, you off already?" he asked.

"Yeah, man, gotta head back to the city with Mister Trundle," I told him. "I'll be back in a little while and we can get together and shoot the shit big time."

"I'm counting on it, Harry. I'll even buy," he said.

"You bet your big-time assistant general manager ass you will," I teased.

"Count on it. Be good, Harry," he said and we shook hands like friends do.

* * *

Ms. Timmons had gone missing for the entire game. Where she went and who she hung out with was a mystery, but much of what Ms. Timmons did was a mystery to me. But she was there waiting when Randy and I got back to the car for the ride back to the city.

"Enjoy the game, Ms. Timmons?" I asked.

She continued to look damn good.

"It's always good when the Schooners win," she said.

"Didn't see you all day. Where'd you go off to?" I asked.

"I was busy with things," she replied.

"Things?" I asked.

"Yes, things, Harry. Some work, some game watching, some more work," she said.

Randy never said a word but he did seem to be enjoying the exchange.

"I guess I'll have to take your word for it, Ms. Timmons," I concluded.

"Guess you will," she continued to make sure she got in the last word as always.

"Harry," Randy finally chimed in. "When we get back to the city I'd like you to check my schedule with Ms. Timmons. Europe beckons again and I will need to be in London early next month for several days. Do you know when this will all go down in 'da sticks' as you call them?"

"Gotta settle a score first, but the plan has already been set in motion for that piece of unfinished business. After that, I just need confirmation that what you and I discussed today has been finalized and I'll be ready to go. The paperwork will only take a few days and the remaining parties that need to be present have been invited with the understanding the time and date will be provided on very short notice. It will be a party they won't soon forget."

I caught my breath and waited for Randy's nod to proceed.

Nod granted.

Ms. Timmons continued to look damn good. Legs crossed with a slight shift in the seat for a better viewing angle, plus the slight hint of air conditioning having a pointed effect, combined for a better than average distraction.

If I wasn't mistaken, Randy was partaking in liberal glances as well.

"Okay," I answered to his nod. "I'll catch a window in your schedule and plan the finale around that timetable. Do you need me to provide you with anything before you come down?" I asked.

"Send Ms. Timmons a copy of the final *paperwork* you talked about so I'll know all I need to know about the parties in question. I'll be sure my end is accomplished in short order and no string will be left untied," he replied.

With a nod to Ms. Timmons, he said, "Have my lawyers in my office tomorrow morning at ten sharp. I'll make a few calls this afternoon when we get back to the office and complete the negotiations. Tell them everything they need will be in their hands before the end of the day."

"Will that be enough time for them to prepare the paperwork needed before ten the next morning? It is Saturday you know," I asked.

"Harry, you have taught me that what needs to be said can be said concisely, whether it be in an informal friendly discussion with friends or in business dealings. A shake of the hands may not be enough but a page or two is more than enough to seal a deal," he said in reply.

I smiled a knowing smile as did Randy, and I could swear I saw Ms. Timmons draw a smiley face on her note pad.

"And as for it being Saturday, business is business and it gets done when it needs to. Business doesn't know what day it is, Harry. It never does."

Chapter 106

We entered Trundle Industries through the garage. Randy rushed off to make phone calls and get his business done. I, on the other hand, got much the better end of the bargain. I accompanied Ms. Timmons to her office to check on Randy's schedule following her behind the whole way. Or should that have been following behind her the whole way. No, it was much better following her behind the whole way.

Randy was right, his schedule was jam-packed as always. The London trip still had that hint of mystery attached to it. If Ms. Timmons knew the real low down, she still wasn't saying. No one person could need that many suits.

"How do the ninth and tenth sound, Harry?" Ms. Timmons asked.

"If that's what he has available, then the ninth and tenth it will be. Perhaps you would like to come down a day early on the eighth to make sure all is in order?" I asked. "You know, check on last minute details, see if anything comes up, get under the covers of the plan as they say," I volunteered.

A hint of a smile, oh so small, crossed her lips.

"I'm sure you'll be able to handle anything that pops up without my help, Harry. Although, it has occurred to me there may be a need to stay an extra day or two to tie up any loose ends that may present themselves. Everything needs to be in proper order and it's important things happen at the right time and place. Don't you agree, Harry?" she asked.

"Time, order and place, but not necessarily in any order. I do agree, Ms. Timmons," I said.

"I'll look forward to it, Harry."

"As will I, Ms. Timmons, as will I."

* * *

As long as I was in New York, I decided to head out to Long Island to check in with the EBIL and say hi to the kids. Bunny was watching my place and I had confidence Mel would handle any problems she couldn't, but it doesn't hurt to check in whenever possible.

"Mel, baby, how's my favorite real estate mogul these days?" was met with a menacing stony glare.

"Call your ex," was all he said.

No Bunny in sight.

"Everything all right over there?" I asked.

"Nothing wrong but you," he replied.

"Me?" I said.

"Yeah, you. She's doing fine, life's moving along without any hurdles to deal with, and you go ahead and fuck it up. And I use the term 'fuck it' in more ways than one," he growled.

"Oh," I said. "She say anything about a recent visit?" I asked.

"Say anything? She say anything? You are a stupid prick, Harry. For a private investigator you aren't very smart, are you? You can't even see the kids setting you up and then you go ahead and flash your dick around in your usual Harry Mickey Shorts 'hump-em & flee-em' manner. Your ex ain't Bunny, Harry. You can't expect to bang her one day and split town the next. Even the kids expected more from you."

"I, ah…"

"You, ah, nothing. Call her, now!" he said finally.

* * *

Calling wasn't going to do it. I decided a face-to-face was necessary if I was going to make this right. Off I went to deal with…something.

The doorbell rang but nobody came to the door. I tried it again and could hear the Airedales barking in the back of the house—even they sounded pissed-off at me.

"Ain't home," came from behind me.

I turned to see the next door neighbor on the sidewalk facing the house.

"She went out around noon with the kids and looked like they were gonna be gone for a bit," he said.

"A bit?" I asked.

"They had a small bag and a cooler with them," he stated.

"Guess I'll try back again. Thanks," I told him.

"No problem, Harry. I'll tell Sherry you stopped by."

I hopped in my car, started down the street, wondering how I was gonna get myself out of another mess my smaller head had gotten me into. Sherry I could deal with. The kids were gonna be another matter altogether.

With nothing else to do, I pointed the HoneyBee south and headed for Mechanicsburg, PA. The ride back would give me time to hash out this unexpected twist in my otherwise perfect existence. That is, excluding a case I thought I had under wraps, a best pal who was drowning with a son seemingly out of control, a mother/daughter 'thing' I had no idea how to end (at least the daughter part) and a future that was turning ugly as time went on.

Life is like a bowl of cherries—it's the pits that'll kill ya.

The one good thing I had going for me was I thought I knew all the bumps I had to face. Time to take control and deal with them one at a time. The case was the number one priority and everything else had to take a back seat for now. Plan and go over the plan. Then go over it and over it, until the certainty of success was all that existed. I had performed this exercise too many times to count and knew we were ready to bring the MechInsCo case to conclusion. I knew it in my heart and in my head. Sitting in the car, going over it one more time, I now felt it in my gut and that told me I was ready.

Better beware. Harry Mickey Shorts is gonna rain down on your heads with a shit storm you ain't never seen before and you can take that to the bank.

Chapter 107

"Tom, its Harry," I said when I called him at home later that night.

"Harry, you back?" he asked.

"I'm back, Tom. Long ride with lots to think about. Everything in place?" I asked.

"Just like we discussed, Harry. My man got me word today he got some real nice cash for certain information he was possessing. Went just like you said it would. Easy as pie."

"Good, Tom. Real good. You hanging okay? Cam?" I asked.

"Been thinkin' about what's gone down so far, Harry, and I been getting more pissed the more I thought about it. Cam's my boy. I love him and he didn't do anything to those people, and that poor lady didn't deserve to be disrespected that way 'cause she didn't do anything to anyone neither. The company's your business now, Harry, and I thank ya for that. But the rest is personal. Real personal," Tom said. "Gotta be fixed and fixed good, Harry."

"I'm with you on all of that, Tom. You know I'm behind you one hundred percent and we are gonna deliver some serious hurt to square things. Won't make them right, but gonna make sure it don't ever happen that way again. On that you have my solemn promise, Tom," I told him.

"Thanks, Harry."

"Now, get some sleep and make sure Cam is together. You and me I trust. I'm counting on you to put Cam where he needs to be and make sure he doesn't do anything stupid when the shit hits the fan. Got me, Tom?" I said.

"Don't worry, Harry. Cam and I will be ready to do our thing when the time comes. You can take that to the bank, my man," he said with authority.

Tom was back, somewhat.

* * *

I proceeded to gather up all the information I had assembled and started the process of documenting the evidence I had against the people who did this. The Web Dudes do such a great job of presenting the information they provide you hardly have to do anything to it. It basically presents itself and, for what they charge, it should.

The systems information I had gathered was a lot more haphazard. There must have been fifty reports of varying size and complexity with no commonality. It was all good stuff that would help nail the humps who did this but not presentable by any stretch of the imagination, even my imagination which can stretch pretty far at times. It's gonna take a long time to corral it and figure out how to put it in 'You can't miss what I've got and you guys are in deep doodoo shape.' Not a real problem, just a tedious process I've done many times before. It may really suck, but it has got to be done.

You start a critical time-consuming piece of a job like this one and you tend to get lost in space and time. The numbers numb your brain and the sheer magnitude of paper and columns of numbers, facts and figures all blur together. The end result is they're in your head and you don't want to take any chances—the bad guys need to go down and the evidence has to be iron clad. Leave a hole and they may have a chance to crawl through.

Not this time. Not after what they did to Tom and Cam and everything else. They are mine and they are going down.

It's all jumbled until that instant when the light bulb goes on over your head and you say to yourself, "Self, you idiot, it was right there. Put this here, that over there, add the summary from the big report with the summaries from the three smaller reports to back it up and it's all there. It was there the entire time and I just had to see it. I saw, I did, and it's done."

Score: Harry Mickey Shorts = 1 ScumBuckets = 0.

* * *

The whole job took me most of the night and I fell into bed just as the sun was starting to come up. I had emailed a copy of the stuff to Ms. Timmons who would run it by Trundle's accounting and legal people to see if they could poke any holes in it. No surprise, they have both areas covered six ways to Sunday including an ex-criminal prosecutor on staff. Well, Randy's got private investigator extraordinaire Harry Mickey Shorts on retainer, why not some legal hotshot as well.

What was a surprise was Ms. Timmons was there at work and emailed back her receipt of the information three minutes after I sent it. The lady never ceases to amaze. I'm hoping the 'never ceases to amaze' will extend to the extra days she will be spending in Mechanicsburg to clear up loose ends after we close down this case. The mere thought of it makes my timber tingle with anticipation.

Picture Ms. Timmons, Wendy, and Harry Mickey Shorts doing the horizontal two-step until exhaustion overtakes both of them and you would be truly reading my mind. Hopefully, that picture will fill my dreams as I hit the sack tonight.

Chapter 108

"Shorts, are you still sleeping?" was what Ms. Timmons said when I answered the phone at eleven am the following morning.

"I was, but I'm not anymore," I answered.

"Well, get up. And if I know you, and unfortunately I'm getting to know you more and more, they are probably wondering where you are at MechInsCo. Correct, aren't I?" she asked.

"I'm up. You're correct as usual and I'll fix that as soon as we are done."

You'll get to know a whole lot more of me real soon sweetie, I thought.

"What have you got for me?" I asked

"The legal people think the presentation is good and the majority of the case is iron clad. There was one hole in the financials that wasn't obvious and might not have occurred to the average criminal. But, and we don't want any buts to exist, if they retain excellent counsel they may have found it and the potential for walking free existed," she said.

"So?" I asked.

"So, it's fixed. The boys downstairs added a new twist using the data you provided and they believe it is now locked down tight. I emailed it to you an hour ago and was expecting you to answer me right away. I now see I was expecting too much and it would have been difficult to do so while you were still asleep."

Our first fight? How sweet.

I was about to remind her I worked all night to produce that information but realized I'd probably be wasting my breath. I also wanted to verbally paint her a sneak preview of what she could expect when she and I got our one-on-one post-work activities going, but again, I was sure I'd probably be wasting my breath.

"I'm on it," was all I managed to get out

"Good. Call me in an hour and let's put the finishing touches on this. Mister Trundle is off to Germany at two and he wants to take it with him," she commanded.

"It'll be done. Let me call work, bring up your email, and check what you sent. I'll call you in thirty minutes," I told her.

* * *

Work was wondering where I was and it seems Crissy had put out an APB for my missing ass. I called Mary Ann and told her, "Long weekend, plus I got in very late last night. Tell Crissy I'll call her as soon as I get myself together." That put off the Crissy crisis.

Crissy was gonna have to be dealt with pretty soon. Fun while it lasted, but all good things must come to an end sooner or later.

The work from Trundle's legal beagles did close one obvious hole I missed. It wasn't the end of the world, but no reason to take any chances when you're attempting to close the lid on the bad guys. It took about half an hour to incorporate the change and plug in one more set of information I had forgotten to include. I emailed the revision to Ms. Timmons and waited to hear back from her.

* * *

"Tom, Harry here. You good, man? Cam solid?" I asked him.

"We're both rock solid, Harry. It's set for seven tonight just as we planned. I do have one question," Tom said.

"What's that, Tom?"

"What if it doesn't go down tonight as planned? What do we do then?"

"We watch, we wait, and we plan the same thing for tomorrow night. Same time, same place, same outcome," I told him.

"Okay, Harry. We both trust you and the plan. Just make sure I get my due, okay?" Tom said.

"You and Cam both, Tom. We're all gonna get our piece of the action and enjoy every second of it," I replied. "Just remember, stick to the plan with no cowboy stunts from either of you. Got it?" I said.

"Got it, Harry. We got the plan down and we'll stick to it," Tom assured me.

"Good. I'll see ya when we discussed. Lay cool for now. Gotta split."

* * *

Ms. Timmons chided me for taking longer than the half-hour I promised, and then told me the parcel was intact. Mister Trundle would have a copy to take with him and the legal minds would make everything look all official and final. If I didn't know any better, I'd swear Ms. Timmons actually complimented me for the work product I produced. It must be the old Shorts imagination working overtime again. Or, maybe I was finally getting through that seemingly impenetrable façade Ms. Timmons hung around herself all the time.

Ms. Timmons not impenetrable—we will see. For now there was work to be done and bad guys to tend to.

Chapter 109

There was a Harry Mickey Shorts QAS—that's Question, Answer, Solution for the forgetful in the crowd—rolling around in my head. I was certain we had the brains behind the case locked up tight with no way out, but behind the brains still remained the brawn. The real bad guys were the scumbuckets who hurt people and thought nothing of it. No conscience to speak of and they don't want one. Just directions, hurt, enjoyment. They are the ones you have to be careful of and make sure when they go down they don't have any chance of getting up.

The QAS finally crystallized in my brain and went something like this: How do you deal with real bad guys? Be like them. Plan, hurt, enjoy, finalize!

* * *

Cam was rehabbing his arm every day and it was coming around pretty good. He was never a strong kid to begin with, so the weight work was good not only for his arm but for the rest of his upper body as well. He was actually back in school and he was either faking it real well or he was actually giving it a chance. That, plus helping Tom with a major renovation project on the house, kept him busy until five pm. every day of the week—Monday through Friday.

The kid might turn out to be okay after all.

An hour workout at the gym and a quick shower normally got him home right around seven every night. Our plan revolved around Cam's predictable schedule and the information Tom had planted with his hometown bud who had a tie to the underground information railroad in Mechanicsburg and surrounding areas. Assuming everything worked as planned, tonight would be the night. If not, I could be real patient when it came to nailing scumbuckets to the wall. There was tomorrow, and the next day, and…well, you know.

Here's the lowdown. Tom had a few cool ones at his local hangout Thursday night and pretended to get a bag on. Everyone knows Tom and how he gets to talking when he's loaded up with suds. So, he tells his bar buddies how well Cam is doing with his rehab and how he's back in school and all. Then he goes on to rehash the whole episode when Cam got his arm busted. Tells 'em, "Cam couldn't remember who the guys were who did it to him. Then, the other day, out of the blue, he says he remembers the guys' faces and a name and we're gonna have him talk to the Chief on Tuesday. That's the first day he can get one of those picture making guys down here to draw them guys' faces. Cam's gonna tell him what he remembers and we're gonna catch them suckers."

The rest was more of the same and Tom laid it on real thick. The trick was his bud with the connections just happened to be sitting in the back of the bar supposedly listening to the whole drunken speech. He already knew all the details 'cause Tom and he had already gone over every last bit of it. It was scripted all the way. His bud was supposed to spread the story of Tom's bar-room talk on Sunday and make sure it got to the right people. Cost a bunch, but it was well worth it. We had Cam locked away out of sight for the weekend and Tom let it be known he was gonna be out at his cabin Monday night until late.

Pretty good plan if the information made it to the scumbuckets who might decide they couldn't take a chance with Cam and would come after him Monday night as we hoped.

* * *

It was now Monday night. Showtime. If I had it right, the two guys with the most to lose would make their play right at seven and make sure Cam didn't get to keep his date with the sketch artist on Tuesday. Cam gets a ride home from the same guy every day and walks up the driveway and past the garage to go in the back door of the house.

Tom and I had been camped out in the shed behind the garage since five-thirty that afternoon. The best chance for the bad guys to get at Cam, yet still remain out of sight until the last minute, was across the yard through the gate that led to the alley. They could keep their car there and hightail it fast after they were done with Cam.

Or at least that's what I thought they would do.

I would.

Tom and I sat in silence for long periods of time thinking our own separate thoughts. Me, I wanted to get these two and then finish the rest of the guys behind this whole mess. Central PA was really beginning to grind away at me, plus the thought of having to deal with the mom and daughter duo depressed me. Good times for sure but, in the life of Harry Mickey Shorts, all good things always seem to come to an end.

Maybe I could get back home and do some coaching and smack the little old baseball around for a while.

What Tom was thinking was hard to guess since he spent a good piece of the time sound asleep. Pretty worried about what was about to go down—I don't think so.

* * *

Tom woke me from my daydream world and pointed to the back fence. It was a bit before seven and a car had pulled to a stop in the alley behind Tom's house.

"Second time around," Tom whispered.

"See how many inside?" I asked.

"Two, I think," Tom answered. "Not positive, but I think I saw two."

"Okay. You know the drill, Tom," I told him. "Stick to it and don't worry about Cam. I told him I'd personally kick his ass if he tried any cowboy stunts like his old man was prone to do."

Tom smiled and nodded.

We heard two car doors close and knew we had at least a pair to deal with.

Cam was at the curb and said goodbye to his friend loud enough for all of us to hear. All four of us. Did just as he was told.

Cam walked down the path toward the back of the house as instructed. As he cleared the garage, the door to the back fence swung open.

"Hey there. Remember us, Cam?" we heard in the shed.

Two guys. One was a wiry string bean of a guy holding what looked like a bat in his right hand. The other guy, older, carrying himself like he was in charge, was pumped and made for punishment. A smallish object was in his right hand

Tom wanted to bolt right then and there, but I held him back to make sure we got what we needed.

"The party dudes. Yeah, I remember. I remember lots, you fuckers," Cam replied.

"Fuckers. He called us fuckers, Sully," the big dude said. "Such language on kids these days. Perhaps we need to teach him not to use words like that or to run his mouth at all when he should be keeping quiet."

"I believe you are correct, Zeke. Be happy to oblige," Sully said.

"Cam," Zeke started, "if you run, we'll catch you. If you run, we'll wait till your old man gets home and teach him a lesson he deserves to learn, too. Then, we'll find you and then you'll be even worse off."

"How about this lesson—you eat shit, then you die," Cam said defiantly.

"Too bad," Zeke said as they started walking across the small yard toward Cam.

I nodded to Tom, he nodded to me, and we both knew it was now party time.

Chapter 110

"Hello, boys," I said as Tom and I stepped out of the shed.

"Well, well, well. Looky here, Sully. We got some company for our lesson time. You boys should have stayed in hiding and saved yourselves a beating you aren't gonna like," Zeke said.

"That a fungo bat there, Sully? I use the same model for infield practice with my team at home. That thing could be dangerous if you aren't careful and start swinging it too close to people," I said

"Come on over here and find out just how dangerous it can be," Sully said. "Cam knows, don't ya Cam?"

"I'll stick that bat up your skinny ass, you beanpole," Cam said.

"Easy, Cam," I told him.

"What's that you hiding there, Zeke? By the way, Zeke short for something," I asked.

"This here is an old fashioned billy-club, cut down to fit my needs. Some lead weight and tape give it a nice heavy end. And the name, kind of a nickname I picked up that stuck. People think I have a pretty good physique from time in the gym. Guess people talked about it enough, it got shortened to Zeke."

"Enough talking, Zeke. Let's get it done and be on our way," Sully urged.

Tom went to take a step forward, but I grabbed his arm and pulled him back. Probably fifteen feet separated us from them, the same distance from Cam to both of us.

"Just a few more questions if you don't mind," I said.

"Make it quick," Zeke said. "Sully and I need to be on our way."

"First, sounds like a New York accent. The city? Second, why the lady and who did it? And third, just Sully beat on Cam or you enjoy wailing on defenseless kids, too?" I asked.

Zeke smiled.

"Okay, hotshot, I'll play. You aren't going to be talking to anyone when we are done with you and these other two. It's going to cost you extra and I do believe I'm going to enjoy it. I'll let Sully teach the old man his version of lesson time."

He thought for a minute, then continued.

Sully smiled at Tom.

"First, Hell's Kitchen originally. Upper East Side now, where the beautiful people play. And play I do, long and hard. The same way I approach my work, as you will soon come to find out. Second, the lady wasn't actually something we planned. Since we missed the kid, we improvised. Sully wanted to do her real bad and I have to admit I gave it a second thought myself. Nice rack, long legs, tight ass. She would have gotten a ride she wouldn't have forgotten any time soon. Do her long and hard, turn her over, and do her again, so she knows how good it truly feels when a real man shows her who's boss," Zeke bragged.

"Yeah, woulda banged her up the..." Sully started.

"That's not necessary, Sully. I believe they get the picture," Zeke said.

Tom twitched but didn't move. A snake waiting to pounce. And kill.

"My friend here gets a little carried away at times. Past history creeps up on you—you know how it goes. To answer your question, we had no beef with the lady. She was just in the wrong place at the wrong time. Scaring her with what I promised to do to her was more than enough, and a picture is worth a thousand words, or so they say," Zeke continued.

"And Cam?" I prompted.

"All Sully, I'm afraid. When he was done, I didn't see any need to continue. The message was delivered loud and clear. You agree? Plus, our directions didn't include any permanent damage, just a further warning," he said.

"From who, if I might ask?" I asked.

"Sorry. Professional ethics," Zeke answered.

"You ain't gonna tell me Jack?" I pressed.

Zeke smiled.

"No, I don't believe I'll be telling you Jack Shit."

That was about all Tom could handle. I had heard what I needed to hear as well.

"And now, even though I have enjoyed our little chat, I believe we have talked enough," Zeke said.

"More than enough," I agreed.

"I'd like the skinny one," Tom said, controlled rage in his voice.

"Me too," Cam chimed in.

"Okay, Tom. He's yours. Me and Zeke will do a friendly two-step," I told him.

With that, Tom stepped in front of me and moved over next to Cam. Sully watched him carefully as he slowly circled to his right. Ever so slowly, Tom reached behind his back and produced a gun the size of a howitzer and pointed it at Sully.

Sully's eyes widened and Zeke looked over with interest.

I bent down and took my gun from my ankle holster and politely showed it to Zeke.

"Sully," Tom said, "put the bat down and kick it over here towards Cam. Hands on your head and don't twitch, 'cause that would cause me to blow a hole in you the size of a small coon."

Sully dropped the bat, kicked it over toward Cam, and put his hands on his head like a good little scumbucket should.

Zeke still hadn't moved.

Cam picked up the bat and walked behind Sully.

"You a righty, Sully?" Cam asked.

No answer.

"I said, you a righty, Sully?" Cam repeated even louder this time.

"Ah, yeah," he finally said.

"Good," Cam said.

With that, Cam swung the bat and connected with Sully's right elbow. The sickening crack was quickly followed by an animal like wail, only to be shortened by Sully's intake of air as the bat connected with the side of his right leg. That blow caved in his knee and he crumpled to the ground in total agony.

Zeke moved his right hand ever so slightly, which necessitated me shooting him in the right kneecap. This seemed to cause some degree of pain as evidenced by his contorted face. I could swear he turned toward me menacingly so, to be safe, I shot him in the left kneecap as well. I was pretty sure there was now a large degree of pain as further evidenced by the anguish on his face and the moaning he was doing.

Didn't scream. He took it like a professional and even held on to his billy-club, too. I didn't think he would be able to use it but Tom took no chances and shot him through the right wrist.

It dropped.

Tom walked over to Sully, took out his cell phone and dialed the Chief's office.

"Chief, we were right. We were accosted and had to defend ourselves in the back yard of my property. You should send some boys and a few ambulances over to my place right fast."

Call completed, Tom turned to Sully and delivered a viscous kick square in the balls.

"Now we're close to even," he said.

Chapter 111

Dell Muoio, Chief of the local police, arrived with Detective Strook and several others. The ambulances were right behind them creating quite a spectacle for Tom's neighbors to enjoy.

The neighbors had heard the gun shots but stayed indoors until they heard the sirens pull up on the street. Guess they figured it was safe to come out then.

Pretty good crowd formed.

"I know some of the details from what you told me this morning but let's hear it from the beginning, Tom," Dell said.

Tom had gone over to the police station and informed the Police Chief of the impending threat these two perpetrators posed to Tom, Cam, and possibly a family friend by the name of Harry Mickey Shorts.

"Just like I told ya this morning, Dell," Tom told the police chief and long time friend.

He then recapped the whole thing from start to finish with a little help from Cam and myself. The menacing nature of the altercation and the dangerous weapons the two guys possessed as firmly attested to by all three of us. Then Tom handed the Chief the tape recorder we had hidden in the bushes right where we expected the two guys would be standing by the back fence. We had managed to capture the whole thing on tape, confession and all. Seems the tape had malfunctioned at the end, right about the time Cam started talking to Sully.

Strange how those machines can break down at the most inopportune moments.

The chief told us to come inside Tom's house so he could hear the tape. When he was done, he told us not to talk to anyone and to meet him at the station.

The emergency people took the two bad guys away with a deputy in each ambulance. The cuffs must have hurt real bad, especially considering what was left of Zeke's right wrist which was hanging like a broken hinge.

* * *

It was past two in the morning by the time we were done giving our statements and they let us leave the station house. Del told Tom it all looked in order even though it seemed an excessive amount of force was used, what with the three of us not even getting as much as a scratch.

Cam had offered to scratch but the Chief didn't think it was so funny.

Don't know why, but it occurred to me Sully wouldn't be scratching his balls anytime soon, either.

* * *

"Harry, I can't thank ya enough, man," Tom said.

"Yeah, thanks dude. It was a kick," Cam echoed the sentiment in his own Cam way.

"Tom, I'm there for you any day, anytime, anywhere. You know it. You too, Cam. That's what buds do for buds," I told them.

"I know, Harry, I know," Tom said.

We shook and Tom gave me a hug meant for good friends. Cam high-fived me and we got in our cars and left.

* * *

One group of bad guys down; one group of bad guys to go. There was plenty to get done over the next few days to conclude the case but the major lifting was behind us and what we had left was damn sure gonna be fun.

Chapter 112

The ringing wouldn't stop. No matter what I tried, I couldn't get it to stop. There was one thing that finally did it; I woke up. The damn phone was still ringing, though.

"Shorts," I mumbled.

"Mister Shorts, Harry. I'm supposed to find out if you are coming in to work today," was what I heard.

"Sure, but you'll have to excuse me. Who is this?" I asked.

"Ah, it's Mary Ann, Harry. Joe asked me to call and he didn't do it very nicely either," she said with a whine.

"Sorry about that Mary Ann. Tell Mister Stoner to calm down, I'll be there in a bit," I told her.

"I'll do that, Harry."

The line went dead.

* * *

The lovely Crissy was chatting up a walking mass of muscles when I entered MechInsCo about an hour later. I was moving, but not very quickly.

"Harry, this is Emile," she said when she saw me trying to slink on through without being spotted.

"Crissy, good morning," I replied.

"Emile is here to install the new equipment in the gym. He has promised to give me a personal lesson on the use of his equipment," she said grinning.

Emile smiled. Unless I was mistaken, I'd bet he was looking forward to showing her all of his equipment.

Replaced by a weight guy. Oh well, it had to end some day and better on Crissy's terms then a messy blow-up. One daughter down; one mama to go.

I continued upstairs and hit Joe's office door just as he was getting off the phone.

"Joe," I queried.

"Harry, come in," Joe said.

I did and I sat.

"I heard some disturbing news early this morning," he started. "Someone told me you were involved in an altercation last night. That's what they said. They said it was an altercation," he continued.

"Altercation? An altercation?" I repeated.

"Yes, that's what he called it. Care to explain?" he asked.

"Who he?" I asked.

"What?" Joe said.

"Who is the he you are referring to?" I asked again.

"The he doesn't matter. What did you do, Harry?" Joe asked.

"If your 'he' explained it was an altercation, why don't you ask 'he' what an altercation is and have 'he' tell you what this particular altercation was?" I answered.

Joe wasn't getting the answers he wanted and he wasn't happy about it. Personally, I didn't give a flying wazoo.

"Harry?" he said.

"Joe?" I replied.

"Are you going to tell me what happened?" he asked, clearly getting more upset with me.

"Joe, boss, I don't have to tell you nothing. But, I will. I was with a friend I've known for some time minding our own business when something went down. I was there, so I helped my friend. End of story," I finished.

"That's your story? That's it?" he said.

"That's what happened," I replied.

I stood and walked out of his office.

Word traveled pretty fast in this town. Two possibilities—the local cops talking to local folk or the big guys spreading the word on what happened to the New York bad guys. The cops, local or otherwise, would be in big trouble if word got out it came from inside their shop, even in Smallsville, USA. That left the obvious.

Show time.

Chapter 113

Every case presents itself differently—unique problems, obstacles to overcome, unusual scenarios, yatta-yatta. In the end though, clues are clues and cases are solved by piecing the clues together until you figure out the who, what, when, where, how and why. When you get to that point, nothing left to do but reveal the bad guys and make sure they get what's coming to them.

Problem is sometimes the bad guys aren't really bad guys, or at least not too-bad bad guys. What to do with them becomes a problem.

It was who, what, when, where, how and why time and I was gonna have to help figure out what to do with the bad guys and the not so bad guys.

* * *

It was now two days later. Two long days of running different final outcomes for our band of no-goodnicks. There was some room for giving people the benefit of the doubt for their actions, but, not much. Some of the people we had to deal with were true scum and they were going down hard.

The purple, ah…I mean *violet* Rolls Royce pulled up in front of Tom's house at 7:30 pm on the dot—right on time. Don't know why I was surprised. M. Randle Trundle does everything to perfection. Always did and always will.

"Time to rock and roll," I said. "Saddle up and let's get us some bad guys."

"Right behind you, Harry," Tom said.

"Me too," Cam said.

* * *

Charlie was standing beside the open door to the limo.

"Harry," he said.

"Charlie, good to see ya," I told him. "This here is Tom and his son, Cam. Good people. Good friends."

"It's a pleasure to meet both of you," Charlie said as we stepped into the back of the limo.

"Tom, Cam, this is M. Randle Trundle. Randle, this is Tom and his son Cam who I've told you a lot about."

"Tom. Cam," he said as he shook each of their hands. "Are we ready, Harry?" he asked.

"Is the Pope Catholic?" I answered.

"Harry, you're good to have around. Not too often, but good to have around," he laughed. We all joined him.

"Ms. Timmons?" I asked.

"All in good time, Harry, all in good time," he replied.

* * *

As Charlie drove, we went over what was about to go down and how we were going to do it. It had been confirmed the players were all there and we had our troops in play as well. When it's right, it's right. This was gonna make things right in more ways than one.

Show time—HMS style.

Chapter 114

Private party being held in the back room of a local restaurant. It happens in local restaurants just like this one every night, of every week, of every month, of every year. For this group, it was going to be their last party together in this kind of a setting. They'll be partying, but not the kind of partying that will bring back fond memories for a long time to come. They'll have memories for sure, that you can count on.

Charlie pulled the Rolls up to the front door and we all got out with nothing but business on our minds. Trundle had arranged for the other members of our party-crashing contingency to be waiting for us when we got there. We all nodded, smiled knowing smiles, and entered the restaurant.

Tom went into the back room first. Local guy in a local place who could have gotten his restaurant mixed up. When I followed and then Cam stuck his gangly body through the door, the jig was up.

"What the…? Harry, this is a private party. You can't come in here," Joe Stoner said as he stood to come around the table. The rest of the people in the room erupted in shouts and angry cursing.

There was the distinct sound of 'Someunafucking bitch' heard within the upheaval.

"Sit down, Joe," I told him. "And the rest of you can all shut up. Now!"

Randle had entered the room with the rest of our crew moving in as well. When they were all in the room, everyone went very quiet. The two giants Randle uses for intimidation were doing their thing and it was working. I'd seen them before and it made me think about sitting down myself.

"Why don't we all sit and get comfy. There are some things we need to discuss and no sense getting all worked up before we get down to the real reason we are all gathered here together. Agreed?" I said.

Mumbling and murmuring from the crowd. Not the answer I was looking for.

"Agreed?" I said with more emphasis.

"Now, since nobody seems to know who invited who to this shindig,

I'll enlighten you. I sent out the invitations and set up this extended family gathering. So, we can dispense with the righteous indignation and accept the fact my friends and I are here to stay. Deal with it."

Mumbling and murmuring from the crowd. Less so, but still there. A bit of recognition on a few faces was beginning to show through.

"I'll introduce the additions to our party first and then get down to the 'who you all be' part afterward. That okay with everyone? Good," I said with continued authority.

A hush had fallen over the crowd.

"You all know the local head gendarme, Chief Dell Muoio. He is here to ensure peace and tranquility at the festivities. His boys are outside should anyone doubt his ability to do so. This gentleman to my left is Mister M. Randle Trundle. The reason for his presence will become clear later on. Oh yeah, the two giants along the wall are with him and they are as good at what they do as they look."

A scan of the crowd showed rapt attention from all.

"Let's move along," I said. "Some of you know Tom Naughton, local private investigator and a close friend of mine. That's Cam next to him, Tom's son. Some of you already know who he is. If you don't, good. Those who do will wish they never did."

Somebody had placed a cool one in front of me. I drank some of it. It was gonna get warm if I didn't and we can't have that.

Yuengling—not a bad local brew.

"Next to Mister Trundle is Jock Woodburn. He's a partner with a guy by the name of Ralph Windel in Windel-Woodburn Enterprises. Ring a bell with anyone?" I asked.

Quiet again.

"Sure you do. Lying good-for-nothings," I said. "Let's move on so we can get to the meat of this get-together. Jock's presence will become clear later on as well. Last, but surely not least in my mind, are the two ladies in our entourage. To my extreme right is the esteemed General Counsel of MechInsCo, Ms. Madeline Metzger, and to my extreme left is Mister Trundle's assistant, Ms. Timmons. Ms. Timmons is here as the second individual representing Trundle Industries as required by the company's bylaws. That will also become clear as we move along."

Tiny murmur, mostly silence.

"Before I begin the introductions of the rest of the members of this gathering, I seem to be wanting. Let's restock and then we shall continue."

As planned, fresh drinks for all arrived at that very moment. Very attractive young lady doing the honors I might add.

Vasimalo stood, the twin towers leaned forward, Vasimalo sat.

Let us get settled and then we shall continue.

Chapter 115

"Okay, ladies, gents, and kiddos of all ages. Sit your behinds in your appointed seats and let's call this session to order. The Honorable—I use the term very loosely, I might add—the Honorable Harry Mickey Shorts presiding. Roll call, please," I continued.

Ms. Timmons liked that one I think.

"Across the table, beginning on my extreme left, we have Joe Stoner. Joe's the accounting manager at MechInsCo and my current boss. Oh, before I forget—Joe, I quit. Next to Joe is his wife, a name I do not know. I do know her sister seated to her left. That's Barb Mueller who was right hand to Joe and fired by Phillips about the time I got to MechInsCo. She did a good deal for Joe, too much as will become evident. Good so far?" I asked the assembled crowd.

No response, not a whisper. I moved on.

Randy seemed to be enjoying his beer and his time with Jock. Ms. Timmons was looking fine and the GC was looking in control as always.

"To continue with the family introductions, next is Greg Boalman, cousin of Joe Stoner and lone reinsurance wolf in the company. He hasn't been with MechInsCo long but plenty long enough as we will see. I believe that is your brother next to you, is it not?" I asked.

Greg was about to speak, then thought better of it.

"Not necessary for you to comment, Greg. If I may, another cousin of Joe brought into the company to work the reinsurance side of the Information Services department downstairs. He happens to be the individual who informed Joe of every report I requested from the system. Silent but deadly, just like a nasty fart. Name. Who gives a rat's ass? Let's move on."

My Yuengling gone, the new love of my eye miraculously appeared with another as if on cue.

"And now we come to the meat and potatoes of this little ingenious and incestuous crew—Billy and Kev, or as I have referred to them in the past, Vasimalo's butt boys. Seemingly non-player nobodies on face value, they actually form the brains behind this scheme and they have the responsibility of watching the dollars like hawks. As we shall see, this little enterprise couldn't have gone down without their particular form of expertise. Oh yeah, before I forget, neither is married to any relative of the extended family at the table. The light of each other's eyes, they form a loving couple happily cohabitating in a nifty loft in Greenwich Village."

Jock cocked his head in their direction, pondered a sec, said nothing.

"Now to the final two pieces of this band of merry men, and ladies. Ralph Vasimalo, current President of Vasco, a New York insurance brokerage firm, and a former international reinsurance broker. Seated next to Ralphy boy is Kevin Mead, ex-president of MechInsCo who is currently living in semi-retirement in Baltimore, Maryland. I will explain his semi-retirement shortly. That is his wife to his left and Mary, her sister, beside her at the end of the table. And lest I forget, Missus Mead's sister's full name happens to be Missus Mary Vasimalo, wife of Ralphy boy."

Oh what a tangled web we weave, when first we gonna deceive the shit outta you. Or something like that.

The shocked faces around the other side of the table all stared at Harry Mickey Shorts in total disbelief. You could just hear them thinking, 'How the hell does he know all that? What else does he know? He can't know it all. What are we going to do now? Run? Hide under the table till they all go away?'

As rehearsed, Chief Muoio said, "Don't even think of moving. Be good and sit where you are and let Mister Shorts continue."

Probably too stunned to actually move, they sat.

Vasimalo glared, Mead's mouth hung open, Billy and Kev held hands under the table, and Barb started to cry softly.

"First, I'm gonna lay out what you all did, how, and why you did it. Assuming there are no protests of innocence from anyone at that point, I will tell you why these people are here with me and what will happen next. That okay with all of you?" I asked.

"Good," I answered without waiting for a response from the other side of the table.

First things first, I had to take a leak.

Chapter 116

Leak out of the way and feeling much relieved, I continued.

"I'm going to try and reconstruct what has occurred and put it into chronological perspective as well as I can," I said. "A long time ago, before Jock Woodburn hooked up with Ralph Windel to form their current marauding machine, Windel bought the reinsurance subsidiary of a New York conglomerate and proceeded to rape, pillage and plunder that company till there was nothing left. In doing so, the president of that company, who had spent his whole life building it into a top notch and well respected international reinsurer, was transformed into a beaten man. Six months later, his company gone, out of work, his psyche destroyed, Vinny Vasimalo committed suicide leaving his family alone and penniless. His younger brother, Ralph Vasimalo, never forgot what Ralph Windel had done to his brother and the Vasimalo family."

A breath, some Yuengling, some thought, then I continued. "The man Windel inserted to take over Vasimalo's company was named Collins."

That surprised a few people around the table who hadn't known that fact. I told you the Web Dudes were the best and leave no stone unturned.

"Many years later, déjà vu entered the Vasimalo world again. Windel had hooked up with Jock Woodburn and continued his ruinous ways. By this time, Ralph Vasimalo was happily married to Mary Tully and had built a successful brokerage company using as a base his experience working in the brokerage world for the brother he had idolized. He had also hired two guys from his brother's old firm—Billy and Kev.

"Everyone with me so far?" I asked.

Resignation had set in on several faces. Question marks remained on others. Even Trundle was a bit fidgety about now.

"To continue, the déjà vu part appeared when a New York corporate raider buys a Central Pennsylvania insurance company and dumps the president and the majority of his senior staff. A president who had spent his whole life building that company and caring for every employee he had ever hired. A president exiled to Baltimore, a broken man, to sit on his boat and look at the water. A president by the name of Kevin Mead.

"Just as Ralph Windel had broken his brother, Ralph Windel had broken the heart of Kevin Mead, Ralph Vasimalo's brother-in-law. More than you could handle, wasn't it Ralphy boy?" I asked.

"Someunafucking bitch deserved to die, just like Vinny, worse than Vinny," he replied. The look of determined hate in his eyes for Ralph Windel was spooky.

"That is the why behind the current apparent failure of MechInsCo. Any questions or anything any of you would like to add?" I asked.

"The how is really very clever. Ingenious in its simplicity and completeness. Kev and Billy masterminded the plan and Vasimalo brokered the deal using VV Inc., the small reinsurance brokerage operation he had formed in honor of his brother. Billy was the president and Kev did everything else. Here's what they did:

"Vasimalo bought the right to place MechInsCo's new reinsurance program by offering to pay higher than normal commissions to place their reinsurance package. That way he could influence placing it where he needed it to be, primarily one company that didn't watch their backs and trusted Ralph, Billy and Kev to protect their interests. Fat chance on that, right Ralphy?" I said.

Killer glare was all I got from him.

"What's he talking about, Ralph? I don't understand what he's saying or doing here in the first place," Ralph's wife said.

"Shut the fuck up, Mary, will ya. You never understood jack and never will. So, just shut the fu…"

One of Randle's boys underhanded a quarter that struck Vasimalo in the middle of the forehead and knocked him clean off his chair.

"No way to talk to a lady," was all he said when the entire room turned to look at him.

* * *

The room finally quieted down and everyone was back in their seats. Vasimalo had a huge welt in the middle of his forehead that brought a big smile to his wife's face.

"Good for you, you good-for-nothing fat piece of shit," his sister-in-law said to him. "Somebody should have put you in your place a long time ago and maybe we wouldn't be in the mess we're in now."

"Fuck you, too," Vasimalo said to her in response.

"Say another word like that to my wife and I'll kick your ass 'till you beg me to stop," Mead told him.

With that, Mead hit him with a wicked backhand that knocked him clean off his chair again.

The place erupted in an uproar and it took Dell Muoio and the two giants to bring order back to the room.

"Settle down everyone," I yelled as the noise dropped to a low roar. "Let's settle down and get this done before somebody gets severely hurt."

Tom was itching to get a few licks in, but I managed to keep him seated and in check.

"Okay, listen up. I'm going to get back to where we were and finish laying out what went down. One more outburst and I'm outta here and you can take your chances with the police and Mister Trundle's two friends here," I said.

That seemed to catch their attention and I was back in control, for now at least.

Chapter 117

"Let us continue," I said. "I believe I was about to say Vasimalo gets his way and he is able to construct a reinsurance program for MechInsCo's growing book of business. Now, here's where the rest of the merry band of thieves gets involved. Barb has all the people who code the policies reporting to her. Multi-talented, multi-functional—that's our Barb. Thus, the direction of the policy information, and more importantly the reinsurance applied to each policy, is all her doing. All is going great until Phillips fires her to spite Joe."

I look at Barb and she's still crying softly.

"So, now Joe has to take over and everything goes legit. Policies get coded as they should and the reinsurance is applied according to the book. The UNK Re. Captive can't be a part of the picture any longer since Joe doesn't have the time to hand select the accounts he wants to flow there. If you follow the management reports, that's when there was a subtle pattern change and I was able to determine how the money was supposed to be flowing through the system."

Look around, everyone is waiting.

"The beauty of the scheme is how you guys concocted the back end. This captive reinsurance company, UNK Re., gets all kinds of policies from mid-range dollars to some bigger premium dollar policies. In just over a year and a half, almost thirty million dollars in premium is funneled into it with what looked like an eighty percent loss ratio. Problem is, when a loss happened on any policy in the captive, it was extracted from the captive, placed back into some other reinsurance company and replaced by a policy of about the same premium size with no losses. Thus, premium flows in and no losses ever 'stick' to the captive. Plus, while the financial reports show a normal ceding commission being paid to MechInsCo for the business, the actual flow of commission dollars is non-existent. Paper money only. Slick, very slick. UNK Re. showed total actual profit in eighteen months of twenty-seven point five million."

Look around, everyone is still waiting. By now you can feel the tension and resignation in the air coming from the other side of the table.

"Nice name for the company, too. UNK Re., short for UNCLE Re. maybe? As in uncle Kevin Mead. As in uncle of Joe Stoner who is controlling this internal heist with lots of help from the rest of the clan."

No response, no denials.

"I thought so," I said.

"How was it done? A nifty computer program, designed by Joe's cousin, who is sitting over there and who worked down in IS, it moved policies with a loss back into the reinsurance pool every night. It used dynamite camouflage to remove any trace of all previous transactions involving any movement of policies back out of UNK Re. Boalman covers any possible questions with reinsurance mumbo-jumbo and, since he's the only reinsurance guy in the company, he doctors up the experience information sent to the reinsurers every quarter. Billy and Kev run the whole financial railroad through their company and can provide assurances of financial correctness, plus mounds of documentation whenever needed. One ass, covering the other ass, who is covering the first ass. Final piece, Joe massages the financial reports and somehow has gotten it past the auditors who certify the books. Still checking, but I wouldn't be surprised if we find a relative at the auditing company."

Look around, everyone's still waiting to see if I got the final piece figured out. A long sip and we continue.

"Where? Where's the money you ask? Where was the money you should be asking? This morning the UNK Re. account was frozen and confiscated by a task force put together to close down this operation. The money is now here and, after the government clears it, it will all be reapplied to MechInsCo's books with every policy properly coded where they belong and reinsurance re-routed to its proper place. The end result should show a nice profit actually coming to the MechInsCo bottom line."

"Ralph," Mead started, "I never should have let you talk me into this stupid scheme of yours. We'd never get caught you said. We'd fix that asshole, you said. I'd have my company back, you said. Well, we got caught, you're the asshole, and my company and all the people who worked there suffered, plus, my family, too. Your brother Vinny is probably turning over in his grave."

Mead shook his head and took his wife's hand in his. With the other, he backhanded Vasimalo again knocking him clean off his chair.

Barb cried softly, Billy and Kev looked in each other's eyes and sighed, and Joe slouched the slouch of a beaten man.

Nobody said a word.

Chapter 118

Vasimalo was back in his chair, again, and the rest of the people in the room were quiet. The floor was still mine.

"So, troops, as there are no objections to the scenario I laid out, the only thing left to do is tell you what's gonna happen now," I started.

"First things first—what happens to MechInsCo? Answer: Trundle Industries has agreed to purchase MechInsCo and will leave the company intact as it currently stands with the following changes:

Jock Woodburn, who has severed his relationship with Windel-Woodburn, assumes the position of Chief Operating Officer at Trundle Industries and Chairman of the Board at MechInsCo. As Mister Trundle's right hand man, he will oversee all aspects of the MechInsCo transition plan.

Collins, Phillips and the rest of the New York invaders are out. Why—general principles, and the fact they couldn't find out where the money was going and why MechInsCo was headed down the dumper.

Ms. Madeline Metzger will assume the position of interim president while a search is conducted to fill the positions of President, CFO, etc. She will also retain her current General Counsel duties and revert back to that position when the other two main positions have been filled. In two years, she will be leaving MechInsCo to assume a senior level position in New York within Trundle Industries.

The remaining positions vacated by the additional people around this table will be filled by local Mechanicsburg area insurance people who value the principles MechInsCo was built on and will be rebuilt on. Also, every effort will be made to find a president with local roots and similar values.

The newly created position of Director of Security at MechInsCo will be filled by Tom Naughton, who will be assisted by his trainee and son, Cam Naughton, upon his graduation from high school.

Any restitution to either insureds, insurance or reinsurance carriers, or any other harmed entity including any assessed fines, etc. will be funded from the assets of those companies presently owned by Ralph Vasimalo to the full extent of his holdings.

* * *

"Questions on any of what I have just detailed?" I asked. "No. Good. Let's continue. Here's what is going to happen to the people responsible for this crime and acts of betrayal on MechInsCo. All of this has been agreed to by the local police as well as state and federal authorities. If anyone protests or doesn't accept what I will now say, they will be taken by Chief Muoio to a Federal holding area to be dealt with by the government. Understand?" I asked.

No responses meant they understood.

"Here is what's going down:

"For what was deemed a minor role, Barb gets a one-year suspended sentence and will commit to one thousand hours of community service of Chief Muoio's choosing.

"Stoner's cousins, Greg Boalman and the IS programming guru, will serve six months in the Camp Hill prison facility and then perform twenty-five hundred hours of community service teaching at a local VoTech school upon their release.

"Joe Stoner will serve two years at the Camp Hill prison facility to be followed by two years house arrest while he commits to thirty-five hundred hours of strictly supervised community service also teaching at the local VoTech school.

"Billy and Kev, you will spend the next five years at a minimum security facility in Connecticut and will be barred from working in the insurance industry for life.

"Mister Kevin Mead, for your part in this crime, plus your incredible gullibility and stupidity, you will serve two years under house arrest while you single-handedly paint every square inch of the inside of MechInsCo's building. You will then be remanded to state prison to serve the remainder of a five year sentence.

"And last, Ralph Vasimalo. For your part in masterminding this caper, ordering the assault on Cam Naughton and causing pain to an innocent lady, and for being a miserable Someunafucking Bitch, you will serve fifteen years in federal prison with no hope for parole.

"Questions or objections?" I asked.

Either too stunned to speak, or afraid to do so, not a word was spoken. The ladies were all in tears by now, while the guys all sat with heads lowered wishing they could bend over and kiss their asses good-bye.

"As we leave this room, you can all consider yourself extremely lucky. Without the assistance of Chief Muoio and Mister Trundle, each of you would have suffered fates far beyond your assigned penalty. Much worse. You deserve it, the people you have hurt would demand it, and I would have seen fit to insist on it in spades. You should get on your knees and thank God every day for the rest of your lives. Now pick up your sorry asses and get out!"

Epilogue

Two days later…

The sun was shining, bats hitting balls, and the sounds of cowhide slapping against leather were everywhere. All was right with the world.

The only exception to the world's beauty was Ms. Timmons leaving for New York directly following our session at the restaurant. Business, or something I'm sure Randy concocted, because he knows everything and he knew what Ms. Timmons and I had concocted for each other. Oh well, it will happen someday. I am Harry Mickey Shorts don't forget.

* * *

Opening day to a brand new baseball season and the Bayport Schooners were playing the Harrisburg Senators at Riverside Stadium. Mister Randle Trundle, owner of the Schooners, was sitting behind first base as the guest of the new ownership group that had just purchased the Senators. Randle was chatting with Todd Vander Woude, past GM of the Senators and now the lead partner in this new ownership group. I knew Todd. He worked long and hard for the Senators and deserved his new role.

"Harry, that the kid you helped in the spring?" Randle asked.

"Both of them—pitcher and catcher," I answered.

"Any good?" he asked.

"Ton of talent in both of them. Raw talent being molded," I said.

"So, if the pitcher gets hammered and the catcher can't catch the ball, then its raw talent showing through. If they both shine, you're the genius who developed that raw talent in short order. About right?" Randy asked.

"Sounds about right to me," I said.

We all laughed. Randy, Jock, Woodie, the GC and acting Ms. Prez of MechInsCo and Harry Mickey Shorts—ex MechInsCo employee and now full time shit bum P.I.

Oh yeah, before I forget. The Senators shut out the Schooners that day by a score of 4-0. The hillbilly pitcher threw six shutout innings, gave up three hits, and struck out nine batters. Ozzie threw out two runners trying to steal second, called a great game, and hit two homers driving in all four runs.

They both shone like stars, so I guess that makes me the genius who developed that raw talent in short order. That about right? You bet your ass that's right.